T0318827

The Shadow City

The Hunters of Infinity Series by Ryan Wieser

The Glass Blade

The Shadow City

The Shadow City

The Hunters of Infinity

Ryan Wieser

REBEL BASE BOOKS
Kensington Publishing Corp.
www.kensingtonbooks.com

Rebel Base Books are published by
Kensington Publishing Corp. 119 West 40th Street New York, NY 10018

All Kensington titles, imprints, and distributed lines are available at special
quantity discounts for bulk purchases for sales promotion, premiums,
fundraising, and educational or institutional use.

To the extent that the image or images on the cover of this book depict a
person or persons, such person or persons are merely models, and are not
intended to portray any character or characters featured in the book.

Special book excerpts or customized printings can also be created to fit
specific needs. For details, write or phone the office of the Kensington
Special Sales Manager:
Kensington Publishing Corp.
119 West 40th Street
New York, NY 10018
Attn. Special Sales Department. Phone: 1-800-221-2647.

First Electronic Edition: October 2018
eISBN-13: 978-1-63573-027-2
eISBN-10: 1-63573-027-9

First Print Edition: October 2018
ISBN-13: 978-1-63573-030-2
ISBN-10: 1-63573-030-9

Printed in the United States of America

My sunshine, my comet—always, forever.

Acknowledgments

I would like to thank my family for their continued support of me. For every reread, listening session, and note-taking, researching, late-night brainstorming gathering—I thank you. For my husband, I thank you for being my constant source of inspiration and support. For our precious child, I thank you for the abundance of love you have filled my heart with: you are my everything. I would like to thank my mother for her presence during this time, without your support I wouldn't have been able to commit to this series. I would like to also express my gratitude for the love, support, and encouragement I received always from my grandmother Toni, and my grandfathers, Christopher and Ralph, and my godfather, John. I would also like to thank Richard Curtis, my constant source of guidance, your patience and support mean so much to me. Finally, I would like to thank Martin Biro and James Abbate for their continued faith in the series.

CHAPTER 1

Azgul

Present Day

In her dream, Jessop wore a linen cloak, identical to one she had first donned in the Blade's mystical pool. He wore dark funerary robes, and he moved quickly, disappearing around corners, catching her eyes in the shadows. She followed him through the maze, wondering where he went, what he thought. She quickened her step, trotting after him, chasing through the dark corridors. She spun around the wall's end, and felt a sudden ache in her abdomen. His arm was around her instantly, holding her close to his body. She looked down, over the sheer linen, and saw between her breasts the hilt of his dagger, his gloved hand still tight around the weapon. Blood soaked the robe, slick and crimson, sticking to her form. She wasn't angry with him; it hadn't hurt that badly. She rested her hand against his chest, and blood leached through her fingers. She looked up into his dark eyes. A tear ran over the star-shaped scar.

"You're bleeding," she whispered, pressing firmly against his chest, ignoring her own wound.

He smiled at her, shrugging casually. "It's only my heart."

Jessop woke to the sound of crying, lurching up in her bed. It had been the same dream, for the hundredth time. Her hair snaked around her neck with sweat, her brow damp and hands clammy. Again, the small cry called to her. She glanced over the large, dark bed where Falco slept, motionless and silent. She rolled off, her feet finding the cool ground, and crossed the room, her eyes navigating the dark with their usual ease. Jeco was sitting up in his bed, his damp dark hair standing on end, his large gray eyes brimming with tears.

She looped her hands under his shoulders and pulled him to her body. "I couldn't sleep either, love." He clung to her tightly, burying his small face under her chin. He didn't care that she was slick with sweat or weary with exhaustion; she was his mother, his protector.

In the darkness, large arms wrapped around her, and she leaned back into Falco, finding the safety in his arms that their son found in hers. Falco was silent in the night, a predatory creature whose abilities amazed her as much in that moment as they had a decade before.

His lips kissed the space where her neck met her shoulder. "Nightmares again?"

"Both of us, it seems," she whispered, her breath travelling over Jeco's short hair.

"What should I do when my family cannot find peace?"

Jessop breathed heavily at her husband's question. It had been a month since Kohl had escaped the Blade, nearly killing her in the process. The Blade had been his home for most of his life. It had been more than a home. It had been his training facility, where he had lived with his Hunter brethren, patrolling the Daharian galaxy on behalf of Hydo Jesuin. The same Blade she had infiltrated and handed over to her husband, Falco. Jessop pushed the thought back, blinking away the image of Kohl O'Hanlon's face. "Find the one who torments me," she ordered.

* * * *

The following morning, Trax arrived early to visit with Jeco, his new favorite resident in the Blade. Jessop had never felt comfortable with anyone except Korend'a watching their son, but Trax DeHawn was different. He was Kuroi and a skilled Hunter capable of protecting Jeco better than most; he was fiercely loyal to the true Lord and Protector of the Blade of Light.

"Good morning, *Hasen-Ha*," she greeted him. His golden eyes shone even brighter as he smiled for Jeco, who reached out towards him. Jeco wasn't simply Trax's newfound friend; Trax was a person of great wonder to Jeco. Jessop watched the two smile at one another and wondered if Jeco could see Trax's eyes as they truly were, as only one of Kuroi blood could see them—*glowing*. Unlike hers and Trax's, her son's eyes did not glow; they were the beautiful, muted gray of his father's.

"*Dey-a, Oray-Ha,*" Trax greeted her in turn, taking Jeco into his arms. Before either spoke further, Falco appeared from the bathing room, running a hand through his dark, wet hair, a warm smile on his face. He immediately approached Trax and offered him his hand. "*Dey-a, Hasen-Ha, aruk 'ta raney'ha Jeco?*" Jessop smiled at Falco's hard-learned Kuroi, listening as he asked what Trax had planned for Jeco that morning.

Trax readjusted Jeco in his arms. "I thought we might attend a morning meditation. Some of our youngest students will be there, as I am sure you remember?"

"*Med-a-shen, Tax,*" Jeco misspoke, studying Trax's face intently.

Jessop smiled at her son, touching his back softly.

"Yes, Master Jeco, we go to meditation," Trax answered.

Falco nodded. "Alright. You know the drill—don't let him out of your sight."

"Not for a second."

Falco cupped his son's head, leaning in to kiss his forehead. "I love you, Jeco."

Jeco smiled, bashful. "Love you, Dada."

Jessop followed suit. "I love you, darling."

Jeco said nothing, instead turning and pushing his face into Trax's neck. It was the third time he had ignored her sentiment since their reunion, and it stung as sharply as the first.

"*Dona teim, Oray-Ha,*" Trax advised. *Give it time.* Falco had counseled the same. She tightened her mouth, nodding sharply, before turning away from them.

* * * *

Falco kissed the back of her neck, winding his arms around her abdomen with ease. "He loves you, Jessop, you're his mother."

"Yes, I am, and I left him. All this time, here with Kohl, in *this* place, I wasn't with him. Or with you."

She had spent so long in the Glass Blade, the training facility for the Hunters of Infinity—the Daharian galaxy's supreme authority—infiltrating their ranks and ultimately becoming the first female Hunter in existence. Her superior abilities hadn't been enough to secure her a position in the Blade. That had only been achieved by winning over the heart of Hunter Kohl O'Hanlon. Kohl had once been Falco's closest friend before he betrayed him. That had been many years ago. Many years allowed for her and Falco to plan the ultimate subversion. Kohl's involvement in the plan had not been a mistake. Any feelings she had developed for him during the execution of their plan—of fooling him to fall in love with her—*those* had been a mistake.

Falco turned her slowly in his arms, urging her to look at him. "What is it that bothers you most?"

Jessop pushed out of his arms, putting necessary distance between them. "What bothers me most? I had to leave. For our plan to work I had to leave Aranthol, and our son may never forgive me for that. *You* may never forgive me."

He inclined his head, confused by her words. "Why wouldn't I forgive you?"

She had said too much. She shook her head, running her hand through her long hair. She needed them to go back to how they were *before*. She needed to be honest with him. But the truth was terrifying. "I slept with Kohl. I had a relationship with him, the whole time I was here…and before him, it had always only ever been you."

"I already know all of that. I'm sorry you had to sleep with him but you did it to secure our son's future, to ensure justice could be claimed. You did it for us," he reminded her, closing the space between them with easy strides.

"Where is that justice now? Hanson, despite his mistreatment of me—*and* of yourself and Kohl—lives! Hydo, who killed my parents, who scarred your entire body, still lives. Kohl…I let him into my bed, Falco, but he let me into his heart, and I betrayed him."

Falco narrowed his gray eyes at her, his long scar flinching across his face. "Never forget, he betrayed me *first*, Jessop."

She knew she had said too much. She nodded, reaching up and cupping his face with her small hand, her thumb resting on the scar tissue under his eye. "Of course."

"I understand the guilt you feel. Your son has been hurt by a plan we hatched for his betterment, and he takes it out only on you. Kohl fell in love with you, as planned, and deceiving him was difficult. But he betrayed me years ago, and more importantly, he tried to kill you, as his false Lord once tried.

"All you need to know, my love, is not whose heart you reside in, but who resides in your own."

He pulled her closer to him, her breast pushing into his chest, the rise and fall of their breathing in perfect synchronicity. "My heart is for only my son, and his father."

He lifted her into his kiss, his warm mouth traversing hers with ease. They kissed with equal parts familiarity and passion. There were no parts of him she did not know, they could map one another's bodies blind, and that kind of closeness allowed for expert navigation. She ran his tunic off his shoulders; he pulled hers off over her head, parting lips for a mere second.

He ran his hands from her lower back, up her rib cage, over her breasts, finally nestling over her neck and jawline, framing her face for his kiss to travel deeper. His tongue moved over hers with deliberation, tasting her slowly. As they fell to the bed, he propped himself on top of her. He pulled away from her kiss and stared down at her. Between her breasts, closest to her heart, was their scar—the twisted fishhook design. Centered in his chest was the exact same mark, and as he hovered above her, the images were perfectly mirrored.

His muscular body tensed as he held himself up on one arm, bringing his spare hand to the mark on her chest. He touched it gingerly, and then covered it with his palm, feeling her heart beat underneath the silvery scar between her full breasts.

She copied him, raising her hand to his and covering it with her palm.

"And the way the two loved each other…" he whispered the start of *their* quote, waiting for her to finish it.

She smiled up to him. "…it was as if they were one."

* * * *

Her head rose and fell with each breath he took, his ribs strong underneath her cheek. He played with her long hair, brushing her strands out with his fingers.

"I love you, Jessop, and I always have," he spoke, touching her temple softly.

She couldn't help but smile, kissing a scar on his rib cage. "I'm not sure about that," she teased.

His fingers froze in her hair. "What do you mean?"

She turned over, resting on his chest, facing him. "There was a time when you thought I was quite the annoyance…simply your responsibility."

He smiled back at her. "We were young."

"Very," she spoke softly against his skin.

"I loved you then, too. I loved you from the start. I loved the way you looked at me…Like you needed me. You needed me to keep you safe, and I needed you to feel less alone in the world. I loved the way your green eyes watched me as I trained. I loved the way you saw my future—*our* future—before anyone else did. I definitely loved you then, I simply didn't know it yet."

CHAPTER 2

Beyond the Grey
Thirteen years ago

Jessop knew she was supposed to be collecting wood, but they already had a bunch sitting right outside their front door. Plus, she hadn't seen Mar'e in days, not since before the Kuroi girl's excursion through the desert, a ritual for all who had reached twelve years of age.

Mar'e had told her it was just a *really* long walk, where they had all followed a tribal elder around, discussing sands and winds during the day, and stars and signs in the night. Jessop wouldn't admit it to the other girl, because it would have brought her too much satisfaction, but she *was* jealous. She was only part Kuroi and that exempted her from tribal rites of passage. Despite this, the elders were good to her, recognizing her and her mother as being of their people. They let them live in the green, walk their lands, visit in their shelters, trade and work with their people. Dezane DeHawn, the true elder, had been a constant source of kindness to her all her life.

"It was very intense," Mar'e concluded, nodding slowly, like she had some newfound wisdom that Jessop didn't.

Jessop shrugged. "It doesn't sound that intense."

The other girl squinted her glowing yellow eyes. "Well, *it was.*"

"If you say so," Jessop chided, getting to her feet. She didn't want to listen to Mar'e talk about the excursion anymore. She should have just gone to find more wood.

"Jessop, you're not Kuroi, you don't know," her friend snapped back, getting to her feet just as fast.

"Who are you, Mar'e Makenen, to decide who is and is not Kuroi?" The voice of Dezane DeHawn startled them both. Jessop spun around to see the true elder standing several paces away, perfectly still as he watched them. His dark skin shone under the bright light of midday, his robes tucked around old lines of well-fortified muscle. His bright green eyes glowed at them both, emeralds on fire. The leader of the Kuroi inclined his head at the young girls. He was older than any knew, but he wasn't *aged*. "Jessop may not be full blood, but her eyes shine as mine do, and her Kuroi tongue is better than all of those her age—yourself included." Dezane spoke to Mar'e, but kept his eyes on Jessop.

She smiled up to the elder, thankful for his support.

Dezane's soft smile turned to a frown. "There are foreign travelers in our parts today. Both of you should get yourselves home, *now*."

Jessop shivered, thinking of the telepath with the dark eyes, the one who always traveled with a younger companion. She kept her gaze fixed on Dezane. "You mean those men with mind control?"

"They are telepaths, and many of them possess telekinesis, yes, but they do not control minds. Your mind can only be controlled if you let it be, Jessop." She knew that in this, as in everything, Dezane was right. But it didn't stop her from seeing the cloaked figure, drunk, yelling at his boy, moving everything from errant barrels to slow-moving people out of his way with just a flick of his hand. It was difficult for her to understand being able to control a whole human body, but not a small human mind.

"Return home," Dezane reiterated. Jessop would have usually hugged Mar'e goodbye, but not today. She offered a tight smile to her friend and a sincere one to Dezane before turning on her heel away from the village.

* * * *

Jessop crossed the desert sands quickly, her leather sandals light on the golden granules. The forest was just up ahead, the one salvation from the dunes. It was an oddity to find a lush forest in the middle of the desert, and many who passed through simply stared at it as though it were a mirage, some false salvation. It was no mirage though. It was her home. Her part of the world with her parents, where no one else lived and no one else entered. One may have thought it would have been lonely being ostracized to the woodlands by the Kuroi, but not Jessop. She knew the soft ground, the trees, the creatures, their shadows and their movements, as well as she knew herself. Plus, she wasn't alone. She had her parents.

Mar'e hated her own mother and father. So did most of the village children it seemed...but not Jessop. Her father, Hoda Jero, had taught her how to track the creatures of both the forest and the desert. He had shown her how to follow the side winding of a snake and the swoops of any bird. He was determined for her to know their lands as well as any full-blooded Kuroi, probably because he knew them in such ways despite possessing no Kuroi blood. Her mother, Octayn Jero, was Jessop's best friend, and the most beautiful woman she had ever seen. She possessed the Kuroi blood, and with it, the same glowing green eyes her daughter had inherited. And she had endlessly flowing fair hair that she let Jessop braid every night after supper.

Jessop didn't need Mar'e, or anyone else. She had her parents, and her forest, and she was fairly certain that was all she would ever need. She ducked into the shade of the trees, curving under a low hanging branch. Immediately, she felt at ease. Mar'e was a spiteful friend. That was what her mother had called her. Her parents had told her much about Mar'e. They had explained that her friend felt Jessop's mixed lineage rendered her somehow inferior, despite her superior skills in all things Kuroi. They had told her this was not Jessop's problem, but Mar'e's. Jessop and the girl had a relationship that swung from hatred to love on a near daily basis, and Jessop shouldn't shoulder the misconceptions of her friend.

Jessop stepped over a fallen branch, and moved expertly around a thick mud pit. She didn't—

Her thoughts were interrupted by the sound of screaming. Her feet stopped. Her heart stopped. And then, all at once, everything started back up again at lightning speed. She took off into the shadows of the forest, weaving through the trees, expertly navigating the treacherous soft ground, swinging over and under, through the thick line of trees. She leapt into the clearing, where her home was nestled against the belly of a mountain. She waited on bended knee, scanning the perimeter. The front door to her house was open.

She didn't know what she was waiting for. Her mother. Or her father. She wanted to see one of them emerge from the house, mid-errand, a smile appearing as they saw she had returned. But she saw nothing. At the sound of her mother screaming again, she ran for the door.

* * * *

Her father was dead. Of this, she was certain. And it made her want to crawl up beside him and die right along with him, resting in his arms. The room was a scene of mayhem. There was the boy—the telepath—kneeling beside her father, and the older man with his hands wrapped around her mother's neck. And there was Jessop, just standing there. She may have breathed, may have moved an inch, and the boy saw her. He jerked his head up from her father, and stared at her with large gray eyes.

"Get out!" he screamed, his face contorting in pain. He flung his arm out and somehow, using those abilities his kind had, made Jessop fly back. She hit the door behind her, sliding down the wood to the ground. She shook her head, getting to her knees. The boy had fixed his gaze on her father, his hands hovering above the older man's chest. Jessop didn't know what he was doing, but she sensed he was trying to help him.

She looked at all the blood her father was bathed in. His entire chest and neck were crimson. The blood soaked the tunic Jessop's mother had just finished for him. It soaked the wooden floor Jessop had cleaned just that morning. It soaked the hands of the boy trying to fix a mortal wound. Jessop couldn't feel anything. She couldn't make sense of anything. She got to her feet and took a small step towards her father and the boy.

With a heavy thud, dishes came flying to the ground, crashing around her mother and the old telepath attacking her. He rammed her body back against the cabinets once more, his hands tight around her neck. Jessop scanned the ground for a weapon, for something to stop the man with, and her eyes fell back on the boy.

"Stop him."

Her voice was small, but it was a command that the boy leapt at. He threw his hands out at his master and focused with intensity, his eyes narrowing, his arms shaking. To Jessop's amazement, the older man was jerked away from Jessop's mother, and thrown into the wall. The young boy began to shake, forcing his master to stay in place against the wall.

"Run! Run!" He screamed his directive at Jessop. But her mother was collapsed on the ground. She ducked around the boy and slid under the giant wooden table, coming to her mother's side.

"Wake up, wake up!" she screamed, grabbing her mother's face and shaking her. There were dark red marks around her small neck, and a wound on her head, staining her fair locks with blood.

"*Run!*" The boy's voice shook through her. She snapped her head up just in time to see the older man break free from the boy's hold. He waved his hands and just like that, he could move again.

The older man lunged at the boy. "You dare betray me for these savages, Falco Bane? Me?"

Jessop turned her gaze back to her mother, who lay motionless. Tears fell from her and landed on her mother's cheek, "Please, *please*, get up." Nothing. No movement. A crashing sound above her elicited the greatest scream she had ever produced. The man had tossed the boy across the table. His body flew into the cabinet and landed abruptly beside Jessop and her mother. He looked at her with his sad gray eyes, blood coming from his mouth, and pleaded with her. "Get out of here."

He then leapt over the table, and Jessop heard a cacophony of destruction behind her. Swords struck one another and the older man yelled at the boy for his betrayal. There was a giant *thud* and the now familiar sound of a body collapsing. She did not know what to do, certain the man had bested the boy. She threw her body over her mother's, holding her tightly to protect her from whatever he had planned. But he never came.

There was a slam of the door and she jolted up. He had left them, even the boy, who now lay in a heap on the floor beside her father. His cloak was spread out around him like black wings, his sword fallen a few feet away from his now open-palmed hand. Slowly, Jessop got to her feet. If the boy lived, they could carry his mother to the village. Dezane would know how to fix this. She crept under the table and crawled to the boy, trying to keep her eyes fixed on him, forcing herself to look away from her father.

"Wake up," she urged, grabbing his hand. He lay motionless. She sat beside him, her hands grabbing his pale face as they had her mother's. She shook him more vigorously. "Wake up, get up." She patted his cheeks, trying to rouse him. She shook him, more urgently, as the distinct smell of smoke began to fill the room. The man had somehow lit a fire. She didn't know how, but flames were rising, with no source, over the walls.

"Get up!" She screamed, shaking the boy. He did not move. She fell away from him, her eyes landing on her father, motionless, then her mother, who was only inches away from the flames. She bolted to her mother's side, grabbing her arm and using all her might to pull her away from the walls. As if knowing her intentions, the flames jumped from the cabinet to the table, onto an overturned chair, following her.

She needed Dezane; she needed help from the village. She dragged her mother as close to the boy as possible, resting her between the boy and her father. She stood and immediately began to cough on smoke. She needed to hurry. She ran to the door and grabbed the wooden handle, pulling with all her might. But it did not budge. Something had forced it shut. She pulled to no avail. She released the handle as flames began to travel over the doorway, closing around her.

She quickly leapt for the window, shoving the burning wooden shutters out, releasing a wave of air that gave new life to the flames. She shielded her face, and while she did not feel the fire, she saw it lick past her. It did not matter; she could not shy away from the flames now, not with so little time left. She grabbed the window frame and heaved herself up, teetering in the box, blind from the smoke, coughing, the smell of charring flesh tickling her nose. She rocked her small body forward but before she could move any further, strong hands grabbed her. Through the smoke she saw the dark, evil eyes of the man. She wanted to scream, but she couldn't. She wanted to wrap her little hands around his throat and take his life away. He said nothing to her, but with a violent thrust, he threw her small body back into the burning cottage. She hit the ground heavily, rolling to her side as she choked on black smoke.

She had never felt this way before. It was more than fear, more than sorrow. This was simply it. Her life would be over, very soon, as she would perish in the fire with her family, and the gray-eyed boy. She crawled to her parents, staying as low to the ground as she could. She knew she was crying, but it was too hot for the tears to reach her cheeks.

She kissed her father's forehead, and rolled over him to reach her mother. She had not moved, had not stirred at all. She kissed her cheek, and embraced her still body. A beam fell from the ceiling, crushing the table behind them. She shook with fear, holding her mother tighter as shingles from the roof fell, travelling in ash and fire, around them.

"I love you," she cried, shaking against her mother's chest. She did not turn from her mother, did not look his way, but she did not want the boy to feel as though he were dying alone. She reached out to her side and found his hand, lacing her fingers through his. He had tried to save her parents; she knew that much to be true. He had tried to save her. He did not deserve to die without comfort.

The flames were closer now. The snapping of wood, the splintering of their home, their lives, echoed all around her. The fire crackled with preternatural rage and strength, attacking the home in all its simplicity and beauty, destroying everything Jessop had ever loved.

She squeezed her eyes tightly shut. She was not afraid of dying; she knew she would stop breathing long before the burns took her. She thought of Mar'e and wondered who would tell the Kuroi girl that her best friend, whom she had been so cruel to, had perished. She thought of Dezane and wondered how he would cry at this loss, and how he would tell his people. She wondered if there would be a ceremony, something done with all of their ashes perhaps.

She burrowed her face further against her mother and thought of the day before this one. The three of them had walked through the forest, her mother had collected fruits, her father had cut a new path for them to reach the reservoir. She had collected small stones and fallen leaves and the odd desert flower as she followed alongside them. It had been a beautiful day.

Suddenly, just as she was falling into their last moments together, Jessop was wrenched away from her mother. She tried to scream, but nothing came out. The boy had risen and he held her in his arms, forcing her small face into his chest. She fought him, somehow finding her feet. He kept an arm around her back, keeping her near. Smoke and sweat had stained his face, dark blood still pooled around his mouth and near his ear. He had his sword in his hand.

His hood had fallen back and he looked at her with a sadness that could have floored her. Suddenly, he threw his sword-wielding hand out before him, and the space where the door had once been was blown away with a deafening explosion, creating a hole in the wall, an escape from the flames. He forced her further away from her parents and she tried to fight him.

She needed to get her mother, she needed to pull her free. He was bigger than her and much stronger. She flailed against him but he barely seemed to notice, forcing her out of the cottage. They fell to the grass only feet away from the flames. She wriggled free, crawling away from him. She tried to blink to clear her vision, but it was an assault on her eyes. Her skin was warm to the touch, her mouth completely dry. The old man was gone.

She leapt past the boy, determined to make her way back through the flames for her mother. But he was quick. He grabbed her ankle, and with no mercy or hesitation, he dragged her away from the inferno. Somehow, she found her voice, and she screamed and screamed. She kicked at him and fought him. She curled up and attacked the hand that held her ankle. In an instant, he fell to the ground on top of her, pinning her still.

"They're gone. They were gone before the flames got them. I'm sorry," he yelled. She knew he was right. She knew what he said was true and she had known it before he freed her, but still, his words were her own death. She buckled over, sobbing tears that barely came, choking on black smoke, fighting him as he kept her safe.

That man had killed her best friends, her parents. She had nothing anymore. She had no one. She wished she had died alongside them.

The boy held her close against his chest, rocking her body slowly as she cried. "You have me."

CHAPTER 3

Beyond the Grey

Thirteen years ago

When Jessop woke, she was by the reservoir, lying on her side. She blinked and a heron flew off the surface of the smooth water. She took a deep breath, rolling to her back. Why was she here? She hadn't planned on going to the reservoir. The sky was changing already—darkening. Clouds rolled into one. There was a dark cloud, or was it smoke? The distinct smell of burning filled her nostrils and she thought she might be ill. She rolled to her side and suddenly saw the boy. With just one look at his charcoal-smudged face, she remembered everything.

She didn't feel fear towards him, though she knew she should. He was one of *them*. His master had killed her family. The thought of it, the smell of the crisp burned wood and flesh, the memory of red fire circling them, it was too much to contain. She rolled onto her side, turning her back to the boy, and heaved. She didn't want him to come near her, to attempt to soothe her. She was thankful to find he didn't.

She wiped her mouth on the back of her hand, noticing how her fingers and arms had distinctly fewer black smoke stains than the boy's. She watched him using his cloak to clean his skin and knew he must have done the same for her. It was odd to think he had cleaned her, tended to her, in her unconsciousness. She took a deep breath, surprised to learn she could. Her chest did not ache with fire damage.

"I healed you," he answered her unspoken thoughts.

Of course he knew her mind; he was a telepath. That was what *their* kind could do. She shot him her most critical stare. "What do you mean?"

He turned back to the water, dampening his cloak once more before scrubbing his neck. "I healed your lungs. It is something only I can do," he answered. His words were very matter-of-fact. He may have sounded arrogant, but Jessop thought he also somehow sounded lonely. As though being singular was the most isolating feeling in the world. She wanted to tell him it wasn't—losing your family was.

She thought of her parents, and her chest fluttered with hope. "If you can heal, then why are we still here? My mother and father," she began, jumping to her feet.

He was on his feet in an instant, standing before her, his hands out to stop her. "I can't...I can't heal the dead."

She looked up into his gray eyes and wanted to tell him otherwise, wanted to somehow talk him into being able to do it, as if that were even possible. "But—"

"I couldn't even heal your father before...His wounds were too grave. I tried. I tried so hard I was too drained to fight. I'm sorry."

She narrowed her eyes at him. How could he be sorry? He had come here and helped ruin her life. "I wish you'd let me die with them."

He nodded down at her slowly before turning back to the water. "I know you do."

* * * *

His name was Falco Bane. As soon as he introduced himself to Dezane, she remembered the man—*Hydo Jesuin*—saying it before, in her home. Dezane had shown up, with his warriors in tow, ready to save them. He said he saw the smoke in the distance—an impressive feat in itself, Jessop knew—and readied his fighters as quickly as possible. They had simply been too late.

Two of the warriors who had known her parents well wept openly, comforted by their comrades. Dezane had silent tears as he stared at Jessop, unable to take his sad eyes off of her. She had hugged him for the longest time, wishing that if the boy couldn't fix this, then perhaps Dezane—a true elder—could. But he couldn't. No one could. They were gone and she was supposed to live without them.

They had made the slow walk back to the village, leaving her scorched home behind. Jessop wasn't really with them though, even if she walked in the center of their group. Her heart was burned to ash with her parents, her mind was soaring above with the falcons, her body was nothing but a mobile corpse. The boy may have thought he saved her from that blaze, but she had died with her parents.

They had made their way to the council tent, where the elders convened on all their important matters. The Kuroi tents were grand structures; fixed out of hide and wood, they stood some forty feet high, many as high as the trees that surrounded her home. That *used* to surround her home.

As they had walked through the village, Kuroi tribesmen she knew stood outside their home tents and wept for her, welcoming back their loved ones who had been too late to save the family that lived in the green. They may have shown her sympathy, but she knew they were grateful it was her family who had died and not theirs. She couldn't blame them. She would have felt the same.

She sat with Dezane DeHawn and the boy in the council tent, as it grew darker and darker around the world. She thought it might be raining, with the slow pattering against the tent walls, but she wasn't sure. She wasn't sure of anything anymore. She rocked slowly back and forth on her haunches, listening to the boy talk to Dezane.

"He has been like this for too long...he acts wholly different in the Blade, but when we come here, it is to torment your people, as you know all too well. It is time for the Assembly Council to learn his true nature."

Jessop couldn't help but notice how he didn't speak like a boy, but like a man. It wasn't just because his voice was deep—it was something else. He had authority, and power, and the confidence that came with true power. He spoke to Dezane like they were equals, though one was a great elder and the other just a gray-eyed telepath.

"You hide your scars well under your cloak and tunic, boy, but I know we are not the only ones that man has tortured," Dezane answered. Jessop didn't know what he was referring to, but Dezane often spoke of things she did not know.

"My scars matter not. There are many who know the truth of my nature, of my destiny. I do not fear Hydo."

Dezane nodded thoughtfully. "It has been spoken about even here. My son, Trax, has told me much about you. The next true Lord and Protector."

Jessop wasn't following their conversation. She was hearing the words they were speaking, and she knew of Trax, Dezane's son who had been raised with the telepaths, but she didn't know what they were talking about—or *why* they were talking about it. Her parents had been killed; nothing they were talking about mattered.

The tent flap hit the back of the canvas wall with the muted clap of hide meeting hide. A young warrior with glowing blue eyes appeared in the dark entryway. He ducked into the tent, and Jessop saw in his hand a flaming torch. As the young man made his way towards the fire pit in the center of the tent, Jessop suddenly stopped breathing. The air in her body simply disappeared. It felt as though something were attacking her, and she scurried back on her palms, knowing she needed to put distance between herself and the warrior. As her back hit a wooden post in the tent wall she knew she was trapped. She grabbed her chest; she could feel her racing heart, panicking as her body fought for air. Her eyes wide though she saw only darkness and fire.

She heard the boy yell, "Get out!"

She saw nothing but the flames, felt nothing but the smoke filling her lungs once again. He had said he had healed her—had it been some trick? Had he been mistaken and she was now dying a delayed death from the smoke?

Her vision disappeared as she fell to the side, her face hitting the dusty ground with a heavy thud. There was a ringing sound, the source of which she did not know. As her chest fluttered with futile attempts to breathe, her fingers loosened their hold on her breastbone. She was going to be with her parents now. She closed her eyes, feeling her chest deflate further and further. Suddenly, strong hands pulled her up. She was being held in someone's arms, her back forced against a chest much stronger than hers.

She could feel a heartbeat—but not her own. *His.* She felt it through his chest, through her back, near her own.

He held her tightly. "Breathe with me," he ordered her. His chest expanded, pushing into her back. His breaths were deep and slow. She somehow opened her eyes; the tent wall appeared fuzzy before her. Dezane was crouched near, but his edges were blurred, and she could not make out the features of his face. She felt the rhythmic thumping of the boy's heart, and it was all she could focus on.

"Breathe with me," he spoke again, his voice softer. And without having to think about it, she did. She breathed with him. Her chest rose as his did, and slowly fell, as his did. They stayed that way until her heartbeat found normalcy, until her vision corrected. Once she'd recovered, he let her go. She turned in his arms and looked into his gray eyes and knew something about him with such certainty, despite how odd it was to know. She knew this boy would always save her.

Jessop knew that she needed Falco, and as she studied his concerned face, the way in which he held her close, her eyes traveled down his neck. Where his tunic was pulled low, she saw lines. Hundreds of silvery lines, all crossing over one another, peeking out under his collar; they were scars.

She knew then that not only did she need him, but he, who held her with such conviction, tight against his mangled body, needed her too.

* * * *

"Did he say when he would be back?" Mar'e asked, readjusting the ochre-dyed shift she wore. Jessop copied her, tightening her own cloth dress. Falco had left her with the Kuroi while he returned to Azgul, the city where his master resided. He had spent several days with her first, explaining to her where the Hunters of Infinity worked, *how* they worked, and why he needed to be the one to confront Hydo. She had asked him how he intended to best his mentor, when he couldn't fight him off the day of the fire. "I had expended my energy trying to heal..." He had let his voice trail off, his gaze fall from her. "It matters not. I can do this. I know my brothers will help me." While she feared his departure, he had spoken of his many brothers in the Glass Blade, where they lived and trained—and assured her he would return safely. He said he thought of at least several brothers who would return with him.

Jessop began to work on her braid. "He just said it wouldn't be long."

Mar'e stared at her skeptically. "He's very beautiful, you know."

Jessop crinkled her nose at the girl's words. She wondered if she and Mar'e were truly friends. She did not understand how the girl spoke to her about Falco so soon after what had happened to her family.

"You think I want to talk about him with you?"

The Kuroi girl sighed heavily. "I don't know what is and isn't safe to talk about with you anymore. I don't know anyone who lost their parents."

Jessop glared at the girl. Mar'e had known her parents. She had slept in their home. She had spoken with them. She had eaten their food. Jessop had expected her to mourn in the same manner she did. They stayed silent for many minutes, uncomfortable.

Mar'e shifted nearer. "I saw you two, the morning he left, walking."

Jessop thought back to that morning. The sky had been gray, like his eyes, and there was a welcoming chill in the desert air. "Once it's done, I'll come back for you. We will make arrangements." He had spoken to her with a soft voice, always dancing around the pointed words. He avoided saying anything about her parents. He simply wanted her to know he would make sure she was taken care of. That his mentor wouldn't get away with his trespasses against her.

"You don't have to feel responsible for me. It wasn't your fault." She had been terrified of speaking the words to him. She thought that maybe, if she told him he could be free of her, he would truly never return. But she didn't want him to return out of guilt. She didn't even want him to return to take care of her. She had the Kuroi. She just wanted him to return. He had shaken his head down at her. "It's not like that." He touched her face softly, his fingertips grazing her temple. He closed his eyes and seemed to focus. Jessop didn't know his kind. She had seen him do much and had heard there was much more he could do that she had yet to witness. All she knew was that she did not fear him. He blinked, opening his gray eyes to her slowly. "You're different. I can't tell what it is…But I know you're like me somehow."

She had stared at the ground, confused by his words. "I don't know about that."

He had raised her chin with his hand, willing her to look back at him. "I do."

Jessop pushed the memory back, returning her attention to Mar'e. "You saw us walking—what of it?"

"You don't even know each other and you act like you have this unspoken bond. You walk with one another as though you'd been doing it for years." Her voice was sharp—jealous.

Jessop narrowed her eyes at her friend. "You don't get it."

"Then explain it to me, Jessop."

"He's alone, Mar'e. Alone like I am alone."

She cocked her head and her dark braids fell over her shoulder. "His family died too?"

Jessop knew Mar'e meant no insult. She simply didn't understand. "No. I don't know. But it's not like *that*. Not that kind of alone. Alone because he's different."

Mar'e nodded, her eyes softening. She looked about the space in the tented room, as though ensuring they were alone. "I *do* know what you mean. He's different like you. Like what the Kuroi speak of."

Jessop didn't know what Mar'e was saying. She crossed her arms over her chest, feeling defensive. "What do they speak of?"

"I'm not supposed to say."

"*Mar'e.*"

"Fine. But remain silent over it. I do not always say you aren't Kuroi because of your bloodline, Jessop. I don't even say it to just criticize you, even though sometimes I know I say it to be cruel…I say it because I have heard my parents speak of it. I heard them talk about how you and your family are different."

Jessop felt her skin prickle at the words. "What are you talking about?" Her tone was angry. Defensive. Mar'e had lied to her before and she was possibly lying to her again simply to feel superior once more. "I don't know any more. That's the truth. All I know is that I heard them talking. Not about how you and your mother were part Kuroi, but how you were part something *else*."

Jessop studied her friend's face. Mar'e seemed excited, as though she relished having secrets to tell. Jessop didn't think the girl spoke the truth. But she thought of what Falco had said to her. She was different. She shook her head, arguing against the thought. Maybe she was different, maybe she wasn't, but if there had been something about her family, her parents or Dezane would have told her. She gruffly walked past Mar'e. "Don't talk about my mother."

*   *   *   *

She didn't understand why the ashes were still smoking. She didn't understand how a week ago, this had been her home, her parents…her whole world. It had burned entirely to the ground—not an intact dish or surviving piece of furniture. No parents. Hydo's wicked magic had given the fire life, a dreadful ability to decimate that which a natural flame would have left simply licked.

She closed her eyes and stepped onto the ashes. She was surprised to learn they were not hot against her feet. Was she numb to new pain now? She kept her eyes shut and raised her hand out before her. In her mind, she saw her front door, her hand wrapping around the lever to open it. She stepped through the wooden entryway, and the smell of fresh flat bread replaced that of charred flesh. Her mother was polishing a dish, her father cutting meat. It was mealtime. They looked to her and smiled. She stepped around the table and approached them, ready to be enveloped in her parents' embrace.

But as her extended arms locked tightly around nothing, she opened her eyes. She was standing right where they should have been, but of course, they weren't. She let her arms fall to her sides. She knelt down and pushed her hand into the hot ash. She wanted Hydo to die—she maybe even wanted Falco to be the one to kill him. But if he couldn't, she would do it. Maybe not today, or even in a year…She needed to grow; she knew she couldn't fight anyone at this size, except maybe Mar'e. But as she lifted her palm and watched the ashes of her life and all that she had loved trickle through her fingers, she knew she would kill him. Given the chance, she would take everything he ever loved, and set fire to it.

* * * *

The fire was moving with a mystical force. The noise of the flames was deafening. The fire hadn't killed them though; *he* had. The smell of smoke was overwhelming. The red of the flame, the way it lit up everything it intended to destroy, filled her with dread.

Jessop. She didn't know who spoke her name, though the voice sounded so familiar. *Jessop.* She spun about the room, though she saw no one. No one but her parents. They were side by side. The fire getting closer. The room collapsing around them. *Jessop!* Someone grabbed her violently—

Jessop woke with a start, scrambling forward. As she crawled away from the pelts of her bed, her hand finding the cool wall of the tent, she realized it had simply been another nightmare. Her heart raced. Her skin was slick with sweat. Her nights were plagued with terror as she slept alone in the tent Dezane had allocated to her. Every night had been the same since Falco left. She was back in the fire. She woke. She thought of how she'd kill Hydo Jesuin one day.

Though Hydo was not the only one who she thought of. She thought about Falco. Dezane had arranged the first leg of the boy's travel, getting him on a Soar-Craft out of Okton Radon. But that was all he could do for him; the rest was up to Falco to figure out. Thinking about him worried her. He was barely older than her, at ten and four years—she couldn't imagine doing what he set out to do. He had powers though, abilities they had taught him, the sorcery the Hunter kind were known for—different from Kuroi power, darker. She hoped that what was said about him was true, that he was the best there ever was.

From what she had seen of him so far, she believed it.

* * * *

Every day Jessop returned to her home. Or at least to what was left of it. Every day she promised herself she would not come the following. That she would say goodbye and mean it. Then the following morning arrived and she was walking back without hesitation.

The ashes had finally stopped smoking. She had taken to sitting among the burned remains, to be near to *them* still. She spoke to them as though they were still there. She pretended they were listening. She told them of her anger, her plans for vengeance, of Falco Bane and the thousands of scars on his body. She had only seen those that stuck out of collars, the jagged ends on the periphery of his limbs, but she knew they were countless. She had not asked, and he had not volunteered any information.

In a few days it would be her birthday. She would be ten and three. "The first one I will have where you two won't be there."

She ran her fingers softly through the ashes. "Dezane weeps for you still," she said, changing the subject quickly. She offered up the information on Dezane, speaking as though she herself did not weep, when she did.

She rubbed her small fingertips together, brushing the ash away. "Many do, still. I suppose many will for a long time."

She crossed her arms over her small body and leaned forward. She had not spoken about what Mar'e had said—not to the ashes and not to Dezane. She had barely spoken to the girl since she had shared her secrets. "I don't want you to worry about me. Dezane cares for me well, and Falco will return for me. He promised he would."

She would have felt foolish saying the words out loud if she didn't already know how absurd it was to be speaking to the ashes of her dead parents. The words were true though. In those first few days, no matter how hard she had tried to fear him, she couldn't. He had saved her and he alone had seemed to understand her pain. Her loneliness.

There were none like him and she understood that he had been treated differently for his uniqueness. She was willing to treat him however he wished to be treated—she owed him that. "He's different, you know. I'm not sure how yet, we don't know each other very well, I guess. But I could tell when I couldn't breathe, and he knew how to fix it. He knows my pain. He's felt it.

"Dezane believes in him too, I think. I mean, *I know*. They talked about his future, and the future of the Kuroi. He cares for the Kuroi, but his eyes are not like ours, Mother. He is like Father, someone who feels comfortable with the Kuroi.

"He's going to be—" but Jessop's words were cut short as her eyes caught the quickest glimmer of metal in the sky. It had disappeared behind the tree line, and within seconds there was the unmistakable sound of a crash.

* * * *

The Soar-Craft was lodged into the sand, smoking. It had left a skid trail for sixty paces at least. Jessop stared at the mangled silver ship, and at the face of the unconscious boy behind the glass windshield. She barely recognized Falco—he was covered in so much blood. Her heart began to race. Smoke was rising from the back of the craft. She knew the Kuroi villagers had heard the crash and would be coming, but once again, they would be too late to save anyone.

Jessop wanted to retreat from the smoke, watching it with an angry suspicion, but she couldn't leave him to die. Not when he had saved her. Not when she needed him so greatly. The doorway to the craft was lodged several feet under sand; there would be no prying it open in time. She eyed the ground around her, looking for something—*anything*—that would help her break him free. She saw nothing, and the smoke was thickening.

She took a step closer. "*Fal—*" Her scream halted as she stubbed her foot on something hot and sharp. She hissed at the pain, but forgot the injury entirely as her eyes fell upon a piece of scrap metal. She was unsure what it was; it looked like a giant bolt, almost too large for her to hold in one hand. It didn't matter what it was or where it came from, though, it could work. She grabbed it up, ignoring the way its heated metal could harm her hand. With an agile leap, she was on the hood of the craft. She knelt before the windshield, her adrenaline too great to feel the scorching metal melding to her kneecaps.

"*Falco!*" She screamed, banging on the windshield with her hand. He did not stir. She drew her arm back, clutched the giant bolt tightly, and punched the windshield with all her might. There was not enough space on the bolt for her to hide her fingers, to shield them from the impact. They crunched unnaturally as they met the glass. Tears welled in her eyes, but the glass had the faintest crack in it, and that urged her to once again wind up.

She hit the windshield again, certain bones were breaking between the metal and glass. "*Wake up!*" On her third strike, he stirred. She saw his eyes, blinking away blood. "*Falco!*" She screamed with urgency and encouragement. She hit the windshield again and again, ignoring the pain shooting up her arm. Suddenly, he was alert, and coughing. Smoke was filling the cockpit.

She hit the shield with all her might, the crack growing like a vein in the glass. She watched him raise his hand out towards the glass. The windshield began to shake, but he was too weak to break it on his own. She could smell the fire and her heart urged her to run. She thought of her parents and knew what the flames could do to him. What they could have done to her if he hadn't saved her.

With every ounce of strength she had in her small body, Jessop slammed the metal bolt into the windshield. Her hand went straight through the glass, shattering bones along with the windshield. She reflexively dropped the bolt onto the dash, her hand limp. Falco lunged forward, leaping out of the Soar-Craft. He grabbed her and they fell from the vehicle. They ran, limping and bleeding, away from the vessel. Within seconds, the Soar-Craft erupted in flames.

He threw his body on top of her, crushing her into the sand. Debris landed all around them, but somehow, they were not hit. She squinted up at his bloodied, unrecognizable face, and knew he was gravely injured. His blood dripped over her freely, pooling around her neck. He would lose consciousness again soon. She pushed him off her and he rolled onto his back.

She ripped cloth from her tunic and forced it against his face. The material was drenched in an instant. She squeezed it tightly over the sand, ignoring the screaming pain of her broken hand, and reapplied it. He had many wounds, but worst of all was one to his face. His beautiful, handsome face had been cut. A giant laceration traveled through his left brow, over his eye, down his cheek.

* * * *

He hadn't lost the eye, which was a miracle. Tribesmen had seen the smoke from the crash and had been quick to come to Falco's aid. Dezane had worked on his injuries personally, using his knowledge of plants and Kuroi magic to heal him. He had applied a thick poultice, covering half of Falco's face. He had worked alone, instructing everyone except Jessop out of the tent. He burned herbs in a small pot, filling the room with a strong and foreign scent. The smell and the heat made Jessop feel ill, but she refused to leave Falco's side. She watched as Dezane rested his hands over the poultice, whispering chants for many hours.

Jessop didn't know how long had passed, but she woke to Dezane softly nudging her shoulder. She had fallen asleep beside Falco. His face had remained heavily bandaged. She looked to Dezane, questions hanging on her lip. He raised his hand to stay her. "He will survive, and his vision will be fine, though he will always bear the scar." She nodded, thankful. Jessop knew some part of Dezane was aware of the fact that she needed Falco. Another part knew that the Kuroi elder sensed Falco's power, and believed he was destined to lead.

Falco's face remained dressed for many days. He did not seem to despair over the cut, his vanity completely abandoned as he suffered an intangible pain. "They betrayed me."

Jessop held his hand softly, tucked between her good one and her bandaged, broken one. She nodded at him as he spoke. They hadn't left the tent in days. Food and water was brought to them. "Hydo hid behind them all...You should have seen the way Kohl looked at me. Like *I* was the insane one. He wouldn't even listen to me."

She had learned that Kohl, the boy Falco spoke of most, with the greatest vitriol, had been his best friend. That it was he who had cut Falco's face. Falco had said Trax DeHawn, Dezane's son, had helped him escape, but barely. He had fought many of his brothers, those who he had originally thought would take on Hydo *with* him. "I didn't kill any of them. Even if they deserved it."

She didn't know what to say to him. She had never killed. She knew nothing of fighting. Despite their bond, they were still strangers to one another, who had led vastly different lives. "Come here," he ordered, eyeing her over with his one uncovered gray eye. She inched closer to where he rested on his cured hides and pelts, ensuring his hand stayed locked in her own.

"Today is the Red Solstice."

She nodded, already knowing what the day was. It was the first solstice without her parents. He brought her wounded hand closer to him, resting it against his chest. "It's my day of Partus," he added.

She cocked her head at him, stunned at the admission. "Mine as well." He smiled softly, nodding, as though he knew that they must have shared a Partus—their day of birth. He closed his eye, covering her hand with his own, concentrating carefully. She felt the bones correcting, the skin repairing. As he opened his eye, he freed her hand. She pulled the bandages off and stretched her healed fingers out, amazed. He had healed her internal wounds the day of the fire—something incredible, but invisible to her eyes. Her hand, though, she could see. She could twist her wrist and clench her fist and *see* the amazing results of his abilities. She could see what beautiful things he was capable of.

"I am thankful for you, Jessop," he smiled. The words one would speak to another on their day of Partus—an honor for one to be thankful for the other's birth.

She took his hand back in hers; letting her freshly repaired fingers lock around his. "I am thankful for you as well, Falco."

* * * *

Jessop rounded one of the many villager tents, careful as she maneuvered pails of water retrieved from the reservoir. Dezane had sent a warrior for her, requesting she speak with him. She had left Falco in the tent they had come to share. He moved with ease, having removed the bandages from his face. His scar was raised and puffy, pink and sore, but his vision, as Dezane had promised, was intact.

"*Dorei Dorei*, Dezane," she spoke the formal greeting, remaining outside his tent until he responded.

"Come, Jessop Jero."

She ducked through the large flaps and found Dezane sitting, cross-legged, in the center of his tent. His hands rested on his knees. He had moved his belongings, pushing his pelts and floor mats aside, and sat directly on the ground. She studied him, wondering what he might have been doing.

"Meditation, Jessop. I think on things for long periods of time. And then I think of nothing for even longer periods." He offered her a warm smile along with his explanation, obviously noting her confused look.

She nodded. "You wished to see me?"

He extended one of his long, slender hands, indicating for her to sit opposite him. She acquiesced, mirroring his position.

He stared at her for a long moment before speaking. "Jessop, I want you to know you have a home here, with the Kuroi, for all your life."

His words seemed abrupt, though they did not surprise her. There had been talk throughout the village, since the fire. Speculation as to whether the boy would take her to Azgul or if Dezane would have her stay with the tribe. "Thank you, Dezane."

"I have spoken with the boy and I know he has great plans. Plans I intend to help see through. If he asks for you to go with him, the choice is yours to do so, but know you can stay if you wish."

She didn't know which plans he spoke of. She didn't even know when Dezane and Falco had spoken, for she had been at Falco's side since his return, but she trusted Dezane. She trusted him to always be honest with her. She tore away from his strong gaze, looking at the ground for a long moment before speaking again.

"I must ask you something."

He remained silent, waiting.

She raised her eyes, forcing herself to look at him. "Am I different? My family…are we *different*?"

His smile remained intact. "Your mother disclosed many things to me, and many things she kept private. What I know is that you are special, Jessop. The rest you needn't worry about."

She could feel her heart speeding up, fearful that Mar'e had been telling the truth. "Special how?"

"That I do not know. Only you can know. Only you can sense what resides within you. Well, you and—"

"And Falco." She finished his sentence.

Dezane nodded. "Yes, I believe Falco can sense it too."

* * * *

Several days passed before Jessop spoke to Dezane again. Falco had initiated the meeting, insisting the three of them speak. "It is the only way for you to be safe, until such a time where you can overthrow Hydo," Dezane added.

"It feels like you're telling us to hide," Jessop complained. She finally knew what Dezane and Falco had been discussing. They proposed the creation of an impenetrable city, a fortress for any who sought to be free from the Hunters. She had listened to Dezane speak for many hours. He assured her it could be done; the city would be fortified by magic from the Kuroi, from the desert, and from places in Daharia she had never heard of.

Falco looked her over slowly. A perfect silver scar traveled through his left brow, over his eyelid, down to the center of his cheek. Mar'e shied away at the sight of him now, but Jessop had found herself staring at him more frequently, more furtively.

"We *will* be hiding, Jessop, but Dezane is right. I will be pursued from this day forth by the Hunters. Word has already reached Okton Radon that I attempted some sort of coup. But we can do more than hide—we can train. I can train you."

She thought of what he proposed. She had seen his Hunter's Blade. He had shown her more of his abilities. He had shown her things she had never imagined. He had told her he could teach her how he fought, how to wield the weapon he carried—how to avenge her parents.

"You wouldn't live alone forever. More would come," Dezane explained.

She didn't voice it, but she had thought that there were worse options than just being alone with him. He had turned away from her, clearly embarrassed to have heard her errant thought. Her cheeks pinked at the realization.

She looked between Falco and Dezane. All of their futures seemed set. She knew the dangerous path she chose when she chose to live her life with the boy. They needed one another, and all of Daharia would one day need him. "What would we have to do?"

* * * *

It was their last night with the tribe. There had been no great feast, no dancing—no spectacle of her impending exit was made whatsoever. She had said a quick goodbye to Mar'e. The Kuroi girl was angry at Jessop's distance and even angrier that she was leaving. She had barely looked at Falco except to grimace at his fresh scar.

"Are you ever going to come back?" Mar'e had asked Jessop.

"I hope so."

"Or maybe I'll find you one day."

"Maybe you will."

Jessop rolled on her sleeping mat. Falco rested several feet away. Though they were in complete darkness, her vision was keen and she knew he did not sleep.

"Yes, I'm awake." Once again, he knew her unvoiced thoughts.

"How do you do *that*?"

"I can just hear you."

"Can you hear everyone?"

She saw him roll onto his back, resting his arms under his head of dark hair.

"Not Dezane. I have heard it spoken about in the Blade—no one can seem to enter the man's mind."

She thought of Dezane and felt unsurprised. If any could resist some mystical power, it would be him.

He moved again, turning to his side to stare in her direction. "I know Dezane told you that you could stay here."

She didn't know if he knew it from reading her mind or if Dezane had told him. It mattered not. "He did."

"Don't."

"What?"

"Don't stay."

"I won't. I want..." She began, but she let her voice trail off.

"You want what?"

She knew he could just hear the thought if he wanted to. He wished to hear her say the words aloud.

"I want to be where you are."

She knew he kept his gaze fixed to her. "I want that too, Jessop."

CHAPTER 4

Azgul

Present-day

Jessop ran down the hall, her linen robe beating about her knees. She rounded the corner, just in time to catch a glimpse of his golden eye and silver, star-shaped scar. She tried calling his name but her voice caught in her throat. She ran after him, tearing down the corridor. She needed to tell him—she needed to tell him he was bleeding.

"*Jessop.*"

Jessop woke to the sharp tug of Falco's hands on her. Instinctively, she clambered back in the sheets, freeing herself from him. He raised his hands away from her slowly. Sweat greased her skin, her hair stuck to her face and neck with a stickiness that stung her. It was the middle of the night.

Falco slowly reached for her, resting his hand on her shoulder. "More nightmares?"

She nodded, sweeping her hands over her face, pulling her hair back from her hot skin. "I need you to find him, Falco."

He lowered his hand from her slowly. "Kohl."

The room was perfectly dark but they saw one another with ease. It was chilly, and yet she felt on fire.

"I broke his heart…he wants vengeance, I can feel it."

She pulled the damp tunic off her body, tossing it to the ground as she moved to the side of the bed. She let her feet rest on the smooth floor and enjoyed the cool sensation. Falco readjusted to sit beside her. He held his hands together, leaning forward to regard her carefully.

"He is no threat to you."

She kept her eyes trained on the ground. "He nearly killed me."

"He caught us off guard. We both know he is no match for either of us. He will bring you no harm."

She snapped her head up to face him, studying his gray eyes in the cold darkness. "Then why do we hunt them? Him, Hanson, the others. Why must we find them if they pose no threat to us?"

The question was rhetorical, but she asked it to remind Falco that she knew his thoughts, as she knew these men. One-on-one, or even three-on-two, they were no match for her and Falco...but that did not mean they bore no threat. They were the fallen rulers of Daharia, and they had many skills and many allegiances.

At his silence, she spoke again. "You have told me many times to not underestimate them. We did just that, the day you arrived, and it nearly cost me my life. We cannot do it again. I want them found and shackled."

He held her stare for a long moment. His gray eyes appeared icy to her, cooler than usual. "You mean you want them found and *killed*, right?"

She said nothing. She saw Hanson's face from that day on the terrace, paralyzed, betrayed. Hydo deserved death; he had murdered her family. But Hanson...she did not know if she could truly sentence him to the same fate as his friend. Despite all he had done, he was no murderer.

"Jeco will never be safe around him. Hanson will always be loyal to Hydo," Falco spoke, answering her thoughts.

She quickly stood from the bed. "Don't do *that*, Falco."

He stood, throwing his arms out with frustration. "I'm sorry—but what choice are you giving me? You've been closed off for days. Since I arrived, if we're being honest, you've refused to open up to me."

She turned from him and rifled through her drawers for fresh clothes. "After months away from my family, I nearly died at the hands of someone I—"

"Someone you loved?"

She turned around slowly. Falco knew her heart, he knew her mind, and he knew she was always only ever going to be in love with him. "Someone I *betrayed*."

He nodded slowly, skeptical. "You cannot tell me he isn't in your heart. He plagues your mind each day and night. I have known you long enough to know you feel no fear—so do not pretend that the preoccupation is because of that."

She ran her hands over her damp hair. "I loved him as I love Korend'a."

"You never slept with Korend'a."

His words were a slap. She turned from him and made her way to the bathing chamber. In the illuminated room she studied the freshly twisted scar on her abdomen. It was a thick knot of mangled flesh. The sight of it, the words Falco had spoken to her, all made her want to be ill. She steadied herself against the mirror, taking slow breaths, wishing her skin were less hot, or the room less cold.

Slowly, she let her eyes trail back to the wound. She had nearly died at Kohl's hands but she couldn't say with complete confidence that *she* wanted *him* dead. If that uncertainty meant some part of her loved him then so be it. Whatever she felt for him, it was not the love that she felt for Falco.

"I'm sorry. That was wrong of me to say," Falco spoke, leaning in the doorway. She watched him through the reflection, their bright eyes locking on one another.

"Sleeping with him was part of *your* master plan, Falco."

"I know."

"Had there been another way—"

"I know."

She studied his face for some sort of sign, some indication that he truly did know her heart still, as he always had. "Can't you understand that I feel I've wounded him enough? He loved me, as you do, and I destroyed him. I do not trust him to roam free, but I do not think he deserves to die."

He nodded but he did not appear in agreement. His perfect lips were tight around his teeth. His muscles tensed as he crossed his arms over his broad chest.

"Can you not understand that he nearly took you away from me? I thought you were going to die, Jessop. Can't you see how I would want him, above all others, to suffer?"

They held one another's stares; contemplating the position their common friend—*enemy*—had put them in. Before either could speak, a small cry called out to them.

"Dada," Jeco wept.

Jessop waited for Falco to go to him.

"Do you want to?" he offered.

She turned, flicking on the water to bathe. "He didn't call for me."

* * * *

The blade was a dark violet color, the hilt made up of shining onyx stones. It was the most beautiful weapon she had ever seen—and its purple edge still bore her dry blood. She cleaned the weapon meticulously, wiping it down until there was no longer any evidence to the fact that it had nearly taken her life. She discarded the cloth and turned the blade over in her hand. It was singular.

We had this made for you, for your initiation.

The last words he had spoken to her.

Her stomach twisted with ghost pains, her skin still quick to remember the feeling of the blade deep inside her. She sheathed the weapon and placed it back on the ground. She had come to the Hollow nearly every day since she had been well enough to walk. Training was when she was most comfortable, wherever she was, *whoever* she was supposed to be, whomever she was with—she felt at ease with a weapon in hand.

"He designed it for you, you know."

She smiled at Trax's voice. He approached the ledge of the Hollow and sat beside her, letting his long legs swing over the lip of the edge. She watched as he picked up the weapon, admiring the hilt, pulling it loose from its sheath to regard the blade.

She watched him turn the blade over. "I'm not surprised."

He sheathed the weapon again, laying it between them. "There are not many who can claim to fight with the weapon that nearly took their life."

She shrugged. "I've never fought with it."

He looked her over with glowing yellow eyes. "Shall we remedy that?"

She contemplated the offer, her eyes darting over the Hollow below—the fire, the burning oil, the ropes and sand…She had last been down there with him. Could she re-enter, with the blade he made her, and claim back a space they had shared for so long? She felt like an intruder, as though this were something she had lost in their dissolved relationship, that this place was something he got to keep.

She touched her hand to her stomach. "It's still too soon."

"*Baruk*," Trax spoke, nodding at her with understanding.

She regarded his glowing eyes carefully; he knew she was lying. He was too reverent to say as much, though. He knew better than most how she felt. He had been with her, her aide-de-camp, her closest companion as she executed the greatest infiltration and deepest betrayal imaginable. He, like many of his kin, had always been loyal to Falco, but that did not diminish the relationships he had built with his brethren in Falco's absence. He too had betrayed those he cared so deeply for.

Trax stood slowly, brushing the dust away from his trousers. "It feels as though we trespass on their land—"

"*Trax.*"

He raised a hand to ward off her defensiveness. "I don't need to enter your mind to know it. I feel it, too. It is important to remember that it is not we who trespass on Hydo's ground, but they who trespassed for so many years on Falco's."

His words resonated within her. As she had known, he felt her difficulties too, as they were his own. She nodded to her friend slowly, silently. Her guilt had torn her sight away from the truth, from the reality of their situation. She had done an unspeakable thing to Kohl O'Hanlon, but it did not change how she felt for Falco, or why she had done it. She now needed to know more than ever that it hadn't changed how Falco felt for her.

She leapt to her feet. "Trax, could you go watch Jeco for me?"

He smiled at her knowingly. "Of course."

* * * *

Jessop threw the door to the Assembly Council room open. Falco was leaning over a table, Urdo Rendo and Teck Fay flanking him, deep in conversation. His gaze tore up to her. "Jessop, Trax came for Jeco if you—"

"Leave us," she barked, crossing the room swiftly. Without hesitation, the older Hunter and the mage left them. They had seen what she was capable of; they did not falter at her command.

"We were actually talk—"

She stopped right before him, ignoring his crossed arms and frustrated stare. "Well, we need to talk."

He took a deep breath. "Alright. What is it?"

She studied his beautiful face, his pale gray eyes and perfect lips, his dark brow and short hair. The scar that Kohl O'Hanlon had carved down one side of his face. "I am in love with you, Falco. I always have been and always will be. Everything I did, I did for you, for Jeco, for *us*. I may have slept with Kohl for our plan to work, but that is not what bonded him and me."

She could see how what she said upset him. His lip tightened at her words, but he forced himself to stay silent and listen to her.

"I watched him breathe at night and he realigned everything he believed in so that I could be a part of his life. While in the end he chose his brothers, for a while it seemed like he might have chosen me. Like I mattered more than everything he had ever been taught. Through all of these things, we were bonded. But did it make me fall in love with him? Never. Not for one moment. Not for a single second. You cannot shatter someone's heart so mercilessly unless it is done for the one you truly love. What I did to him,

I did for you. What matters now isn't whether I want him dead or alive, but whether you can see past the bond we forged at your behest."

His face softened but he said nothing. She rested her hands on his chest and still he did not move.

"I only want *you*. I know it will take time for me to live with what I did to Kohl, but that means nothing for us. But if you don't want me too—"

Her voice cracked at the thought. If Falco couldn't see past what had happened between her and Kohl, then so much of what she had done was for naught. If she had reclaimed a throne for a lord who could no longer love her, for a son who did not recognize her any longer, then...

He had his arms around her so suddenly it trapped her breath. His mouth found hers with ease and hunger, his fingers working over her tunic, grabbing her, propping her up on the table. With equal craving, she grabbed at him. She kissed him deeply, pulled him closer to her, felt the heat of his chest against her breast.

"Of course I want you. I'm so sorry," he whispered into her hair as she kissed his neck.

She raised her arms for him to pull her tunic free. "As am I."

* * * *

Jessop pulled her vest tight around her muscular frame. The leather ran smoothly over her tunic. The dark breeches tucked around her legs well. She traced her fingers over the Hunter's sigil on her breast—*Falco's* sigil. She would eventually don different attire. She wouldn't always dress as a Hunter, but for the time being, it felt surprisingly good to once again wear the leather. She leaned over and pulled on her black boots.

With expert hands she wove her dark hair into a plait, letting it fall down her spine. She dampened her fingers in the bowl of water before her, patting down any errant strands. Finally, she reached for her blade. She did not stop to admire the hilt, she did not hesitate with a flash of Kohl's face in her mind. She did not think of how he had designed this weapon for her and her body did not ache as it remembered being impaled. She simply grabbed it, a weapon—*her* weapon—and sheathed it at her hip.

"Mama." Jeco's small voice surprised her. She turned from her reflection and saw her son standing in the doorway, Falco behind him. He looked up to her with big gray eyes, and slowly, he smiled. His dark hair was messy and his face a pale blush—he had just woken.

Falco rested a hand on Jeco's shoulder, his eyes beaming at Jessop. "You're forgetting something."

She arched her brow at him. "Oh?"

From behind his back he revealed her leather back holster, her two needlepoint daggers resting in their slender sheaths. She hadn't seen her former weapons, let alone wielded them, since Aranthol. "Falco," she whispered as she reached for them.

She swung the holster on with ease, until the hilt of each blade appeared just above her shoulders. She reached up and ran her fingertips over the hilts, and with expert ease, she freed the weapons, spiraling them over her shoulders, circling them about her fingers with skilled, memorized movements. The small weapons sung out as they sliced through the air. She spun them back and flicked them into their sheaths.

She stepped towards Falco, reaching for his hand. "Thank you."

He nodded silently, and with his free hand he traced the outline of the sigil on her chest. "You're in uniform."

She nodded. "I am your Hunter."

He pulled her closer. "You are my everything."

As Falco kissed her, Jeco wrapped his small arms around her leg, hugging her tightly.

CHAPTER 5

Aranthol

Ten years ago

Jessop ducked under his strike, lowered herself to the ground, and spun, one leg extended. She knocked him to the ground, but he rolled in a backwards somersault, returning to his feet, in sync with her. She squared off with him, fists high at the ready. She wore nothing more than a cured pelt vest and breeches, and across her exposed flesh she had bruises and cuts. He had gotten her side with his blade, and she felt the blood flowing quite freely over her hip.

He was not unmarked though. His lip bled profusely, his bare chest was swollen with bruising, and there was a cut over his muscular shoulder—a new scar amongst one million old ones. "We've been at this for three hours," he remarked as they circled one another.

She smiled at his words, "Falco, we've been at this for three *years*."

It was true. Aranthol, the Shadow City he had built for her, had been their home for three long years. Their city was grand—black buildings and stone streets, an eternal night sky filled with stars overhead. Falco had forged the city with the Kuroi people, building a dark fortress for her to live in with him. Their home was a grand palace, made entirely of onyx stone. It was dark and majestic. It had grown rapidly, drawing in many who fled the Daharian galactic authority—the Hunters of Infinity. It would have overflowed with newcomers if they had the choice, but citizenship was an exclusive right issued only by Falco.

Since leaving the Kuroi and residing permanently in Aranthol, they had trained for hours on end, every day. In the beginning, it had been easier, as it had just been the two of them. It hadn't stayed that way for long. Aranthol was a thriving shadowy metropolis of Daharia's most wanted. Which was not to say the inhabitants were entirely corrupt—they weren't—but for the most part, they were wanted by the Hunters or ostracized from their communities for their oddities. Finding time to train had become increasingly difficult for Falco, as lording over a city such as Aranthol required constant vigilance. Falco was their leader, and he earned his mantle daily.

She had seen him challenged by every man, beast, and machine that had viewed Aranthol as something they might like to control, and he had never lost. He had never even come close to losing. He had always offered an alliance before death. Should the bested individual swear fealty, they could live under Falco's rule. And in three years, his fair approach had worked hundreds upon hundreds of times. Jessop's back was a reminder of the time it hadn't.

"We have a council meeting to attend," he sighed, lowering his blade. Jessop knew they were busy that afternoon. Newcomers who wished to reside in Aranthol would be presented to Falco and herself. No one could enter without a recommendation from a current resident. They believed the choice was up to Falco—they believed all of Aranthol was ruled by him alone, but that was not so. Jessop could decide whatever she pleased; Falco reminded her on a near daily basis that the city was his gift to her. She did not wish to rule, though. She wished only to be with him and work on their plan for the Hunters.

She sheathed her blade. "Must we?"

He smiled at her softly and approached her. He rested his hand against her side and healed her quickly. His powers had grown exponentially. In teaching her Sentio, he had gained a greater grasp on his gifts than either of them had thought possible. While Jessop had learned many of the wonders of telepathy and telekinesis, she could not heal. They still had never found another who could. Yet, as he smiled down at her, fixing her wound, his shoulder began to heal itself, forming a tight silver scar as his flesh mystically mended back together.

"You amaze me," she smiled up at him. She reached up and slowly cupped his face with her hand, running her thumb over his scar, just below his eye. His hands coiled around her abdomen, pulling her closer to his warm body. She turned her face up to him, her heart beating wildly as she offered her lips to him.

He grazed her nose with his, and his bottom lip barely brushed over hers, before pulling away. "We can't," he spoke, but he did not let her go.

She ran her hands over his chest. "We both want this."

"It's too soon. Too soon after what happened to you." It was what he said each time they got too close.

"It's been nearly a year, Falco. I'm fine," she insisted, pushing her body against his as if the heat she emanated for him could be enough to convince him.

She *was* fine—for the most part. If she closed her eyes, she could still see the white eyes of the mage. She could feel his eerily smooth hands grabbing her, his mind prying through hers, immobilizing her. She could feel the whip, sharp as a knife, cut the deep lashes into her back.

He had run his hand over her freshly marred back, painting the blood down her spine. "I can see why he covets you so," he had whispered to her.

And she had known what he had intended—but Falco saved her. As she had known he would. He was all she had ever had faith in. She had never heard screams like those she heard from the mage.

He pulled away from her. "Do you think I don't want you? Of course I do. I'm in love with you, I've been in love with you since we were children."

"Then why won't you kiss me? I understand if everything *else* is too much, too soon. I know what damage the mage did to the both of us—it is *me* he attacked—but it does not change how I feel for you."

"Yes, it was *you* he attacked—to harm *me*. We've never even kissed and all of Aranthol knows you are my weakness, my love."

She took a step closer to him. "What of it? You think if we give in to our feelings, if we were together in more than just words, it would somehow make *you* more vulnerable?"

"Yes!"

She crossed her arms over her chest, glaring at him.

He ran a hand through his dark hair and looked at her with wide eyes. "You're already all I think about."

If we give in, how could we possibly carry on with our mission? How could I ever function without touching you every second of every day? He pushed the thoughts into her mind.

She uncrossed her arms. "But we're in love." She said the words matter-of-factly, for they were *fact*.

He shook his head at her. "We need more time."

She turned from him, knowing she needed to clean up before the council meeting. "You need more time, Falco. I know what I want."

* * * *

Jessop and Falco had a standard for who was and wasn't allowed to reside in Aranthol. While their first mission was always to provide a sanctuary for those sought after by the Hunters, they still needed a community that would be loyal. They wouldn't align with any who hurt the vulnerable, though it was difficult to know for certain. Jessop looked the two raiders over slowly.

They ran an illegal transport service, moving goods unchecked across Daharia. They were both wanted by the Hunters for their trespasses. The taller of the two had only one eye, while his companion had half a face made up of metal. *What sort of goods?* She pushed the thought to Falco.

During these meetings, Falco sat on his throne, forged of galaxy rock and scrap metal. Jessop stood on his right-hand side, while Corin, Falco's advisor, stood on the periphery of the makeshift platform.

Falco crossed his arms, readjusting in his seat. His hair was damp from bathing, and his black tunic stuck to his skin. "What goods do you move?"

Jessop looked up the walls of the grand room. Made entirely of onyx, the room was the entryway to their home. Five hundred men and women could fit in the space comfortably. The walls stretched some sixty feet high, and shone like black glass. Her favorite part of the chamber was that it bore no ceiling—she could view the perpetually black night, and all the glorious stars, whenever she pleased. If it rained, it rained on them; if there was resulting chaos, then there was chaos. She loved the home Falco had built her, the world they created, that they governed. If she wanted chaos, it was hers. They had possessed both vision and power from such young ages, and they were young still, unbridled and ambitious, building a world in their likeness.

She didn't know how long he would keep her at arm's length though. They had shared chambers since the incident. In the beginning, she thought it was just because she hadn't wanted to sleep alone, but it didn't take long for her to realize that Falco didn't want her out of his sight.

Jessop didn't quite know when things had begun to change for them. They had built Aranthol and lived there alone, as young friends, for the longest time. Dezane had visited them frequently, bringing updates on Hydo Jesuin and the Hunters of Infinity. It had been incredibly lonely, living with the scars of their shared past, leaning on only each other.

Jessop remembered sitting under the dark sky, staring up at the one building in Aranthol— *their* palatial home. Their dark castle. She had looked into the sky as the rain began to pour down on her and she had screamed. She screamed with her eyes tightly shut, her hands clutching her face, willing, with all her might, to take the image of her lifeless parents out of her mind. She screamed as she writhed in pain, seeing the fire and the blood. She beat the stones beneath her with angry fists. She pulled her hair and thrashed wildly against her living, ever present nightmares. She screamed until she couldn't scream any longer. Until she collapsed against the wet stone. Until Falco scooped her up in his arms and carried her in from the rain.

In the beginning, everything had been overwhelming. It wasn't just the two of them for long. Dezane began to send all those who sought a reprieve from the Hunters, and more and more arrived, each somehow more dangerous than the last. It wasn't until Jessop realized that none were capable of besting Falco that she could ever relax. After three years, they still ruled, and wherever she went in her city, she went with an air of authority. She was feared in her own right, but Falco's imposing nature is what truly kept them all at bay.

"Whatever we are paid to," the taller one answered, pulling Jessop back to the moment.

Jessop squeezed Falco's shoulder. He nodded. "You'll move no slaves."

"But—"

Falco raised his hand, silencing them. "No slaves, and your residency is probationary for several months."

The two slowly nodded in agreement.

Falco leaned back in his throne. "Good. Find my man Corin later this day, and he will assist you with your residency documents."

Falco kept a ledger of any who came through Aranthol. When she had asked him why, he had but one response. "Conscription."

* * * *

Jessop left Falco to discuss matters with Corin. She had never had any interest in leading Aranthol. Just like Dezane, she had always known Falco to be a trueborn leader. She had faith in him, and she did not envy his position of power. She thought of their earlier exchange and wanted to put it out of her mind. She couldn't just spend her life between their chambers and the Pit, their training arena.

Leaving the castle was easy, and she had free reign over the Shadow City. Leaving it without any guards attending her was somewhat harder. She had roamed the city unattended before the incident with the desert mage, but since then, Falco had made sure she rarely had a minute alone. All who knew her face knew her skill, and knew Falco's love of her. If they were too dumb to fear her, they were at least smart enough to fear him. She had tried reminding Falco of that time and time again, but he wouldn't be persuaded.

It was the same love he had for her that kept him at arm's length. She wished she could force him to see reason—whether they were together in more than words did not matter to those who sought to harm them. His love was motive enough. Unless he intended to stop loving her, she would always be a target. Despite Falco's concerns for her, they both knew she wasn't a very vulnerable one.

She finished brushing her dark mane back, braiding the top so it would stay out of her eyes. She turned from her reflection, secured her usual weapons—two daggers, each the length of her forearm— in their harness, strapped in a diagonal cross over her back, and made her way for the door.

She rested her hand on the wall beside her doorframe. Closing her eyes, she focused on the energy surrounding her. She felt through the black walls, breathing slowly, concentrating vigorously. Falco had taught her well, but her skill for Sentio, though great, still lagged behind his own. She could *feel* the two guards on the other side of the wall. That was how Falco had taught her, in the beginning. To shut your eyes, and use your mind to seek out others, like you were in a dark room trying to feel with an outstretched hand. In the beginning, it had been beyond futile. She had been certain the Hunters were right—perhaps Sentio couldn't be grasped by women. And then, Falco had employed a new tactic.

He had blindfolded her for their training. They had gone onto the rooftop of the highest building in Aranthol, her eyes covered, and he had told her to stop him before he stepped off the ledge. When she rushed him, targeting his presence with any small sound, he had struck her. He did not harm her out of malice, but necessity. They fought, and she lost. Again and again. Until she could fight without eyes, until she could find him without sound, until her mind was the greatest weapon she had. Blinding her had given her true sight.

Finding had been the first step to mastering Sentio. Manipulating had been the second. Altering the cognitions of another human, suppressing their ability to move because you could suppress their ability to *want* to move, had been no easy feat. Reshaping energy so that the inanimate was under your influence or forcing a guard to see an empty hallway when you stood but a foot before him were skills that took a lifetime to master. Yet Falco had already conquered them all, and he was dead-set on Jessop following in his lead.

She entered the minds of the guards, using a great deal of concentration to work over two minds simultaneously. The ease of the work wasn't solely based on the skill of the one who mastered Sentio, but of the strength of mind of the one who could fall prey to it. She found their vision, and could see their view of the dark, black hall. She saw one gaze over the onyx walls, the other staring at the black marble flooring.

Only when she was certain she had fixed their perception did she dare open the door. She hesitated, halting in the middle of the two sentries for but a moment. She could stop a knife midair with easy confidence, but she was still sometimes uncertain about the more advanced maneuvers. When they made no gesture to suggest they could see her, she quietly closed the door behind her and ran off down the hall. Certain she was in the clear, she flung herself around a tight corner, only to bump straight into another guard.

The guard stumbled back, shaken. Jessop found herself staring at a set of glowing green eyes, identical to her own. She huffed heavily, "What are you doing here, Korend'a?"

Korend'a was a Kuroi guard whom Falco had hand selected to work in the castle. He was tall, with dark skin pulled tightly over sinewy muscles. He straightened out his black robes, reminiscent of Kuroi warrior attire, and looked her over quickly.

"I maintain the safety of the castle, Jessop. I do tend to walk around here."

She studied his face, finding herself wondering for a brief moment how old he was. Maybe as young as three decades, maybe as old as six—the Kuroi were a stunningly youthful people. "*Hada'na nei hey'wa,* Jessop?"

He asked her how she had been faring. Korend'a had been the only sentry to help Falco get rid of the remains of the man who had attacked Jessop the previous year—he had been the only one to know what had nearly happened to her. He had been the only one, aside from Falco, to ever see her back.

"*Dand'e dore dona,* Korend'a," she responded, insisting that she had been well. "I promise," she added when he kept his glowing gaze fixed on her.

"I believe you."

They stood in silence for a moment, and she used it to think of a way to get past him. Korend'a did not have a weak mind. He had the powers of the Kuroi, but more than that, he had her respect. She would never wish to meddle in the mind of one she cared for.

"I must be going—"

"Let me accompany you."

She raised a hand. "Not necessary, Korend'a."

He remained in her path. He looked her over slowly, and she knew he sensed her intentions to be alone in the city. Sentio was not a gift of the Kuroi; what they could do was something quite different, and unnamed. They had a power they claimed to have inherited from the earth, one that lived in the sands as surely as it lived in their blood. Falco had theorized that it was her Kuroi lineage that made her capable of mastering Sentio with such ease. She had never thought it had been with ease.

"*Norenay,* Jessop."

Necessary.

* * * *

They walked through the dark streets in silence, and Jessop had to admit that even though she had sought isolation, being with Korend'a wasn't dreadful. He didn't harass her or stare at her; he didn't stop to speak to anyone in the bazaar. He moved through the black market of their high street with utter disinterest, winding toward the Gahaza Square with silent composure. It made *her* want to pester him, if anything.

She could tell simply by looking at him that he wasn't evil. He wasn't cut from the same dark cloth that all of those who roamed up and down the street were. She was certain he wasn't even sought after by the Hunters of Infinity. But there was something about him...He lived with guilt, in true isolation, always present but constantly, somehow, absent. She could see in his eyes that there was a life he had left behind, a life he missed greatly. He had wronged someone, perhaps. She believed she could ascertain the reasons by force, if she entered his mind quickly enough, but she wouldn't. She knew it would be wrong to do so, and to use abilities just because she had them seemed like an abuse of power.

Jessop halted by a wooden stand, running her fingers gently over the silver talismans being sold. She eyed him quickly before speaking. "How is it you came to work for Falco?"

Korend'a kept one hand on his sword, the other behind his back. "I have worked in your castle for two years, and you have only thought to ask me this now?"

"I tend not to make small talk with the guards."

"What would you call this?"

She dropped the necklace she had been holding and stepped back into the busy street, carrying on with her walk. If he didn't wish to tell her, she wouldn't press him.

"I killed two Kuroi, amongst others," he spoke suddenly, his voice soft.

She turned around to face him and saw his face harden, awaiting her reproach. She was surprised at his confession. For a Kuroi to kill one of their own was the greatest of trespasses amongst the tribe. She had anticipated a history of slighting another, not murdering.

"And Dezane DeHawn let you live?"

His lips were tight with regret. "I killed the man who murdered my husband...and I also killed his entire travelling party. Dezane knew I had been wronged, and while there is no excuse, he offered me the opportunity to live out my life in the Shadow City, instead of dying beyond the Grey."

She nodded slowly at the tall man. She could not blame Korend'a for his actions, not when he so clearly punished himself for them. "And when you moved here, Falco chose you to serve in the castle."

"He said he wanted someone who understood love was worth killing for."

Jessop thought of the guilt she saw in Korend'a. She thought of Falco. She thought of her mother and father, and of Hydo Jesuin too. "Is it?"

"For me, it meant losing my home, my people, the right to live the way I wanted for the rest of my days, all to avenge the one I loved."

She stared at him, captivated. Korend'a had long ago done what she intended to do herself. "Well, was it worth it?"

He looked down at her with dark, certain eyes. "Absolutely."

Before she could speak to him further, Jessop felt a hand latch onto her shoulder. "Excuse me, lady?"

She shook the hand off, turning to face whoever spoke to her. Korend'a was at her side in an instant, and had pushed the man back several feet. Jessop sized the man up. He had one eye and ragged hair, his dark clothes matching those of his companion, one with a face made of metal. They were the men from the assembly that morning, the two who ran the illegal transport service.

Jessop looked from the one-eyed man to his robotic companion, to the larger group of leather-clad denizens they had congregated with. "What do you want?"

He clasped his hands together, his one pale eye rolling around as he looked her over. "I recognized you from this morning, Miss, and couldn't help but ask if you could do me a kindness?"

He moved to take a small step closer to Jessop, but Korend'a immediately had his hand out, keeping the man at bay. Jessop knew the trader had been drinking—she could smell the ethanol on his breath. Jessop was many things, but a woman of the people was not one of them. She could fight at their sides, but she could not stand and speak with them in the streets. It had nothing to do with their station or demeanor—it was about *her*. She didn't want friends, she didn't need any companion other than Falco, and she didn't like talking. She most often wished to speak to no one except Falco or another Kuroi.

"I don't grant favors," she answered, brushing past the man. He quickly got back in her way, and at his gesture, Korend'a unsheathed his sword. The group of men, many of whom Jessop recognized as other local dark traders, stood behind their cyclopean frontrunner.

She took a slow breath, trying to recognize everything she was feeling. Falco had told her to control her emotions, lest they control her. She hadn't been forced to deal with any menacing citizens for a year. She felt challenged by the man, and angered by his disrespect, but she did not feel fear, for the fight was something she had long since learned to love. Though she recognized how greatly outnumbered she and Korend'a were, she felt adrenaline—excitement. She knew her heart raced not simply out of anticipation, but out of concern for Falco. If she fought in the town bazaar, he would know, and he would be angered.

She drummed her fingers against her thigh, trying to suppress her exhilaration. On a deeper level, Jessop always wanted the fight. She had an irrepressible rage that could only be quenched through combat, the memories that once shook her with terror in her sleep now fueling her every strike. But she was not a barbarian—she clung to civility and composure, to restraint and control. "Remove yourself from my path, or have yourself removed, trader. Any issues you have with Falco Bane's ruling, you take up with him."

The man did not move though. Instead, he half-smiled at her. "If you could just speak to your Lord on—"

"He is *your* Lord too and as long as you stand in the Shadow City you live under his ruling. Now get out of my way," she ordered.

She could sense his strike before he had even begun it. Slowed by feebleness and intoxication, his hand moved toward her face at a glacial pace. Hastened by skill and adrenaline, secretly pleased he had started something she would gladly finish, she unsheathed her daggers with expert speed. She pierced the palm of his hand before his slap connected, forcing her blade through his calloused skin, impaling metacarpals and flesh, bursting through the other side with a plume of blood and a shrieking wail from the trader.

His scream set them off. Three men leapt at Korend'a, who moved about them like a shadow, slicing and ducking and weaving—untouchable. Two lunged past their wounded leader and made for her. She ducked a strike, elbowed a jaw, turned, and with perfect fluidity executed a roundhouse kick on one. He flew back and knocked his companions to the ground. She knelt, dodging another strike, and slipped her blade into the thigh of another. He cried as she pulled the blade free from his torn muscle and flesh. She stood and flung both blades out, instantly killing two of the traders. Using Sentio, she called the blades back, and in an instant, her fingers were wrapping around their leather-bound hilts. She turned one blade inward so it ran parallel to her forearm, and kept one extended out. As another man lunged at her, she punched him with the hilt of the inward facing dagger, before slicing him up the gut with the other.

They fell from her, afraid and angered. Korend'a pulled his sword free from the chest of a trader. She listened to the gushing flow of blood escaping the cavity. All about them the high street had diminished into chaos. Some screamed and fled their curios—some gathered to watch. She no longer cared if Falco had been beckoned—she relished in her fight. Let them see her anger, she thought, let them see she wouldn't be threatened by them. The man who attacked her the year before, a famed and dark desert mage, had not lived to see another day. Neither would these seditious traders if they didn't yield to her.

By the mayhem surrounding her, she felt as though she had gotten her message across. The one-eyed man had found his feet and was lurching towards her. She threw her blade, and using Sentio, froze it midair, the tip hovering just a half inch away from his eye. He didn't dare move, and his paralysis was infectious—the remnants of his gang stood frozen.

"Gather your living and leave," Jessop began, but before she could say anything further, the passersby in the street began to kneel, ducking their heads low to the ground. She could feel *him* behind her—Falco had arrived.

"What is this *mutiny*?" he asked, his deep voice travelling over the street. She did not turn to face him, not daring to pull her focus from her blade.

"My Lord—she attacked us, killed my men, her and her manservant!" The one-eyed trader yelled past her, his voice filled with vitriol and terror.

She could hear Falco walking slowly towards them. "Firstly, he is no 'manservant.' Secondly, she attacked you? Unprovoked?"

"M-my Lord, we wanted to just speak with her. I thought I could ask her to speak to you about t-the s-slaves, s-seeing as she is y-your l-lady, isn't she?"

Falco actually let out a small laugh, his breath brushing over her hair as he came up behind her. "She is my *everything*," he growled, his voice deep.

Without hesitation, his Sentio cut through hers as he took control of her blade and plunged it into the man's eye. He leapt past Jessop, pulling the blade free from the screaming trader, and quickly stabbed him in the throat. He spiraled under the arm of another merchant, quickly piercing him in the armpit before leaping up behind him and snapping his neck. He pulled the blade back, pirouetting about the group of dwindling survivors. He sliced and stabbed and snapped. Blood flew about him like paint, flicking over his face, covering his hands. None could strike him; none could anticipate his next move. Falco's abilities, the way he danced with a weapon, immobilized his enemies. He fought with a true unparalleled ability and an almost arrogant sense of ease—knowing he had no equal.

Jessop watched him with shock, silent. This was not the first time he had killed in the street, nor even the first time he had killed for her. He had ended the lives of many who had entered Aranthol. She was shocked because of his public declaration.

He crouched over the body of the last trader, staring him in the eye as he passed. Then slowly, he rose, turning to face Jessop. He stepped over fallen bodies, navigating the street, slick with blood, with ease. A splattering of blood covered his perfect face. His gray eyes held her, and just as his opponents had felt, she was frozen by him. He was singularly the most intoxicating person she had ever known.

She felt a hundred eyes on them, but his were the only ones she cared to see. He reached out and pulled her into his arms, careful with the dagger. And then, in front of the entire high street crowd, in the middle of a blood bath of fallen slave-traders, he kissed her.

CHAPTER 6

Aranthol

Six years ago

"You're eight and ten years, Jessop," Falco reminded her. As though she needed reminding. It had been over five years. Five years since they had forged Aranthol, five years since she had been beyond the Grey, five years of life with Falco. Five years without her parents, whose deaths remained unavenged.

She ignored him, stepping into the water. The warm cascade fell heavy from the ceiling, like a waterfall. She lathered her body with the imported wedges of salt and fat. She rubbed the cleaning concoction over her breasts, up her neck, down her stomach and thighs.

He stepped into the water with her. "We should celebrate such a Partus," he pressed, running his hands over her back.

She glared up at him. "You are two decades today— why shouldn't we celebrate that?"

He shrugged, pulling her closer to him, his large hands resting on her hips. "If you wish to celebrate me, I won't stop you," he smiled.

She ran her hands up his muscular form, letting them rest on his chest. She still couldn't help but stare at the scars. She thought of the first night he had spoken to her about them. He would not say much, but she knew Hydo had been the one responsible.

She knew it had something to do with a rite of passage, and while he wouldn't confirm anything, she had figured it involved young Hunters surviving a beating so terrible it could convince any to abandon their position within the Blade. She assumed that only those who could endure, without surrender, could carry on to become Infinity Hunters. She had run her theory past Falco before, and while he didn't confirm it, his silence told her much.

She had lost count more than once before, trying to number all the marks.

"It has been many years, Falco. You have an army, a loyal nation, you have *me*, what more are we waiting for?"

He covered her hands with his. "Jessop, you cannot do this every year. I understand the Red Solstice is a reminder of all we lost, but we cannot storm the Glass Blade unprepared. We need a plan."

She let her hands fall from him. "Then why aren't we making a plan?"

He pulled her closer to him, his lips trailing over hers. "Believe me, I am."

* * * *

She found him in the Pit, sparring with Korend'a. The Pit was the training space Falco had designed within their palatial home, and it was aptly named. A massive hole had been cut into the onyx flooring, like a giant pool made of black glass. In the Pit, there was limited room to escape, forcing you to engage your fighting partner. There were no fancy weapons, no hideaway spots, no surprise treachery. You simply would slide down the edge of the steep wall and fight. No distractions.

Jessop could remember the first time she had trained with Falco in the Pit. She had slid down the sloped wall and put up a terrible defense for mere minutes before calling it a day. He had crouched low and leapt with ease out of the hole, back up to higher ground. He had sat on the lip of the Pit, waiting for her to figure out how to get herself out.

After many attempts at carefully crawling up the slick black onyx only to slide back down, she had figured it out. She had run at the sloping wall full speed ahead, no fear, no inhibitions, and keeping her feet wide, managed to scale it with the swiftness required to escape. That had been long ago, before she could move like Falco.

Jessop paced around the edge of the Pit, watching Falco. Both men wielded two blades, but those were not the only weapons in use. Three additional swords were attacking Falco, controlled by invisible forces. Falco had begun to use Sentio to train himself more and more. Sweat dripped down his bare chest as he twisted and turned, his arms never ceasing to move, his wrists twirling his weapons about him, forming a constant shield.

Korend'a was a beautiful fighter. Over the years they had spent together, Jessop had trained with him often and engaged in several very real fights by his side.

He was masterful with a blade, and quick as one of the many sandstorms she had experienced as a child beyond the Grey. For most, he was untouchable, but next to Falco, he seemed mediocre at best. As she circled the Pit, watching Falco fend off five blades, she thought of his ever-growing skill. She had truly become his last able opponent, but she knew that while her skills were peaking, his were advancing ever more.

Korend'a attacked mercilessly and Jessop knew there were few alive in Daharia who could have defended themselves against the man. He had a long reach and a singular focus, never tearing his gaze away from his target. Korend'a never hesitated, never blinked, never took a moment to think of his next move—he simply executed it. And it wasn't enough.

Falco spun about in circles, his blades never stilling, his footing never faltering. The sharp cry of his star glass blade beating back the steel forged weapons was melodic; the graceful precision of his turns and deflections was intoxicating to her. She watched him and knew she could stay watching him for a lifetime. In fact, she intended to. She knew it when they were children and she knew it on her eight-and-tenth day of Partus—she would spend her life with an eye always on Falco Bane.

She halted by the edge of the Pit. "May I cut in?"

They stopped at once, Falco dropping the three ghost blades to the ground. Korend'a smiled up at her. "*Baruk.*" *Of course.*

She smiled back. "*Sevos,*" she thanked him.

Korend'a sheathed his weapons and inclined his head to Falco. Falco offered his arm to the man and they shook. "*Sevos f'ara harana,*" he spoke. He was thanking Korend'a for the fight, though Jessop could hear the misplaced inflection.

"*Sevos far'a harana,*" she corrected him. With an easy leap, she flipped forward into the pit.

"*Far'a,*" Falco repeated.

Korend'a nodded. "Any time, my Lord." With a final smile to her, the Kuroi warrior leapt from the Pit.

Jessop listened to the sound of his footsteps disappearing down the hall. She leaned down and picked up two of the discarded blades, spinning them in opposite circles around her body.

"You have been speaking Kuroi for five years and still it trips you up," she smiled to him, her eyes dancing over his strong chest.

"It's difficult to learn a new language late in life," he answered.

"Yet, you persist," she said, taking a fighting stance opposite him.

He stretched out his neck before taking his own position. "Always."

She sliced through the air with both blades parallel to the ground, her right arm keeping one blade just above the other. He leapt back, spun about and engaged—their blades singing as they clashed.

She kicked him in the chest, sending him flying back against an onyx slope. She took aim and thrust one blade, but he deflected, sending her point into the wall with a shrill clash. He pushed off the wall and with a flick of his wrist he turned his hilt inward, so that the blade protruded from his underhand. He moved like a storm, turning and twisting, his blades curving about him in perfect circular motions. It was a maneuver of his that many found hard to best.

She struck at the opportune moment, her sword halting his. With two blades locked against each other, they fought with their left hands, weapons dangerously close to one another's bodies. "To be a good fighter, you have to be hungry for the fight," he mused.

With a swift pull, he disarmed her active blade. She didn't hesitate. She turned into his body, reached up and grabbed his wrist, her fingers grazing over the hilts of their locked blades, and flung him over her shoulder. She had to use all of her might, but his strong body flew over her bent one, and left her holding both her own sword and his.

She leapt at him as he lay on the ground, taking aim at his throat and abdomen, standing on his blade-wielding wrist. He smiled up at her, sweat trailing down his neck, glistening over his chest. With a force she couldn't resist, both of her weapons were flung out of her hands. His Sentio was magnificent.

She smiled down at him, disarmed. She took her foot off his wrist, and instantly he grabbed at her legs. Her knees buckled as she landed on him, mounting his strong frame. His hands moved up her thighs slowly. She looked over his gray eyes, filled with want and anticipation. She ran her hand over the long scar that cut through his face. She traced his lips with her fingers, slowly moving them down his throat, onto his chest.

She leant over him, kissing him deeply. Her lips worked firmly against his, tasting him, hungry for him. His tongue moved against hers with a teasing pace, and she dug her nails into his arms. His hands worked over her tunic, tearing at the material until it fell from her body. He kissed her neck and collarbone, he drew her breast into his mouth and she felt his want for her.

They rolled to their side, both of their fingers working quickly on the other's clothes, no longer novice with one another's forms. She kicked off her boots as he pulled material from her. She lay back on the black onyx floor, naked. He stepped out of his boots with careful deliberation, removing his own breeches slowly, never taking his eyes off her. Resting beside her, he let his hands travel her body as he locked gazes with her. His strong fingers brought her to life, they trailed over her hips, up her thighs, and as they found her, she leaned forward and bit his shoulder. She moaned against his hot skin, her body alight with desire. She wanted all of him. She rolled him onto his back, locking her thighs around his hips, arching her back as she took him. Falco cursed under his breath at her rhythmic movements, taking her hips and rolling them against him with his strong hands. As she moved with him, she heard a *clink* of metal. Every weapon in the Pit was levitating several feet above the ground.

She looked down to Falco, knowing he did not move the blades on purpose. She found the extent of his abilities amazing, the extent of his dangerousness rousing, never faltering, not even when they made love.

* * * *

Jessop continued to stoke the fire, her back to Falco. She could feel him staring at the nape of her neck. She looked down to the iron rod. It was long and sleek, and it thinned out into a small turned wire at the end, perfect for burning fine lines. She had seen the Hunters' sigil on Falco's neck thousands of times—if she could have done it herself, she would have. She needed him, though.

"I don't understand why this is necessary, Jessop. We don't even know when we could execute the plan," Falco reiterated, shifting in his seat on their bed.

She turned from the fire to face him. "Falco, you told me your plan and I believe it will work. I know what I need to do, when the time comes. But they will need more than my word. They will need to see scars—"

"You *have* scars," he argued.

"It's not the same. You said so yourself—they will ransack my mind, they will inspect my body. We need to be convincing."

He ran his hand through his dark hair. "The plan is still formulating. You've known of it for several hours and have already acquired some torture device that you want *me* to use on you."

She crossed the room and knelt before him, taking his hands in hers. "Your plan is perfect. But in order for it to work we cannot overlook the details. Branding me creates a memory of pain and torture, it creates a scar for them to see, and it sends a message."

He arched his brow at her. "Oh, and what's that?"

She squeezed his hands tightly. "That you're coming for them."

He held her stare for a long moment, before abruptly standing from the bed. "If you feel the need to mark yourself then so be it, but it won't be at my hand."

She leapt to her feet and stood between him and the door. "Falco—this is *your* mark. You are the true Protector of Daharia and the Blade of Light, you are the rightful leader of the Hunters of Infinity. You are the only person fit to mark me with this sigil."

He looked down at her with concern. "How can I take your pain away if I am wielding your branding iron?"

She ran her hands up his arms. "You can't. The memory of this act needs to be real. You, me, pain."

He nodded slowly. "Then let's get this over with."

* * * *

Jessop rested on her stomach, watching Falco in the darkness. They had gone to bed, but neither slept. Though heat was a pain Jessop rarely seemed to feel, the branding had been excruciating. Thankfully, Falco had been fast about it. As soon as he was done, he had tended to her wound, lessening the pain. They had dined in their chambers and made love once again. While her neck still stung, she felt sated. The morning had started like every other, a reminder of years gone by.

He had told her his plan and it was perfect. She had the looks and the abilities to execute it. They both knew there were those loyal to Falco within the Glass Blade. She didn't know how long it would take to win over their trust, but she knew she could do it. She *would* do it, however long it took. She would have the opportunity to watch Hydo Jesuin grovel at her feet, to hear him plead for life as she considered all the ways she might kill him.

Falco had told her they would have to wait, they would have to be patient for a while longer. Her Sentio was strong—but it needed to be tested further. A weakness of the mind was more dangerous to their plan than a weakness of the body.

Falco rolled onto his side to face her. "Can't sleep?"

"I'm thinking about our plans," she answered.

"I do not care for them as much as you do. I hate the thought of risking you."

She reached for him in the darkness. "He killed my family, Falco. There is no risk too great to stop me."

"You will have to conceal your abilities from them. They will have never encountered any like you before."

"Aside from you," she reminded him.

They watched one another with ease, their eyes having long since adapted to the shadows.

"Are you afraid?" he asked, finding her hand with his.

She thought about his question before answering. "You know I do not feel fear," she reminded him.

"Your adrenaline is too directed at your fight, and at Sentio, to allow you to feel the emotion…but you could, if it truly seized you," he explained.

She thought on his question, his explanation of her. She hadn't felt fear since she had been much younger. Falco had explained her fearlessness through understanding her abilities, and while he was right, she knew that wasn't the only reason she had ceased to feel the emotion. She was unafraid because she had him. Even when the Oren desert mage attacked her, some part of her had known Falco would get there in time.

She would never forget the sting of the leather as it ripped into her flesh. And she would never forget the sounds he made as Falco tortured him. She would never forget the way his inky blue eyes turned white as death took him.

Jessop reached for Falco's hand in the dark. She lived without fear because she lived her life with him.

"I am afraid of being away from you," she admitted.

I am always with you. He pushed the thought across her mind. She appreciated the sentiment. He could be in her mind in an instant, and she in his. It kept them, in a way, always together.

"It's not the same. I haven't lived a day without you by my side since childhood."

"I know," he spoke. His deep voice was soft and contemplative. He relied on her presence as greatly as she did his.

He pulled her close to him, their bed linens bunching up around their legs. She rolled onto his body and rested against his chest. She closed her eyes and listened to his heart beating. She knew that she could do this forever, that she *would* do it forever.

"Jessop," he spoke.

She kept her face pressed into his chest. "Yes?"

He ran his hands over the scarred skin of her back. "I've been thinking about something."

She waited, suppressing a yawn.

"I've been thinking that you should be my wife."

She smiled against his warm skin and sat up slowly. She ran her hand over his cheek, grazing his scar with her thumb. "I've been thinking the same thing."

* * * *

Corin officiated the ceremony and Korend'a was the only guest. They had chosen to marry in the middle of the night, in their grand hall, under the brilliant stars and shadows. While they observed few otherworld traditions, they did dress and ready separately—and Jessop wore a gown.

Corin had brought it for her, mentioning having found it in a shipping container passing through customs. Jessop was not a woman for gowns, but the one he brought to her was quite remarkable. Even Korend'a had insisted she wear it. The dress was entirely black and glittered like the night sky—thousands of shimmering crystals sewn into the massive skirt and train. The bodice was simple, sleeveless and black, with a slit down to her navel.

"There's more," Corin explained, shuffling slowly over to her and Korend'a. Jessop wasn't quite sure how old Corin was, with a silver beard that he tucked into his waist belt and thick star glass spectacles, but she knew he was old enough to remember things from a lifetime before most. He leaned on his walking stick and held out his hand. In his weathered palm were hundreds of tiny crystals. The three of them proceeded to stick the crystals in her long mane of hair and around her eyes, finding the small shimmering gems had an adhesive coating.

Jessop wouldn't admit it aloud, but as she regarded her glistening reflection, the way her dark hair trailed over her bare shoulders like the shining spiral arms of a constellation, she felt perfect. Falco had thrown his hand over his heart upon seeing her enter the hall with Korend'a. His dark hair was still wet from bathing and while he wore only his black leather vest with a high popped collar, black breeches, and boots, he seemed more handsome than ever to her.

Korend'a had kissed both of her cheeks upon handing her to Falco. "*Ura kora daneha,* Jessop." He had told her she was most beautiful.

She squeezed his hand tightly. "*Sevos,* Korend'a."

Falco looked at her from head to toe. Slowly, he grazed her lips with his thumb. "You are a Night Queen."

Corin had provided them a formal ceremony, despite the late hour. He spoke to them of their commitments and their bond, to their shared life story. He told them a history of the marriage bond and even performed portions of the ceremony in perfect Kuroi tongue. He then gave them an opportunity to speak.

Falco smiled at her softly. "My entire life, I had been alone in my mind and in my heart, in my abilities and in my day to day living. I was told that I was the only one like me, and, in truth, I was devastated to hear it. Then I met you. I met you and you resided instantly in my heart—for you were my match in every way. Even before you ever wielded a blade or pushed a thought, my soul recognized yours, and I simply knew who you were, and who you would become. I knew instantly who I would be for having you at my side. I knew I'd be whatever you needed; I would be whomever you wanted.

"From the first, I would have laid down my life for you. You have been my lifeline to a world that told me I had none of my kind to know. You have been what no other could be—my equal. Whatever you choose to do with your life, do so knowing you have my love and protection. My heart, my life, and my blade, are yours."

Jessop squeezed his hands tightly, suppressing the tears his words brought forward in her. She knew he had never spoken so candidly in front of Corin and Korend'a, or any other. She smiled at him softly. "Falco...I feel like we have already shared a lifetime. We met as children, and despite our young ages, you were never a child. You saved me, again and again. And while I loved you for that, you truly won my heart when you taught me how to save myself. You saw in me more than who I was; you saw who I would be. The day I lost my first family, I gained my second.

"You didn't just save my life, Falco; you gave it meaning. Loving you kept me sane. In a world where all was lost, we found each other. I loved you then, I love you still, and I will love you always. In a world on fire, we found our solace in the Shadows."

Falco mouthed the words *I love you* back to her. With their vows complete, Corin instructed them to swap wedding bands. Korend'a handed her the one they had chosen from the market—a simple black band. She turned, ready to place it on Falco's finger, when she saw a dazzling stone in his hand. The ring was made up of a giant, shining black stone, surrounded by weaving ropes of white crystals. It was beautiful. He opened his other palm and revealed a simpler band, made of black crystal. "For easier day to day wear," he smiled.

They dressed one another's fingers in the jewelry. Corin smiled at them both. "In this life and the next, you are now paired. Never before have I known two so destined to live as one."

CHAPTER 7

Azgul

Present-day

"Even with only half the army arriving from Aranthol, that's still thousands more than Hydo and Hanson can muster," Jessop spoke, looking over the large map Falco had laid out before them.

He readjusted Jeco on his hip. Their son was still most at ease with his father, but he would bring his toys to Jessop in the evenings and talk with her. He remembered her; he was just slow to trust her again. "We don't know that. Who really knows how many remain loyal to him, despite our presence in the Blade?"

Urdo Rendo placed his hand down on the table, his eyes darting over the map slowly. "Daharia is home to hundreds of thousands…Nearly a third of the population is Kuroi, and even if they are far out beyond the Grey, we can count on them. Hydo has spent his tenure here in the Red City, infrequently leaving its borders after you—err—left." When no one spoke at Urdo's words, he continued on.

"I wager the majority of his allies are here, or in surrounding regions. Many in Haycith, his home…but after the display you two put on here, word is out. Everyone knew Falco was heir apparent before, but no one knew what *you* could do," he explained, eyeing Jessop with equal parts fear and admiration.

Falco stood up straight, placing Jeco down on the table. "They've seen nothing yet. Jessop is singular."

She reached for Jeco's hand, smiling as he grabbed hold of her finger. They had spent days discussing battle tactics, fielding reports from the scouts who hunted for Hydo, Hanson, and Kohl, strategizing and trying to find out what their rogue enemies had planned. It consumed them all—having taken the Blade, they now needed to *keep* it, and trying to gauge where the loyalties of a nation lay was near impossible. Yet this was not all that was on Jessop's mind.

When she wasn't trying to figure out where Kohl O'Hanlon was and what he was plotting, she thought only of Jeco. His safety meant everything to her. Ensuring the security of the Blade was paramount, but no matter how many guards stood watch, she could not leave Jeco alone. He had to always be with Falco, herself, or Trax. More than anything, she wished Korend'a could join them in the Blade, but he was governing Aranthol in Falco's absence. He was whom they trusted most with their son and their city.

"Certainly," Urdo agreed. Jessop found the older man's eyes on her, narrow with curiosity.

She did not blame him. She had lived amongst the Hunters for quite a time, convincing them daily she was skilled only in blade and not in Sentio, only for them to see what was likely the greatest demonstration of Sentio in all their lives the day Falco arrived. They did not trust her. While they swore allegiance to Falco out of a belief that he was the true Lord of Daharia, a conviction based on memories of his childhood abilities and shared history with Hydo, they did not swear that same allegiance to her. Falco had never lied about his skills or intentions—Jessop had.

"And have we any news on our missing brother?" Falco pressed, referring to Kohl.

Urdo exhaled slowly, bad news travelling on his deep breath. "Nothing. Trax said there have been whisperings, beyond the Grey—some well-known mercenaries spotted traveling together. But no sightings of O'Hanlon."

Jessop watched the way Urdo spoke to Falco. She didn't blame the brothers who stayed for trusting Falco—but their trust in him did not earn her trust in *them*. She had no brethren, she had no army. She had wronged many, more than just Kohl, and she possessed neither the time nor constitution required to make all the necessary amends.

"They'll be arriving by end of day," Urdo spoke, his words pulling her back.

Falco nodded slowly. "Is their camp ready? And do we have enough provisions?"

Urdo seemed to be performing calculations in his mind. "Camp is ready...As long as half your army stays in Aranthol, yes, we should be fine for several months at least."

Jessop flicked her gaze between the two, trying to discern whom they spoke of. Falco turned to her. "You'll want to be there when they arrive, I imagine?"

She chewed the inside of her lip, embarrassed to have lost track of his conversation. Before she could answer though, he spoke again. "I hear Dezane will be bringing them in. It will be wonderful getting to see him after such a long time."

Jessop smiled, realizing who was arriving in the Red City. Perhaps she had been wrong; she did have more allies than she thought. She had the Kuroi.

* * * *

The camp was quite unlike anything Jessop had ever seen before. Behind the Blade stood two towering buildings with few to no finished walls, simply stone floor after stone floor—a docking station for public Soar-Craft. Falco had commissioned new docking stations to be built south of the Blade and commandeered the current ones for his camp. Without any real solid walls, one could see thousands of canvas tents neatly arranged in rows on each open floor. Falco's army had taken over one tower already. There were multiple levitating platforms permanently located outside each floor of each tower, and on the ground below. All that was required was to step onto the platform and utilize a lever to be taken up or down.

As they traveled up the tower, Jessop's eyes flicked over the soldiers. Even though they were her husband's army, Jessop knew they were an unsavory folk; a mess of men, creatures, and machines. Most of them had been hunted or had bounties on their head. They stuck largely to their subgroups, which were defined by illicit profession or region, and there was often intergroup fighting and killing. But they had two things in common; they were all indebted to Falco, and they all had a penchant for violence. They were a formidable army that could be led by one and one alone.

"The Kuroi will not want to associate with them," Jessop spoke, looking up to Falco as they traveled higher up the side of the tower.

The Kuroi were a distinguished people. They abstained from drink and activities of ill repute. A highly select and proud tribe, with ancient traditions and skilled fighters. Jessop knew she held a bias towards them—they were her first family, and she shared their blood—but she did not speak out of bias; the Kuroi wouldn't wish to reside with Falco's army.

Falco kept his eyes trained forward, assessing his troops as they passed. "Hence the second tower."

She did not know if it would be enough to simply keep their quarters apart. Or if that was any real solution at all…They were expected to fight together, but couldn't live or train together. "They need common ground, Falco, if we expect them to fight side by side."

He looked down to her. "They have it. You, myself, Jeco. We are their common ground. You are of the Kuroi, as I am of my army; Jeco is of them both. They will fight for their rightful leader."

She nodded. "Fight, I am certain they will. It's cohabitation I am less convinced of."

"Like I said, two towers."

* * * *

Jessop walked at Falco's side, halting their conversation every so often as he stopped to greet members of his army. They had established their encampments throughout the tower, and Jessop was unsurprised to find many had already formed tents for gambling, drinking, and trade. It was simply their way.

She grew weary of their walk through the tower, her mind set on the arrival of the Kuroi. She could not push him on though. Falco had forged an army from nothing, he had earned the respect of all those who followed him, and he would not disregard their loyal presence in Azgul. She watched as he embraced a soldier with curls of dark hair and one dark eye, a man Jessop did not recognize. The man's leathers were worn, but not cheap, and his skin was marked with many scars and many ink drawings. She carried on down the rows of tents. Many inclined their heads to her as she passed, recognizing her and all she had accomplished on behalf of their leader. Some simply stared, confused by her presence. Jessop was accustomed to both forms of regard; she was a woman in a world of men.

As Falco fell back in stride beside her, she spoke. "How much longer until the Kuroi arrive?"

"The streets will be cleared for their arrival at sunset," he answered, waving to a passing combatant.

Jessop nodded. "Good." She pictured Dezane's face in her mind. It had been too long since she had spoken with the man who helped change her and Falco's lives. He was as much a parent to them both as any could be from a distance. Though he did not raise them in the traditional sense, he had guided them throughout the years. His presence, and that of his warriors, would be of great comfort to her, as Korend'a and Trax's presence had always been. Even if one could not immediately tell she was of their people, for she did not have the dark skin of the desert tribes, she had their eyes, their dark hair, their culture, and their language.

Falco flashed his gaze down to her as they walked on. "Once everyone is settled, we will need to discuss who is fit to become a Hunter."

Jessop stopped walking, grabbing his wrist to halt him. "What are you talking about?"

He smiled over her shoulder, acknowledging another comrade, before turning his gaze back to her. "We need to fill the ranks, Jessop. We lost many disloyal Hunters the day we took the Blade."

His voice was soft and low, and he spoke to her as if his claim was obvious. She had spent several hours walking about a militia of the most dangerous men in Daharia, waiting for an army of one of the oldest tribes in their galaxy. Skilled fighters, experts in their craft, menacing and capable, regardless of whether they were of the Kuroi or Falco's outcasts. None of which made them Hunters, however.

"Falco, Hunters are trained from birth. Sentio cannot be learned after adolescence. You know, better than most, that none here are destined to be Hunters."

He cocked his head at her, his gray eyes unblinking. "Are you suggesting the Hunters are superior to everyone else who follows us?"

She thought on his words. "Not superior. But not the same either."

He crossed his arms. "You became a Hunter. The first woman to ever do so."

"Yes, I did, but can you choose any man here— or in Dezane's army— who could best me in a fight?"

He stared at her with frustration. "Jessop."

"You can't, can you? Because you know what it takes to become an Infinity Hunter is not what it takes to be a soldier. Hunters are something different."

He nodded at her slowly. "Maybe that was true before, but we need to be inclusive now. This is a new dawn for Hunters."

She grabbed his arm and brought him closer to her, needing to keep her voice low. "Falco, you cannot take thousands of the most dangerous men in Daharia and tell them they now are the enforcers of the law—they cannot have that kind of trust or power."

He narrowed his eyes at her. "And what of the Kuroi? Such a noble people, surely they are worthy of the title?"

She crossed her arms over her chest. "However noble, they do not simply inherit the Hunter title because we took the Blade. I agree with you that we need to fill the ranks once again, and I believe that there may be some throughout your army and some throughout the tribe that could wear the sigil, but we cannot simply title all of these men Hunters. It would be a dangerous move. Disrespectful to those Hunters who chose to stay with you, and disingenuous to all those who have come to follow you."

His eyes softened. He exhaled slowly, running a hand over his dark hair. "You're right. Everyone needs to get settled first and we will figure the rest out soon enough."

She smiled softly up to him, taking his hand back in hers. Falco could be rushed in his decision-making; he had a notorious temper that was not restrained by contemplative thought. She knew, though, that when presented with sound reasoning, he could be swayed. If not by Corin, Korend'a, or Dezane, then by her. She always had his ear.

"I heard news of something," he spoke, his tone already lighter.

They turned back to their walk, weaving through tents and smiling at passing soldiers. "Oh?"

He glanced down to her. "Dezane DeHawn will be arriving with an old friend of yours."

* * * *

As Falco had said, the streets had been cleared, but that did not stop the Azguli from finding ways to watch the arrival of the Kuroi warriors. Men, women, and children sat perched in windowsills, lined up on levitating fueling station pads, peeking out of doors, and watching from rooftops. As the red sky shone more brilliantly—their version of a sunset—the Kuroi arrived. They had come on Soar-Craft, but the vessels had landed outside the city limits. The warriors walked through the twisted apricot stone streets, a haze of red dust gathering at their leather-sandaled feet. Before you could see them, you could hear them.

When the Kuroi warriors marched, they sang their battle songs. Thousands of men huffing heavily, their combined breaths sounding like a great, dangerous beast, a predator approaching. Every so often, one would sing out in the Kuroi tongue.

"*Far'a harana, vande far'a sei, far'a daku, vande far'a sei.*" Jessop closed her eyes, listening to the call. *For the fight, we come for you, for the death, we come for you.* There was no doubt that their music was menacing—she could imagine the fear thousands of Azguli felt hearing it for the first time—but to Jessop, it was beautiful. For others, this war song meant death; for Jessop, it meant the arrival of her kind.

She stood with Falco, Trax, Urdo, and a handful of others on the lowest terrace in the Blade. Jeco was on her hip, listening keenly to the war song. She held him tightly, *"Far'a harana, vande far'a sei, far'a daku, vande far'a sei,"* she sang. He listened intently, his gray eyes wide with interest. He understood many words in Kuroi, having been spoken to in the tribal tongue often since his birth, and it was Jessop's intent that he would feel as at peace with their people as she did. When he heard the war song, he would not feel fear but security, knowing his people came to him.

She looked out to the street, watching as the band of warriors appeared amidst the metal and stone buildings. Their dark skin glistened under the red sky, mahogany markings painted over their bodies, disappearing under their ochre-dyed robes. Some held giant shields made of hide, some had their spears—ranging from five to ten feet in length—in hand, others kept them strapped to their backs. Some carried short, thick blades, sheathed in oiled leather around their hips. Their dark hair was braided back, their eyes narrowed on the path ahead as they chanted. They moved as a single unit, singing, breathing, marching, as one.

And leading them was none other than Dezane DeHawn—Trax's father. Dezane seemed unchanged to her. His hair was braided back and his body was also covered in the ochre war paint. His green eyes shone brilliant as ever. His body, though much older than all who marched in tow with him, was still in equal form—strong and sinewy. He was as tall as Jessop remembered, and his shoulders still kept tightly back with every proud step. Despite his age, he was stronger than all those he marched with, and all those who watched him. Dezane had one of the strongest minds in Daharia, fortified by years of meditation and practice; it was near impenetrable. While his body could be seized by another's Sentio, his mind could not.

Jessop looked to Trax, knowing he had likely not seen his father in a very long time. Trips back beyond the Grey to deal with raiders and illicit activities did not ensure a meeting with his tribal leaders. Dezane was equally occupied, often travelling to meet with tribesmen, attend gatherings, and provide dispute resolution. Trax's jaw was tensed but his lips moved in time with the heavy breaths of his Kuroi brethren, and his eyes stayed on his father. Soon, she and Falco would go down to meet Dezane and welcome him into the Blade while his warriors were escorted to their tower to be fed and tended to. Trax would watch Jeco while they brought his father up. As he neared Jessop, she handed her son to him carefully, all three of them keeping their eyes on the approaching Kuroi.

Trax leaned closer to her, keeping his voice quiet. "Who walks with my father?"

Jessop narrowed her eyes on Dezane and those who walked in line with him. At his side, marching in tow with the warriors, was a woman. Jessop cocked her head. The Kuroi were liberal in many things, but she did not recall hearing of any female warrior. She crossed her arms tightly over her chest, wondering how she had not come to hear of such a woman, given her own unique station.

The Kuroi woman was a great beauty, with long braids that reached her hips, full lips, painted dark skin, and glowing yellow eyes. She carried a short sword on her hip and a spear on her back, clearly a warrior.

Jessop was about to tell Trax that she had no idea who walked with his father, when suddenly the yellow eyes of the woman, from so far away, locked on Jessop. She knew in an instant who had arrived in the Red City. Stunned, Jessop managed to nod slowly to the woman, who stared up at her with an unblinking concentration. Jessop couldn't believe it.

"That, Trax, is Mar'e Makenen."

CHAPTER 8

Aranthol

Two years ago

For the third night in a row, Jessop couldn't sleep. She rolled over in the large bed she shared with Falco. It had been several weeks since their fourth wedding anniversary, a time of year they usually reserved for one another, but they had both seemed busier than ever before. They had worked on her Sentio daily. Falco would sift through memories, pushing thoughts at her, trying to enter her mind without her knowledge. Fending him off had been exhausting in the beginning, but she had been capable of it. After years of practice, she could close her mind to him whenever it pleased her. He said it was a rare skill she possessed, but that did not impress her or fill her with a sense of pride. She and Falco were known rarities.

When they weren't working on Sentio, they were in the Pit, and if they weren't in the Pit they were convening with Corin or welcoming newcomers to Aranthol, all the while enhancing their security checks. They knew that protecting their home would never be more important than in the coming months. They performed random searches in the streets, home checks in the boroughs, and they implemented more thorough customs processes. They had spent night and day preparing for her impending departure, and the time had finally come. She was truly exhausted—and yet, she did not sleep.

She had stressed daily over the passing time—when they had first formulated their plan, she had thought it would be executed in weeks. Years had passed, and each day had brought more intense training. Each day she learned that she had not been capable of the plan the day before.

Each day she learned that by the following, she would be more prepared. In the recent weeks, they had both known that the time had come. Her mind was a fortress, her sword hand unparalleled. Though she knew Falco worried still, often thinking of Hydo and the man's renowned skill, she did not feel fear—she felt ready and trapped. She did not want to voice what she already felt so certain of in her heart. Her body was changing, and she was the only one to have noticed.

Falco rolled over, his hand finding hers in half-sleep. She squeezed his fingers tightly. The plan was brilliant. She was supposed to infiltrate the Blade and win over the trust of the Hunters, the only woman to ever attempt such a feat—the only woman likely capable—and when the moment came, she would grant Falco access to the Hunters' home. Then, together, they would take the Blade. It would be a violent affair, but his brothers would come to see reason. He was the *true* Protector—he was their destined leader.

She looked past Falco, to where his Hunter's blade rested beside their bed. She knew that she was supposed to take the weapon as her own and start the process that would change their lives forever. She knew that everything they had worked so hard for had been within their grasp. She lowered her free hand to her stomach. She felt anger, and something perhaps resembling fear. She knew the plan would have to be postponed again, if not entirely abandoned…She felt the tears streaking her cheeks, pooling between her skin and the cushions. She had put off speaking to him for as long as possible. She squeezed his hand tightly.

"Falco," she whispered. With ease he woke, never a deep sleeper.

"What is it?"

Her thumb brushed over her navel, her fingers grazing against the smooth skin of her stomach. She thought of the Blade. She thought of vengeance. She thought of the reaction Falco would have when he knew—

"You're pregnant," he whispered to her.

* * * *

He was laughing at her. Falco, who nearly never cracked a smile, was openly chuckling. She slowly looked over her shoulder to see him. His wide smile pinched his face as he tried to suppress his amusement.

"What is so funny?" she growled.

He stood and came around the side of the bed, standing before her. "Just let me help you up."

She ran her hands over her swollen abdomen. "I don't *need* help." She chewed her lip, knowing that was possibly the first time she had ever lied to Falco. She was three full moons away from birthing and she had never been larger in her life. Her stomach protruded so far out that her breasts rested freely upon it. The scar of where her belly cord had once been had grown outward. Her legs were certainly fuller, though she had much muscle to rely on to carry her newfound weight.

Her back ached with an unceasing pain. If she attempted to rest in any position other than her left side, surrounded by soft cushions, she felt ill, as though all her organs were misplaced. Her hair, however much shinier, needed to be constantly pulled atop her head for she couldn't stand the heat it brought on her neck. Her skin was as dry as that of a foreigner in the desert lands. She hadn't slept since she first fell ill with pregnancy nausea. She woke abruptly in the night, for no reason it seemed, just to think about the life that grew inside her.

She longed for their child to be born for many selfish reasons. She wanted to reclaim her body—to eat and drink and train as she had done every day for years. She wanted to *see* the child, to actually lay eyes upon the baby and know it was safe and well. She lived in constant fear that something she was doing was harming the baby. She had grown neurotic about the foods presented to her. Falco had even employed a taste tester, to check each meal prepared for poison.

Most selfish of all though was Jessop's concern for her marriage. While the child was everything that was good to them, and they had never been more excited for a new future together, she knew how her body had changed. Falco and she had possessed a fiercely physical relationship—whether they were sparring or falling into bed together, they clung to one another's forms. They each relied on their own physical power to fight, and to love. They would rely on it to keep their child safe, though they both knew a child born of them would possess unparalleled abilities.

Falco had insisted he loved her fuller form, though he touched her with caution. He knew her breasts were tender, her back sore, her body tired from sleeplessness and the dedicated growth of their young one. Jessop knew the toll taken on her form was well worth it. She had never imagined loving anyone more than she loved Falco, or even in the same measure, and yet, as soon as she had felt her infant kick firmly inside her, she had felt just that. She had known instantly that the baby would be what stopped her and Falco from leading completely selfish lives. Everything that they had once planned for themselves, they had since modified for their child. Their future was designed around ensuring the baby would have every opportunity, every privilege and security. Still, in a small and seemingly trivial way, she worried about her large frame and newfound fragility.

She looked up into Falco's eyes and reluctantly raised her hands to him. He grabbed onto her gently and pulled her off the bed. She rested against him, safe in his strong arms. "I need to bathe," she explained.

He kissed her forehead. "Let me help you then."

She held his gaze for the longest of moments, wondering if her pride was worth the risk of him actually acquiescing to her claims and not helping. She knew she was wrong.

He smiled softly. "I insist."

She nodded, walking with him to the bathing chamber.

She pulled at the strings of her tunic. She had needed an entirely new wardrobe. Nothing of her former collection could contain her new form. Falco had commissioned the designs, ensuring she wore the finest his money and power could purchase. She thought it was a waste of coin to invest in such finery—she wouldn't need these clothes again. She tried removing her clothes discreetly, without any slow seduction. She felt swollen and unappealing.

He stood behind her and closed his hands around hers. "Jessop, I wish to lay eyes on my wife." His voice was deep, serious but soft. She knew that while he still longed for her, it was she who struggled.

He ran his hands over her shoulders, gently around the sides of her breasts, and rested them on her bump. "You are perfect," he whispered against her neck.

She looked down, keeping her eyes on his hands as they traveled over her swollen stomach. "It is hard for me...for you to see me this way."

"What way? You have grown to carry the child we made together. Your body has moved bone and muscle and organ to accommodate our baby. I had never thought it possible to love you, or *want* you, more than I did before...and yet, here we are."

She turned in his arms, resting her head against his chest. "I love you, Falco."

"And I you, Jessop."

* * * *

Jessop squatted low, pushing her back against the foot of their bed, exhaling heavily. The early hours of labor had arrived and she spent them with Korend'a. The child hadn't been due for another ten days at least. Falco had needed to see to an illegal shipment stopped at customs. A brawl had broken out and several citizens had been killed. He had been gone for hours, and though Korend'a had sent word for him, they had heard nothing in return.

"*Horen'da hei?*" She demanded, reaching for Korend'a's hand. He helped her back to an upright position and she kept her firm grip on him.

"I don't know where he is, *Oray-Ha*, but I imagine he will return soon. Corin knows you have entered labor; guards have been dispatched for him. He will be here."

She studied his soft eyes. If she had to be with anyone other than Falco, she was glad it was Korend'a. She had spent many months with plagued sleep. She would have nightmares of delivering their child without Falco present. He had insisted she was wrong, that he would be by her side for the entirety of the ordeal. Neither of them could have known, when he was called away in the middle of the night, that she would be delivering early. However unintentional, she felt angered still.

She had been angry with him for his absence and also with Hydo, more during her pregnancy than ever before. He had robbed her of the people who should most be at her side during such times. He had robbed them of seeing her grow into a woman capable of giving them a grandchild. He had set her and Falco's lives onto the course they had traveled, and in that way, Jessop found it possible to blame him directly for Falco being summoned to his customs dock in the middle of the night.

The pain came in a wave. It tore through her entire body, rippling through her muscles, gravity forcing the child into its descent. Her knees buckled as she grit her teeth. Korend'a held her steady.

"Breathe through the pain, *Oray-Ha*," he advised, holding her upright. She rested her forehead against his chest. "Where is that *blasted* medic?"

"Here!"

The elderly man with a beard to rival Corin's appeared. He was blind in one eye and had a scar across his old face, but despite age or injury, he was touted as being the best. Falco had asked if she would prefer he find a female medic, willing to search outside of Aranthol for one, but she had declined. She had been raised as a sole woman amongst men in the Shadow City. She didn't need a female friend, a female guard, a female servant, or a female medic. She had lived as one of the men for many years; she hadn't anticipated childbirth changing that feeling of belonging so greatly. Yet, as she clung to Korend'a, she did find herself longing to be in the company of a mother—any woman who had undergone such torment. A man couldn't truly know if everything were going according to plan, could he? He couldn't see her pain and ever claim to have experienced the same.

She dragged Korend'a into a squatting position, keeping her arms on his shoulders for balance. The medic made his way over to them, carrying a large satchel. He placed the bag on the bed and began ordering instructions to the guard in the doorway. He needed to sterilize his instruments and requested hot water be brought to them.

Jessop eyed the old man from her crouched-down position. "Tell me, physician, how many children have you helped bring into the world?"

He seemed to be doing a mental calculation. "Perhaps close to several hundred now, my Lady, but none so important as the child of the Banes."

Jessop dug her fingers into Korend'a, knowing another wave was approaching. "I need a medic, sir, not a sycophant."

The old man nodded sharply. "Of course, my Lady. I only meant the child of the Arantholi Lord will be great indeed."

"I know what y—*arghh!*"

"Breathe, *Oray-Ha!*"

* * * *

He was perfect. He had pale gray eyes, circled in dark lashes, and he took to her breast without hassle. Falco rested beside her, staring down at his son with unblinking intensity. "I told you I wouldn't miss it."

She rolled her eyes. "You came running through the door at the exact moment."

Falco kissed her shoulder. "I'm sorry."

She ran a finger softly over the baby's cheek. "You saw him breathe his first. That is all that matters."

He reached over and touched the boy's small face. "And I will love him long after I breathe my last. As I do his mother."

Jessop smiled but she did not take her eyes off of her son. The agony of bringing him into the world paled in comparison to seeing the rise and fall of his chest as he breathed. She knew that the love she felt for him as he grew inside her these many months had only multiplied with his arrival. She thought no longer of the toll he had taken on her body. Instead, she saw only his perfect skin, his father's eyes, the curve of his lip, and knew all she had done she had done to fashion his form.

She knew in an instant that she would have done it all over again. They had never discussed a family. Orphaned at such young ages, they were the only family one another knew, the only family they needed. Yet their son was the greatest joy either had ever known. "Jeco Bane," she whispered, holding him closer to her beating heart. They had decided the name together—a combination of their own forenames.

"Jeco *Jero* Bane," Falco corrected.

She turned to him. "You honor my parents."

He smiled at her softly. "Our son does."

* * * *

For months after Jeco's birth, neither Falco nor Jessop slept. Whether their son slept or woke, cried or rested, they were watching over him. During the days, Korend'a would be at their side, tending to the child as though he too were the boy's parent. Falco had increased the guards so that wherever the boy went, in the arms of Jessop or Falco, he was accompanied by four additional Kuroi guardsmen. Korend'a had helped in choosing those for the assignment, insisting he vet all the options.

Jessop had known as soon as they found out about the pregnancy that their plans had been indefinitely delayed, and as she held her son in her arms, she could not imagine ever leaving his side. Yet, they could sense his power already. He was a child who rarely cried, he had a calming effect on all who neared him, and he was pensive, even in such infancy. "He deserves all of Daharia," Falco had said.

He was right. Their son would be the leader of their galaxy. He had great power and deserved a position from which to rule, and it was up to her and Falco to carve that position out for him. He was the son of the true Protector of the Blade of Light—they knew his destiny. "And all of Daharia he will have," she agreed.

CHAPTER 9

Aranthol

Eight months ago

"He's sanctimonious...Even as a boy he walked around with this holier-than-thou attitude. So bloody moral all the time," Falco sneered, rolling onto his back and lifting Jeco up above him.

"Yes, he's self-righteous, isn't he, little man?" he continued, his voice mimicking that of a child as he stirred laughter from his young son.

Jessop stared at Falco. He had told her everything there was to know about Hydo Jesuin, the murderer of her parents and Falco's former mentor. She knew that Hydo had a liking for green eyed-women and the drink, but that he saved his deviousness for regions beyond Azgul. He kept up appearances always, he made rational decisions when sober, and he was a master with a blade. Falco had no issue disparaging the man, but he made a point of telling Jessop that the Hunter Lord had won his mantle fair and square—his abilities were not trivial.

He had then told her of Hanson Knell. Hanson was as scrupulous as he was naturally suspicious. He had never taken to any women and Falco had speculated that the Councilman had no interest in any physical relationships. "He's above it all, or at least he seems to be," Falco had said. Jessop would not be able to rely on her physical appearance to win him over. And there were more, Falco had said—other Councilmen who harbored more disdain for women than lust.

But he for whom Falco had reserved the most vitriol was Kohl O'Hanlon, her way into the Blade. Falco had described a pious, self-satisfied sycophant, with the skill required to best most of his brethren, but never Falco. "And definitely not you; you could carve him lip to loins if you wished." Jessop had shrugged off the sentiment—whom, aside from her own husband, could she not best with a blade?

Perhaps Hydo. The thought had crossed her mind. The man was revered, undoubtedly skilled. Jessop feared him not though. He was old, he was unsuspecting, and he had grown too comfortable in his seat of power. She imagined the Hunter Lord hadn't even had reason to take up the blade in decades…at least not since Falco had confronted him.

"How do you know he'll want me?" she asked, turning her mind back to Kohl O'Hanlon.

Falco lowered Jeco between them. "Because since childhood Kohl has wanted everything that is rightfully mine. The only reason he would turn his back on me as he did was so that I would be expelled from the Blade, thus clearing a path for his own success."

She ran her fingers over Jeco's soft head of hair, lulling the boy to sleep. "I don't want him to want me."

Falco rested his hand on Jeco's small chest, looking over the sleeping boy with love. "Everything we do, we do for him now. Don't you know that the thought of what you might have to do kills me inside? I know what this plan entails."

"Then we can think of another plan," she rebutted, trying to keep her voice low so as to not wake Jeco.

"I've tried. We have spent years thinking this through. The ruler of Daharia must hold the Daharian Blade of Light—that is what Daharians will respond to. We could rain fire and war down on the Blade—we have the armies to do just that—but it means nothing if we don't have five living Hunters to get you or me access to that weapon."

"What about Sentio? I could force their hands with my mind."

"They would die in battle before letting their minds be infiltrated."

She ran a hand through her dark hair. She knew he spoke the truth. They had contemplated every plan, they had discussed every potential eventuation, and they knew what needed to be done. This was a war that needed to be started from within the Blade, and of the two of them, she was the only one capable of getting in. She lifted her son from the bed and moved him to his bassinet. She would do anything for her family—anything to see Hydo pay. Even if it meant winning over the heart of some stranger just to break it into a thousand pieces.

* * * *

Jessop paced the room, slowly rocking Jeco back and forth in her arms. She looked into his eyes, which had only the faintest Kuroi glow, and wondered if he saw hers as only one of Kuroi lineage could. Falco had never seen her eyes glow green, though he had often said they shone with a supernatural brightness.

She could not fathom leaving her son. He was but a year and a half, he *needed* her, and Falco needed her too. She had been prepared to go, before. Before the pregnancy, before Jeco, before realizing that her heart lived inside the small chest of her only child.

She sensed Falco as he opened his eyes. She could feel him when they were in the same room, feet apart. They had become extensions of one another.

"Did he wake you?" he asked, scooting to the end of their bed.

She shook her head, knowing his eyes had grown keen in the darkness as well and he could see the gesture.

"Jessop, he will be safe with me. Do you think Korend'a will ever let him out of my sight, or his, for that matter?"

His voice was teasing, but he spoke the truth.

"He's my son, Falco. How can I part from him? It's like asking me to leave behind my heart," she explained.

He stood and walked over to her. She watched the curve of his muscle, twisted and taut as he took each step toward her, always moving with graceful agility. Her eyes trailed up to his and her heart swelled with love and longing. He was the father of her child, the love of her life, her greatest ally. He took Jeco from her and placed him slowly back in his bassinet.

He took Jessop's hands in his and pulled her close. "Everything you are doing is for him. You risk several months, maybe a year, of distance, to ensure a lifetime of rightful power for him. You legitimize his claim to the Daharian galaxy. You restore me to my *rightful* position, to prepare the Blade for Jeco one day."

She nodded. "I know. I just feel as though my heart is breaking."

"I will be with you every step of the way. Here," he whispered, touching her temple softly. "And here," he lowered his hand to her chest, holding it firmly over her heart.

She ran her hands up his chest and kissed him. His lips were warm against hers, his body emanating heat. He ran his hands through her hair and drew her closer to him. "Your bravery will change our lives, Jessop."

She remembered the fire; its heat, its arching flames and thick smoke. "As yours once did, long ago."

＊ ＊ ＊

Jessop spun Falco's blade about her, twisting its hilt, growing comfortable with its weight. She would take his Hunter Blade with her when she left, as tangible evidence of her claims. The blade was perfect in weight and balance. She had fought with many weapons, nearly always opting for her two needle-shaped daggers, but she knew Falco's weapon was quite special.

Falco circled her, two swords twisting in opposite directions around his body. "Every Hunter fights with a Hunter Blade. Forged by the remaining sediment of star formations, the glass is harder than any substance found in our galaxy. The blade is designed to reflect its owner—strong, capable, deadly."

Jessop flicked the weapon about, marveling at its beauty. She had never fought with Falco's blade. The hilt was somewhat big for her grip, but she had the strength to wield it nonetheless. The blade sung through the air and she thought of the many times she had deflected its deadly edge in their sparring sessions. She looked up from the Pit to Korend'a, who held Jeco in his arms. "What do you think, Korend'a?"

He nodded down at her approvingly. "It suits you, *Oray-Ha*." Jeco struggled against Korend'a arms, growing frustrated as a spectator to his parents training. Jessop lowered the blade and crossed the Pit, knowing he needed her.

He wriggled his little hands free and held them out towards her. "Mama," he called, and as he closed his small fingers into tight little fists, Jessop felt the Hunter's Blade lurch free from her grip.

"Jeco, no!"

The blade flipped through the air, commanded inadvertently by Jeco. Jessop felt as though her body were draining of blood, her heart frozen, her eyes wide with horror. Suddenly, the blade froze mid-air.

Falco had his hand turned out, having taken hold of the blade, cutting through his son's abilities. Jessop leapt in the air and grabbed the hilt, quickly sheathing the weapon. She crouched down and pushed off the onyx floor, leaping up onto the lip of the Pit to take Jeco in her arms. Korend'a quickly handed the boy to her.

She looked him over, uncertain what she thought she might find. He had never done such a thing. Sentio was something that needed to be taught and they had never...He was powerful already. Falco was at her side in an instant, examining their son with an equally critical eye.

She pulled Jeco closer to her chest as she looked to her husband. "How could he do that already?"

He was silent for a long moment, stroking Jeco's dark hair softly. "He's destined to rule. His abilities already showing through simply indicate the speed at which he will overtake even us, Jessop."

She knew what Falco said was true, and she knew what it meant. The time had finally come. She needed to leave her son, her husband, her closest ally, and make for Azgul. If Jeco could already pull a blade free from her, there was no telling what greater abilities each day would bring. Were any outside of Aranthol to ever learn of him, they would hunt him down simply for being a Bane. Jessop couldn't imagine the danger if Hydo learned the child of his enemy was born with such skill.

"It's time," she whispered, kissing Jeco's head.

* * * *

She rested her head against Falco's shoulder, their bodies still intertwined, slick with sweat, tender and electric all at once. Their hearts, as always, beating as one, their scars—a woven design of the letters of Jeco's name—touching one another. She kissed his collarbone as she sat up, needing to see his face.

His gray eyes were soft and sad, framed by dark lashes. She ran her finger over the scar that cut down his face, running her thumb over his bottom lip. "Leaving you is breaking my heart," she whispered, her voice cracking over the words.

A tear trailed down his cheek, tracing his scar. He grabbed her hand and brought it back to his mouth, kissing her fingers. "It's killing me just to think about it."

She cried in his arms. He held her tightly and they rocked back and forth, swaying one another into a soothed comfort. They stayed that way for many hours, declaring their love for one another again and again, whispering their despair, clinging to one another, as they always had, as they always would.

Eventually, Korend'a brought Jeco back to them. She held him the entire night, forgoing sleep, watching him as he dreamt. She had never entered her son's mind, feeling as though it would be a betrayal, but she often pushed thoughts at him. She told him of her love for him. She showed him images of her life with Falco, she shared with him the sense of safety and protection that she had always known with his father.

"The world may say and think many things about us, about *him*, but we know the truth. We know one another," she had told him. She knew Jeco was born into a time where Falco Bane was the most feared man in

Daharia. She knew that if they stayed in Aranthol for all of their lives, not only would they be forgoing their rightful positions of power, but they would be raising their son amidst the constant lies, gossip, and ridicule. If Jessop did not act now, Jeco would be regarded as the dangerous son of a traitor, instead of the rightful successor to the Daharian Blade of Light, born to the most skilled Hunter to ever live. She had the opportunity to correct the narrative of his future, if she were to act while he was still young. Leaving broke her heart, but it secured his future.

* * * *

Jessop hugged Korend'a tightly, "*Had'away hei*," she whispered, telling him to watch over Jeco.

Slowly, he released her. "*Baruk, Oray-Ha*," he offered with a tight smile. It was late in the night and they stood at the far edge of the city. The Soar-Craft was small but well-engineered, prepared for her to travel the distance to Azgul without needing to stop.

She kissed her son once more, holding his sleeping body tight against hers. "I love you with all that I am," she whispered. She handed him to Korend'a, certain she could feel the fibers of her heart tearing. She told herself she was doing this for him; again and again she whispered the mantra inside her head.

Falco pulled her into his arms, holding her firmly against his chest. She felt with each heaving movement that he was forcing back tears. They had always been with one another, always lived as one, since Hydo had set everything into motion so many years ago. She needed him as he needed her.

"You are everything to me," he whispered.

She kissed him. She ran her hands over his short hair and around his shoulders. She touched his face and chest and hugged him tightly. She kissed his neck and mouth and felt the fire of despair rising up in her throat.

"It's always been you, Falco. It will always be you. No matter what."

He nodded, his eyes dark with tears. "Do what you must."

CHAPTER 10

Azgul

Present-day

Jessop embraced Dezane, holding him tightly in her arms, trying to focus on the reunification instead of on the unyielding stare she felt from Mar'e. In her periphery she saw the woman, her old friend, greet Falco. "You grew into the scar." She smiled, bowing her head low to him.

He offered her a small smile and gestured to her weapon, "I remember your dislike for all things grotesque. I must admit I am surprised to see the path you have clearly chosen."

She rested her slender fingers on the hilt of her short sword. "This is a different time. The Kuroi have no issue with women taking up arms."

Falco inclined his head. "I said I was surprised by your choice—not the Kuroi's."

Before the two could speak further, Dezane released Jessop from her embrace, turning to Falco. The two took arms, embracing quickly. "Dezane DeHawn, you are most welcome in the Red City," Falco smiled.

Dezane nodded slowly, looking up at the Blade. "Words I never thought I would hear before meeting you, young Falco."

As they spoke, Jessop turned to Mar'e. Her young friend was no longer quite so young. Of course, just like Jessop, she had grown up. She was undeniably striking, with full lips and arched brows. She wore her ochre robes fitted and donning a weapon somehow suited her—regardless of however capable she may have been with it. But Jessop saw the same look, the one that had been there in childhood. Mar'e regarded her with contest in her eyes, forever viewing Jessop as competition instead of comrade.

She could see it in the way she stood so near to Falco, in the way she had positioned herself in Dezane's life—Mar'e was as ambitious as ever. Jessop knew she must have become quite skilled in either spear or speech to have come to be in Dezane's favor.

Jessop offered a brief embrace to her old friend. "Mar'e Makenen, I am…surprised."

Mar'e looked her over with surprising warmth, squeezing her tightly despite the briefness of their embrace, and for a moment, Jessop felt remiss for dismissing her old friend as unchanged in her youthful malevolence. "Jessop Jero, the years have been good to you."

Jessop brought her hand to her hip, flashing her black wedding band. "It's Jessop *Bane*."

Mar'e smiled, "Of course. I had heard as much."

Jessop instinctively took a step closer to Falco. "And it is still Mar'e Makenen, is it not?"

The woman's smile faded. "Yes. Still Makenen. My time training and serving Dezane has kept me quite busy. Too busy for concerns about a wedding ceremony or children."

Jessop smiled as her friend smiled. She kept her tone light, as Mar'e did, but she knew the other woman was taking a jab at her. Mar'e was certainly unchanged, but little did she know Jessop was an entirely different person from the girl she had once known.

* * * *

Jessop had bombarded Dezane with questions as they made their way up the Blade and towards the Assembly Council room. While she and Dezane conversed in Kuroi, Mar'e held Falco's ear in the common tongue, asking him almost as much as Jessop asked Dezane.

"*Baruk*, we always knew this day would come. The Kuroi have never lost faith in Falco," Dezane answered as they turned down another glass corridor.

"Never," Mar'e was quick to add, smiling to Falco. Falco remained silent, his eyes catching Jessop's. *She's unchanged,* Jessop pushed the thought his way. He inclined his head ever so slightly in agreement.

Jessop had to admit the Kuroi elder, dressed in his warrior garb, looked out of place in the modern environment of the Blade. She knew he would have new attire waiting for him in his room, as all his troops would in their tower. Their robes would not suffice for the weather in the Red City; though not cold, it was not the warmth they were accustomed to beyond the Grey.

"Father," Trax's voice startled Jessop, drawing her gaze forward. Trax stood several inches taller than most men, but his wide eyes, the way in which his mouth remained slightly parted as he stared at his father, presented him in a youthful light. Jeco was asleep in his strong arms, his small head resting peacefully against the Hunter. She approached her friend and took her son from his arms, quickly stepping out of the way and allowing for Trax to embrace his father. They embraced tightly for a long minute, releasing one another with reluctance. She knew the father and son should speak in private. Meeting with the Assembly Council could wait.

"Falco, Trax can show Dezane and Mar'e to their quarters. Why don't we reconvene for supper?"

Falco walked around the Kuroi elder and took his place at her side. "I agree. Dezane, it is most excellent to have you in the Blade. Trax, Mar'e, we will see you shortly."

Mar'e bowed her head low but kept her eyes on Falco. Dezane smiled warmly, but Jessop could see the exhaustion in the older man's face. He had traveled far and would need rest. Tonight, they would regain their strength; tomorrow, they would strategize a new future for Daharia.

* * * *

"She likes you," Jessop spoke quietly as she lowered Jeco into his bed.

She turned from the sleeping boy and found Falco undressing. He pulled his tunic off, revealing his body of silver scars. Muscle built upon scar, scar built upon muscle. He continued to undress as he made his way to the bathing chamber.

"Falco." She pressed, following him.

He adjusted the water. "Yes?"

"I said she likes you."

He stepped under the heavy downpour. "Who?"

Jessop leaned against the doorway, her arms crossed over her chest. "What do you mean *who*? Mar'e. She couldn't take her eyes off you."

Falco ran his hands through his wet hair. He tilted his head back and let the water rush over his face. When he looked at her, water droplets clung to his dark lashes. "She likes antagonizing you, as she did when you were younger. It had nothing to do with me then, it has nothing to do with me now."

Jessop shrugged. "Maybe. Or maybe it has everything to do with you."

Falco stepped out of the water and approached her, his eyes fixed on hers. "You saw much of her body today, in her robes."

Jessop crossed and uncrossed her arms. "Yes, what of it?"

He rested his wet hands on her shoulders, his fingertips rubbing her neck. "Though she holds a blade, Mar'e Makenen bears no scars."

Jessop hadn't really looked, but she trusted Falco was right. "That may just be a testament to her skill."

"What it testifies to is a history she does not share with me. It was not Mar'e Makenen who lost flesh for my cause." At his words, his hands traveled over her back, her lash scars.

His hands danced over her hips, up her stomach. "It was not Mar'e Makenen who carried my son for so many moons, bringing me my greatest joy."

He rested his palm against her most recent scar—Kohl's stab wound. "She did not nearly die to ensure my place in the Blade and the rightful future for my son."

Jessop smiled softly up to him, inching her body closer to his. He moved a loose strand of hair out of her face. He tilted his head low, his lips nearing hers. "I don't care if she couldn't take her eyes off me. My eyes are always only ever on you."

* * * *

Jessop woke early the following morning, making her way through the silent Blade, down to the Hollow. Dinner the previous night had been for the most part enjoyable; Dezane and Trax had held the group captive with many stories of their family, much reminiscing and an even greater amount of catching up. Jessop and Falco recognized many names out of their long-shared history with the Kuroi tribal leader, but Jessop found herself most amazed by Trax. They had mind-shared early in their friendship, but neither the insight into his past nor any conversation he had ever had with her had reflected such a joyous demeanor as the one she had seen that night; a recollection of some happier past long since left behind.

She delighted in seeing him reunited with his father, who was so like a father to herself and Falco. Mar'e hadn't even managed to agitate her. She spoke to Falco and made her small barbed comments, but Jessop wouldn't be provoked. Not when she had waited so long for the Kuroi to arrive. She had learned that Mar'e served as an advisor to Dezane, information that surprised Jessop. Dezane openly spoke of Mar'e, her growth and maturation. As he beamed with pride, Jessop felt a twist of discontent in her stomach. Dezane had favored *her* in childhood. She hadn't thought that in her absence, Mar'e would have been the one to take her place.

To Jessop's annoyance, she found the Hollow to be occupied, by none other than Mar'e and Trax. Jessop watched them silently from above as they sparred. She knew Trax's skill, but witnessing that of her former friend was most captivating. Mar'e had been trained well. She wasn't the most poised fighter, relying on strength and aggression over grace or skill, but she was good. She lunged with force; she threw her body low and leapt high, grunting and hissing with each move. Trax was her superior, undoubtedly—but she made him sweat.

Jessop crossed her arms over her chest, watching the two as they darted about the Hollow. They ducked through the ropes, leapt about the levitating platforms, and circled the fiery pits. Finally, as Mar'e swung too eagerly, Trax disarmed her. Slowly, Jessop clapped for them. Startled, they both jolted about to see her. With an easy flip, Jessop dove into the Hollow. She landed firmly on her feet, bending her knee to absorb the impact, one hand on the black gem hilt of her blade.

She smiled tightly. "Trax, do you have a second round in you?"

He smiled back at her, but before he could answer, Mar'e spoke up. She took a keen step towards Jessop. "I'll duel you, Jessop."

Jessop eyed the woman slowly, and suppressed a bemused smile. "Absolutely not."

The bright-eyed woman cocked her head to the side, her mess of long braids falling over her shoulder. "And why is that?"

Jessop narrowed her gaze at her old friend incredulously. "No insult intended, Mar'e, for I have seen your skill, but you simply aren't capable."

Mar'e took a step back, glowering. "That's not—"

Before she could say another word, Jessop was in her mind. She had spent so long concealing her abilities, her true nature, that acting with deliberation and power once again was liberating. She answered to no one. She wouldn't continue to be disrespected by anyone, least of all by a long-since-abandoned friend.

Jessop smiled at her slowly. "You were saying?"

The Kuroi woman's full lips trembled as she tried to answer Jessop; her glowing eyes widened. Jessop watched as Mar'e struggled for her sword, unable to move a muscle, trapped in her own body by Jessop's mind.

Jessop reached out slowly, one finger extended, and stroked Mare's cheek. "Reach for your sword, friend."

The woman grunted inaudibly, angry and shaken, trapped by paralysis. Jessop uncoiled her hand and cupped Mar'e's smooth cheek, letting her thumb run over her quivering lip. She took a step towards her and leaned as close as possible, her lips grazing Mar'e's warm, dark skin as she spoke. "You are not competition for me, friend. Not with the blade, not with Falco." "Jessop," Trax spoke, urging her to let up on Mar'e.

Slowly, she pulled away from Mar'e, smiling at her as she freed her. Mar'e stumbled, her hand fumbling on her hilt, her body shaking. She had likely never been under the control of Sentio before and Jessop couldn't deny relishing in upsetting the other woman.

Mar'e glared at Jessop. "That's not true, if—"

Before she could speak further, Trax interrupted. "It *is* true. Mar'e, none of us could truly fight Jessop, none but..."

"None but *me*."

Falco's voice surprised them all. Jessop looked up and saw him standing at the lip of the Hollow, Jeco in his arms. She had been too occupied by Mar'e to feel his presence.

Falco shifted their son in his arms. "Trax, would you please look after Jeco? My wife needs a sparring partner. A *capable* one."

Jessop noted how Mar'e stirred at Falco's words; he knew of their conversation already. She knew that the extent of their abilities could be very startling for some. Trax leapt from the Hollow floor, graceful and silent as he landed beside Falco. Mar'e gave Jessop a wide berth. Once out of arm's reach, she scaled a long, worn rope, quickly finding her way out of the Hollow. As Trax took Jeco in his arms, Mar'e moved around them, eager to leave.

"Mar'e," Falco stopped her. She slowly turned to face him, her glowing eyes wide.

He smiled to her. "Stay and watch."

She shook her head, already pivoting away. "Actually, I would rather—"

Falco shook his head slowly. "It's not a request."

Slowly, Mar'e nodded. Falco smiled to her once more, and then leapt from the edge. He landed directly beside Jessop, so close that their linens grazed, but both knew his positioning had been deliberate. He ran the back of his hand over her cheek. "Well enough to spar, my love?"

Jessop kissed his fingers as they passed over her lip. "Indeed." He smiled as he backed away from her, his hand falling from her face to his hilt.

They circled one another slowly, the excitement pulling a smile across Jessop's face. It had been long—*too* long—since they had trained. She did not let her mind wander to her wound, to the scar Kohl had left on her. She remained focused, enjoying the rush of adrenaline, the anticipation building inside her.

Falco took easy steps backwards, his eyes never leaving hers. "Blades?"

Jessop nodded. "Blades." She needed to try out the new weapon, the weapon which she had so longed for and had so nearly ended her life. He changed footing, pacing counterclockwise. "Sentio?" She smiled at him smugly, "Give it your best shot." He smiled back at her. "I think I shall."

Without another word, Falco shot his hand out and Jessop felt a wave of force pushing against her chest. She spun out, unsheathed her blade, and cut through the mystical energy with ease. Falco met her blade with his own, the two weapons crying out as they found one another. Jessop spun again, connecting a closed-fist back hand against Falco. She went to strike, but he blocked and forced her back with his blade.

They moved with unparalleled speed and precision, executing movements that would have left a lesser opponent stunned or dead. For every strike, there was a counter; for every move, a parry. Neither slowed, neither stumbled. They moved like a desert storm, a tunnel of wind ripping the world around them apart. She kicked him back and he flipped away; he lunged and she ducked; they fought not just sword against sword, but hand against hand. They covered the entire Hollow grounds—leaping across fiery pits, over floating platforms, scaling the walls and sliding across the ground.

Sweat drenched their linens, their brows, and both grew quick of breath after the long duel continued. For a time though, Jessop forgot about Mar'e. She forgot about their audience, she forgot about Kohl O'Hanlon and how he had nearly killed her. She forgot that the place they lived in had ever belonged to anyone but them. She forgot that they had a war to wage, and men to find and capture, men to find and kill. She forgot it all—because that was the effect Falco had on her. When they fought, as when they made love, the world was only theirs.

* * * *

Jessop was so embroiled in her fight that she never heard the conversation between Mar'e and Trax. As the Kuroi Councilman rocked Jeco back and forth in his arms, Mar'e watched the fight with wide-eyed shock. With gasps and shakes of her head, she finally turned to Trax.

She stared up at him, their yellow eyes connected. "They're…terrifying."

Trax nodded slowly. He had seen much when he mind-shared with Jessop, but to watch her fight with Falco, it was more than what he had seen that night in Okton-Radon, more than what he had ever imagined. They were unstoppable. Relentless in their assaults, they moved faster than any he had ever seen. He remembered Falco as a young boy, how impressive he had been then. His abilities had never peaked, it seemed, for he had grown stronger and more capable in his exile than anyone could have fathomed. He could only think of the terror one would feel facing either in a true battle. He nodded to Mar'e slowly. "Imagine how Kohl O'Hanlon feels knowing these two are coming after him."

Mar'e had heard the story—Dezane had told her what had transpired in the Glass Blade before their arrival. "He doesn't stand a chance against them."

Trax thought of Kohl and all that his fallen brother had endured at the hands of Jessop Bane. Kohl should have accepted Falco's offer, to remain in the Blade and follow the rightful rule. He should have done a lot of things differently. But Trax had seen the way Kohl looked at Jessop; he had truly loved her, and he probably still did, even if it was masked as hatred. He turned his gaze back to the fight. The way Jessop moved with Falco, the way they acted as one, their eyes always on one another...

He readjusted Jeco in his arms. "Kohl never stood a chance coming between them. No one did."

Mar'e cocked her head up to Trax. "I meant coming up *against* them, not coming *between* them."

Trax turned to the Kuroi woman. "You'll learn this quickly, Mar'e, as I did; as Kohl O'Hanlon has—when it comes to those two, there's no difference."

CHAPTER 11

Jessop woke early to bathe Jeco before her morning training. She had slept well thanks to her spar with Falco. It had been one of the first nights she hadn't had a nightmare about Kohl. His absence in her dreams did not remove him from her waking thoughts and she found herself distracted as she readied Jeco for the day. She had thought about the night Kohl had taken her up the Blade, to watch as evening fell on Azgul.

"I would keep all your secrets, if you let me," he whispered, leaning closer to her.

His hand found the back of her head softly, and she could feel his thumb brushing against her affectionately as he tilted her face up to him. The intensity of his golden stare nearly made her forget...everything.

Just before his lips found hers, she remembered herself. She rested a firm hand against his chest, stopping him from kissing her.

"Maybe one day you will," she whispered.

"Jessop?" Falco's voice pulled her back to the moment. She finished dressing Jeco, pivoting on her knee to look up at her husband.

"I called your name twice," he explained, staring at her intently.

"I was distracted," she explained, lifting Jeco into her arms as she stood.

While Falco was too busy to spar with her, he had agreed to watch Jeco. She walked past him, towards their own bed. Jessop intended to find Trax for a morning training.

Falco took Jeco from her and sat him down on their bed. "You'll be in the Hollow?"

She tightened her vest. "Yes, if Trax can train; otherwise I will come join you sooner."

"Are you alright, Jessop?"

She nodded quickly, "I'm fine."

"Is it Kohl? I thought you slept well last night."

She kissed him quickly. "I slept fine. It's nothing." She quickly kissed Jeco and turned from them, making a swift exit. Before he could ask her anything further, before he could enter her mind and see all her memories of his disloyal brother.

As she made her way down the corridor, she passed a room of young Hunters-in-training. She rarely saw the children, as they were never without their instructors. She wondered if Jeco should be joining such classes soon, or if his training was best left to her and Falco. She saw the young boys in their black linens and small vests with the Hunters' sigil emblazoned on their chests, attempting to levitate miniature blades. They must have been five or six years of age, and only half of them had managed the task. Jeco, though half their age, was already far superior.

She carried on, taking a bullet down several floors before reaching Trax's corridor. Jessop had found a new route to Trax's chambers, one that did not require passing Kohl's old room. She couldn't bring herself to enter that space—*his* space. Where everything meaningful between them had transpired. She knew that no matter how powerful she was, no matter how many stood in her army, no matter how great her love for Falco, she could not forget how she had wronged Kohl O'Hanlon. Jessop was not a sympathetic woman—she felt little for others, as others had always felt little for her—but not when it came to Kohl. There was much between them still—he had loved her, and he had nearly killed her.

She knew, no matter how Falco pressed the issue, she didn't want Kohl dead. Even if some part of her sought vengeance for his mutiny, deep down, Jessop knew he didn't deserve to die. Death came easily for her and Falco—they had killed so many. But she knew that Kohl was not like the others who had tested her patience or questioned their rule. Kohl didn't deserve what she had done to him.

"Jessop."

Mar'e appeared from around the corner. Jessop froze, slowly crossing her arms over her chest, noting that Mar'e came from the direction of Trax's room. "Mar'e."

The two stood in silence. Jessop couldn't help but see the face of thirteen-year-old Mar'e, her eyes so unchanged. She remembered how close they had been, but knew that even then, their closeness had been tainted by her friend's superiority complex. Jessop knew that no matter how much power she wielded, whom she had married, or the size of her army, Mar'e

Makenen would always believe herself to be superior to Jessop—for she was full-blooded Kuroi.

Mar'e readjusted her stance, placing her hands on her hips, her shoulders held tightly back. "I was hoping to see you. I wanted to apologize."

Jessop couldn't help but hide the surprise in her face, knowing her arched brow gave her away. "Oh?"

"I was wrong to treat you as I have, both in childhood and during my time in the Blade. I spoke to Falco inappropriately and I greatly underestimated you, your abilities…and your marriage." She lowered her golden gaze for a brief moment, seeming ashamed.

Jessop lowered her arms and then re-crossed them. Mar'e had never apologized to her, not in all the years she had known the girl. Jessop had intentionally frightened her in the Hollow to demand respect, but never had she imagined evoking remorse.

"*Sevos*, Mar'e. I appreciate it," she nodded to her old friend.

Mar'e offered a tight smile back, clearly made as uncomfortable as Jessop was by the sincere conversation. Aggression was simply easier for some, far easier than sensitivity. "*Baruk*, Jessop. I would appreciate the opportunity to start over. If we could start anew…"

Jessop cut her off. "Of course." She didn't need to force the other woman to carry on. Jessop was not one for second chances, but she had been truly surprised by the apology Mar'e offered. The least she could do was be gracious.

Mar'e offered her a small smile. "Were you looking for a sparring partner?"

Jessop inclined her head slowly. "Mar'e, you know you can't spar with me." She meant no insult, but didn't understand why Mar'e would volunteer after the display Jessop and Falco had put on for her.

"I cannot best you, this is true, but refrain from Sentio and stick to the blade, and I promise I will at least help get your heart going," she offered.

Jessop wanted to decline, knowing that the training she required Mar'e was not capable of participating in. But she also knew alliances were important when you had as many enemies as she did. She smiled tightly and nodded, pivoting around in the direction of the Hollow.

* * * *

"So, he loved you," Mar'e concluded, sitting opposite Jessop. They had sparred, but not for long. Mar'e, despite her best efforts, could not keep up. During their rest they began to discuss how their lives had fared in all their years apart. Mar'e had never taken a spouse, though she had options. She had found that her position in Dezane's life was all-consuming, and that she could not abandon him in order to start a family. Jessop found that Mar'e had grown true affection for the elder, her loyalties to him stronger than her wish to have a family. Jessop had told her of her life with Falco, of Aranthol, Jeco, and how she had come to overthrow Hydo. Which of course, had brought up Kohl.

Jessop nodded slowly, her hand immediately reaching for the scar on her abdomen. "Yes, he loved me."

"I imagine he still does."

Jessop locked eyes with her old friend. "He tried to kill me."

"We all know what they say about love and hate."

"Regardless," Jessop spoke, readjusting her position so she could lean against the cool wall. "I could never love him back."

Mar'e arched a well-defined brow. "Even though you slept with him?"

"I did what I had to do for my family. Falco is my everything, as is our son. I would do it all over again if it meant securing Jeco's future."

Mar'e shifted in her seat. "All of it? Would you even let him stab you?"

Jessop took a deep breath, thinking of the wound he had inflicted, knowing how close to death she had come. "I deserved it, I know that. But if he ever tried it again, I'd kill him in an instant." Only as she said the words did Jessop actually know them to be true. She wouldn't agree with Falco; she wouldn't kill Kohl for his trespasses against either of them. That did not mean she would ever let him trespass her *again*.

Mar'e looked at her with a perplexed stare. Jessop knew it was complicated. Perhaps too complicated to explain to anyone. She ran her hand over her scar. "I won't kill Kohl for his attempt on my life, not after all I did to him. But if he comes after us—my son, my husband—I would stop him."

Mar'e slowly got to her feet and offered Jessop a hand up. Jessop took her hand, standing and stretching out.

"And will he?"

Jessop looked back to her friend. "Will he what?"

Mar'e shot her an obvious look. "Will he come after you?"

Jessop saw his face, his pale-yellow eyes and blond hair. His star scar. She thought of the nightmares she had. Of the memories that plagued her. She could close her eyes and remember his hand on her face, how quickly he had become devoted to her. She saw the way her treachery had destroyed him. She had seen his heart break. "Undoubtedly."

* * * *

Jessop turned the corner and nearly collided with Falco. He had Jeco in his arms and a stern look on his face. "Where were you?" he demanded. She ran her hand over Jeco's soft dark hair. "In the Hollow—as I told you I would be."

Falco nodded. "Right. Sorry. Look—we need to get to the Council Assembly room."

Jessop noticed the strain in his voice, the tension in his face. She knew something was wrong and found her way into his mind. He welcomed her presence, their eyes locking as he showed her all he knew. Jessop's heart began to race.

"Korend'a," she whispered, pulling free from the images Falco shared with her.

They rushed to the Council Assembly room and found Urdo, Trax, Dezane and the others waiting for them already. While all of the men speculated in harsh voices, wondering why they had been called by Falco, Dezane sat at the panel table in silence. His wide eyes looked sadly down at his hands. Jessop couldn't help but stare at him, wondering if he looked so despondent because he had somehow foreseen such an event happening.

Jessop took Jeco from Falco, moving into the corner of the room where she could watch them all as they sat at the panel. Jessop was still keenly aware of her position in the Blade. The only woman to ever don the Hunter mantle, the one who had tricked them, betrayed them…The one their true Lord and Protector was married to. She didn't need to sit at the panel table to remind them of her presence, to be revered…or feared. She commanded great attention from wherever she stood.

Falco crossed his arms over his chest. "Everyone, sit, please, we do not have time to spare."

"Mama," Jeco cooed, pulling at Jessop's braid.

"Shh, darling," she silenced him, kissing his hand away.

Falco waited until the room was completely still before speaking. "Aranthol has come under attack. As half of my army has come to the Red City, the Shadow City was left vulnerable. A resistance is being held by our closest friend and advisor, Korend'a, but they will not be able to hold off the attackers much longer."

Jessop scanned the faces of the men. Most of them appeared unconcerned, having spent years associating Aranthol simply with the outlaws they hunted. Had they heard six months ago that the Shadow City was under siege, they would have rejoiced.

Urdo leaned forward, his hands clasped together on the desk. "How have they gained access to your city? We, in this room, spent many years trying to learn a way; it seems odd another could do it so quickly."

Falco nodded, and began to loosen the strings of his tunic collar. "We hid the city for many years through mage magic, and when our son was born, we implemented the same system you have here in the Blade. A mystical mark that would act as a key."

Falco drew his tunic low, showing the scar in the center of his chest, fresher than the hundreds of others it laid atop. It was a shape formed entirely out of the letters of their son's name, and only a small handful of Arantholi bore the mark—residents and those on probation needed to be escorted always by a marked member of the guard.

"How could we have never realized?" Urdo shook his head.

Dezane finally spoke, his deep voice low. "More importantly, how did another realize it sooner?"

Falco fixed his tunic and once again crossed his arms over his chest. "I imagine the leader of this attack realized it after seeing the scar on Jessop."

Jessop ran her hand over Jeco's ear, feeling shame for some reason. She did not want him to hear that the fall of Aranthol might be, in part, her fault.

"How do you figure? Jessop has been in the Blade for…" Urdo let his voice trail off, realizing.

Teck Fay spoke, his cloak low over his face. "Who leads this rebellion against your homeland?"

Jessop pushed away from the wall and stood beside Falco. She looked over the Council, readying herself for whatever reaction they might have. "Kohl O'Hanlon does."

The small group of men immediately erupted in speech—some hurling questions at Falco, others turning and speculating amongst themselves. Jessop entered their minds with ease and trespass, not needing to seek permission, should any even notice her. Trax was relieved to learn Kohl lived, Urdo was keen to engage in a war, and Teck thought only of the mark Falco had displayed and of the mage magic used to conceal the Shadow City.

Falco waited patiently for their outburst to settle. They had all been hunting Kohl and the others since Falco's arrival. Jessop understood that it would be a relief to learn that their fallen brother lived, as Trax clearly felt, but relief for his beating heart was all they were permitted. Jessop knew Trax was not a sympathizer to the old regime, that none who sat in the room were, but they had to always be vigilant to prevent their old camaraderie from influencing their actions.

After several minutes, Falco simply cleared his throat, and they were all silenced once more. "There is more to know."

He waited a long moment, his gray eyes slowly traveling over them. "Korend'a has reported that a wave of soldiers, many simply hired weapons, is headed toward the Red City—being led by none other than Hanson Knell."

Urdo stood, while Teck seemed to retreat further into the shadows. Trax appeared shocked, an expression Jessop wasn't accustomed to seeing on her friend. Urdo came around the panel table. "Knell would never use mercenaries."

Falco locked eyes on the older Hunter. "Wouldn't he? With no Hunter army to command and a disgraced Hydo to protect?"

Urdo narrowed his eyes on Falco, contemplating the possibility. Trax shifted in his seat. "Of course, the reports we heard before of mercenaries being spotted…"

Urdo crossed his arms over his chest, a look of disappointment in his eyes. "Regardless, I maintain my previous position. Mercenaries or not, Hydo and Hanson do not have the forces necessary to combat us."

Jessop shifted Jeco in her arms. "Even if they recruited from Haycith?"

Urdo shook his head, but he seemed less certain. "I doubt it. We recruit from Hydo's home town. There are many loyal to him, but not enough to forge a standing army."

Falco crossed and uncrossed his arms. "Well, a standing army they seem to have. Two, actually. We all know Hydo Jesuin comes from one of the wealthiest families in Daharia. Money can buy soldiers. Those soldiers have already set upon the Shadow City; the rest march on Azgul as we speak."

Jessop hugged Jeco tightly. There was only one fear in her heart, and that was something happening to her son. Falco was untouchable, and she could enter any man's mind with more proficiency than any person in existence, but Jeco was just a baby. He looked up at her with his large gray eyes and smiled.

* * * *

They had adjourned their Council meeting, allowing a recess for everyone to digest the information Falco had shared. Aranthol was under attack, and Azgul would soon face the same threat. Jessop had ignored the news, forcing herself to simply attend to her son without any distraction. She played with him and fed him his supper. She was disappointed when he fell asleep so quickly, and for the longest time she simply held him tightly in her embrace.

As the hours passed, she finally allowed herself to contemplate the reality of the situation. She knew what the solution would be. Despite every one of them taking their leave from the Assembly Council meeting to deliberate on options, expected to return with fresh ideas, she knew— *they all knew*—what the solution was.

She found Falco bathing, watching his strong, scarred back turn under the pouring water. She knew he sensed her before she spoke. "You know what must be done."

He turned under the water, fixing his gray stare on her. "There are other possibilities."

She held his gaze. They both knew there weren't. She tightened her vest and readjusted her sheath at her hip. "All that is left to decide is who will stay and who will go."

He stepped out from under the water and approached her, pulling her into his wet embrace. "We could find another way."

She offered him a soft smile. "Not if we wish to see both cities survive. Not if Korend'a is to have any hope of a rescue."

He said nothing, but his eyes grew darker. She knew he held back tears, as she did the same. She rested her small hand against his face, covering half of his long scar. "You must stay here and defend the Blade. It is the priority."

He nodded, turning his face in her hand to kiss her palm. "You will take what is left of my army and any more you need."

She shook her head. "No, I will be taking Dezane's army with me. He will want it that way."

He raised his hands and cupped her face. "Jessop...Kohl will be waiting for you."

She knew as much. "He'll surrender or he'll die on my blade, Falco."

A single tear escaped from his dark eyelashes. "Swear it. I know how you feel about this and I cannot let you go knowing he could...knowing you might let him best you. I need you to swear it. Swear you will kill him."

She pulled him into her embrace, holding him steady to comfort him. She remembered in Okton Radon, when she was terrified of losing Kohl, entirely committed to ensuring he survived Falco and his raiders. It had never been out of a lack of love for Falco, but a lack of hatred for Kohl. Her lips found the warmth of his neck, damp with water. She kissed him softly. "I swear it."

CHAPTER 12

"I will go with you," he spoke firmly, the first of the group to say anything.

Jessop shook her head at her Kuroi friend, "No, Trax. I need you here with Jeco."

He nodded slowly, concern growing in his eyes. They had reconvened and Jessop had told them of her intentions. She would take half of Dezane's army to Aranthol; the rest would stay here and protect the Blade, along with Falco's troops.

"If Falco or Trax cannot travel with you, I volunteer to serve at your side," Mar'e spoke. She had been absent earlier in the day but Dezane had updated her on the situation. Jessop nodded slowly to the woman. While they had seemed to find more common ground, Jessop was unsure if she needed her on this mission, for fear that her old friend might be more of a distraction than a necessary sword-hand. She couldn't focus on saving Aranthol, fighting Kohl, and keeping Mar'e Makenen alive.

Jessop tightened her grip on Falco's hand. Jeco slept in his lap, his small face nuzzled into Falco's chest. "Thank you for your offer. I will consider it."

"If you take my army, I will be at your side," Dezane spoke. Everyone turned in their seats to regard the older man. His bright green eyes shone, contrasting with the dark shadow across his face. He wore the black tunic and leather of the Blade, but he kept his ochre robe on top of the clothes.

Jessop immediately shook her head. "No, Dezane, you must stay here." She kept her tone soft, though her order was clear. She had never commanded Dezane DeHawn, nor did she wish to, but she truly required his presence in the Blade.

The Kuroi elder narrowed his eyes on her. "Why is that?"

Jessop leaned forward in her seat. She needed him in the Blade for many reasons. Dezane was a strong, true elder. His mind would not be easily corrupted by Sentio and that made him invaluable at the Blade.

"Your mind is not an easy one to enter. That makes you a rarity in these parts. Here is where you are most needed."

He readjusted in his seat. Jessop could feel Trax's eyes on her. The Kuroi were a brave people and most skilled in battle. Going to fight was an honor, and yet, she knew Trax feared for his father's life. She knew he would be grateful to have him stay beside him in the Blade.

Dezane kept his green eyes locked on her. "Are you sure it is not simply because you fear the frailty of an old man fighting at your side?"

Jessop rose, holding his stare. She made her way slowly around the table until she stood at his side. She placed a hand on his shoulder, *"Harana vei kora met hasan, Mesahna."* She smiled down at the old man, thinking her sentiment to be most true; *Fighting with you would be an honor.*

He clasped his hand over hers. "For me, as well, young one. But if you wish me to stay, I will not fight you on that."

She nodded. "It is what I wish."

They held one another's stares for a long moment, until Urdo Rendo broke the silence. "Fine—you don't want Trax or the elder, you're not taking your husband's army—I will go with you."

Jessop eyed the Hunter up—he was a formidable warrior, with a reputation that spanned across Daharia. Despite his age, he was skilled, and however gruff he may have been, Jessop liked his candor. Slowly, she nodded. "Okay."

Urdo nodded thoughtfully, pleased to see she didn't protest his joining her campaign. "When do we leave then?"

Jessop looked back down to Dezane. "When will your troops be ready?"

Before he could answer, Mar'e spoke up, causing Jessop to turn. "I can have them ready in two days' time. And *I* can be ready along with them."

Jessop looked from Mar'e to Falco and pushed her concerns across his mind. He softly shrugged his shoulders. *She's made it this far with her soldiers— let her carry on.*

Jessop turned and nodded to Mar'e. "If Dezane permits it, you may accompany."

Dezane sighed heavily. He seemed tired, weary of a war that had not yet happened. "I permit it."

Jessop looked about the room. In two days, she would lead an army of Kuroi to Aranthol, with a great Hunter and a former friend at her side. There were many others she would have chosen to go to battle with first, but as her green eyes fell to her son, she knew that she had chosen well. Jeco needed the most capable at his side for his protection.

* * * *

Urdo spent the following day drinking in an Azguli tavern. "You never know when a drink might be your last," he had told her as he made his way towards the docking bay. Mar'e spent it with the Kuroi warriors, making preparations for battle. Jessop spent it with Falco and Jeco. She stood beside Falco, leaning against the wall on the terrace where they had so recently executed their coup. She stood feet away from the place where she had nearly died. Though the grounds had been scrubbed clean since then, she felt as though she could make out the traces of her blood.

Jeco toddled about the terrace, slaying imaginary beasts with his small sword. Every time he dropped the weapon, he used Sentio to bring it back to his grasp, and as his small fingers found their way around the tiny hilt, he would look to Falco and Jessop for approval, which they gave with ease. Their boy was truly remarkable.

"Like his father." Jessop smiled, wrapping her fingers around Falco's hand.

Falco was lost in his thoughts. His brow was woven with concerns, his jaw tight. She turned and snaked her arms around his waist, watching as he kept his gaze on Jeco. "Falco, what is it?"

His gray eyes darted over her shoulder, following their son as he played. "I fear what is to come."

She almost laughed at his words. "You and I fear nothing. Nothing but Jeco's fate, of course."

He shook his head, closing his eyes for a long moment. "That's always been you, Jessop, not me. The fire destroyed your sense of dread or trepidation, and the confidence you have in your abilities reinforced that fearlessness. But I have always lived with fear. For Daharia, for you, for Jeco, for the warriors I lead."

Jessop felt at odds with his words. She knew them to be true; Falco was the most capable warrior in all of Daharia, and coupled with his inherent bravery, he seemed truly fearless. But he had not lost the sense of feeling the way Jessop had. Somewhere in Daharia, Falco had a family, he had men to lead, and he had connections with people and places. Jessop had only Falco and Jeco. He feared more than his wife, for he had so much more to lose.

She turned from him, letting her gaze fall to Jeco. "You were born to live with great responsibility, Falco. Of all the things you must occupy your mind with, do not let me be one of them. Battle approaches the Red City too, and you must keep our son safe."

He ran his hand over her back, both of them watching as Jeco levitated his sword in the air, captivated by his own abilities. "It's not just you I fear for. It's Aranthol, our people, this war that is looming…So many will die, and it will be my fault."

At his words she turned back to him. "That is a lie. It's the fault of Hydo and Hanson. Of Kohl. You gave them every opportunity to submit. Whatever deaths occur, the blood is on their hands."

At his silence, she took his hand in hers once more. "As for Aranthol, and our people, have a little faith."

His gray eyes studied her face. "In what?"

She cocked her head to him, as if the answer were obvious. "In me, my love."

* * * *

Jessop spent the night holding Jeco as he slept. She could not believe that after such a short reunion they once again would be separated. She couldn't imagine him in the Blade as a battle was fought in the streets of the Red City. She couldn't imagine him being anywhere *near* a battle, especially in her absence. For all of the fear she had ceased experiencing in her day-to-day life, she felt it for Jeco tenfold.

She did not stir as Falco roped his arms around her, his head peering over her shoulder to gaze on Jeco. "It is my fault you must be separated again," he whispered. His voice was quiet and low, filled with sadness.

She rocked her son slowly, keeping his small body tight against hers. "It's not. What we do we do for the destiny of our family—for your reign, and for his."

"I know. We fight these wars so that he won't have to, so that he can inherit the Blade of Light without question when the time comes."

She turned her face slowly, grazing her cheek against his. "Like you should have been able to. I look forward to few things, Falco, but seeing Hydo Jesuin bleed out is one of them."

At her words, she laid Jeco down in his bed. He knew of their world, but he was still so young, and she wanted to shield him from all the darkness she could, for as long as possible; even the darkness that filled her and Falco.

Falco ran his hands down her arms. Taking her small fingers in his, he led her out of Jeco's attached room and back to their own chamber. "Hydo's blood will stain your blade before this war is over."

She smiled in the darkness, running her hands over his chest. "Tell me what you look forward to." Her voice was an order, filled with tension and longing.

Slowly, Falco ran his hands over her shoulders and under her neck, brushing her long mane of hair away from her skin. His fingers pulled at her tunic and she raised her arms, allowing him to remove it. "I look forward to my wife returning from battle."

Their mouths locked instantly, hands roaming over one another, pulling clothes away, exploring the territory they were both so familiar with. As they fell to their bed, Jessop pushed her breast against him, his hands warm on her hips, their matching *J* scars lining up perfectly.

* * * *

They had left early, when the red sky was still a dusky crimson and few were in the streets. Several of the largest Soar-Craft the Hunters kept in their fleet carried them to Bareduk, the nearest weigh-station to Aranthol. From there, they would travel on foot for one night before reaching the Shadow City. Dezane, Trax, Falco, and Jeco had seen them off. Jeco had cried, finally understanding, with a child's sense of urgency, that she was leaving again. It had broken her heart to walk away from him, hearing his muffled sobs against Falco's neck. She had told herself again and again—she did this for him.

"That's why Hunters don't have families," Urdo had said, leading the way onto the Soar-Craft. She had shot him an icy glare, warning him off the topic, but she knew he meant no insult. She also knew he was right. It was selfish to lead the lives they led with children. Her situation was different though—she had never dreamed of becoming a Hunter, she had never thought she would have the child of the true leader of Daharia, a boy so powerful he lived without equal. She had been forced onto this path—by Hydo. He had taken her family, he had betrayed Falco, he had ensured that all of this would come to fruition.

"What would happen?" Urdo's voice wrenched Jessop back to the present. She turned in her canvas-covered seat to face him.

He cleared his throat. "What would happen if I tried to enter your mind? I've never seen anyone so stuck with their thoughts."

She eyed him slowly. He was being serious and it did not surprise her. The Hunters had discovered much about her, but not all, and it left them curious. "Feel free to try."

She didn't move, she didn't sit up or brace herself. She knew that if Hydo couldn't trespass her mind, if Falco couldn't find a thought she did not want him to find, then none could. Perhaps Jeco, one day. She felt the strong pressure against her temples as he fixed his stare on her. She could tell instantly that he was a master of Sentio. His mind found perfect focus on hers, and were she anyone else, she knew her walls would fall under his fixed gaze rapidly, and everything inside her would lay vulnerable to him. But she was not any other, and her walls would not fall. She felt the pressure of his attempts and nothing more.

She watched his eyes narrow, she could sense his blood pulsing, a vein protruding from under his brow. He strained, while resistance was easy for her. Suddenly, she bolted up in her seat. She leaned forward, grabbing his hands with hers, fixing her stare upon him. She pushed back and while he was quick to resist, he could not keep her out. He had a strong mind, surprisingly unweakened by age or drink, and she knew he would be a formidable target for any other. She broke through his walls with ease, though, and found herself walking through his recent memories. Drinking in a tavern in the Red City, training a class of young Hunters, polishing his blade. She did not search for more, for she was not interested in unveiling his secrets or betraying his privacy—she simply performed a demonstration of her abilities.

She released her hold on him, leaning back in her seat. He stared at her, unblinking, clearly shaken. "Not even Hydo can enter our minds like that."

She nodded. "I know."

"Falco?"

She nodded.

"And your boy?"

She turned back to him. "Jeco has little understanding of his abilities, though Falco and I are certain they are already destined to outshine ours. He can move blades with his mind and he is barely two years of age."

Urdo shook his head, leaning back in his seat. "It amazes me that Hydo knew, all these years, the truth. He deceived us."

She studied his face, intrigued by his admission. "Not all view his actions as deception apparently. Hanson and Kohl, many of the others—they heard the truth and still they left."

Urdo stared straight ahead, his eyes seeming to recall an old memory. "Falco Bane was a terrifying boy, you have to understand that."

Jessop shot him an angry glare. He raised his fingers lightly, as if to show he meant no harm. When she readjusted in her seat, relaxing ever so slightly, he continued to speak.

"We were *all* skilled, we were *all* told at one stage or another that we might be the next Lord. We all came to learn we wouldn't be, in the Hollow, during the rite of passage—earlier for some. But Falco—he was just different. Hydo brought him to the Blade, this small boy with dark hair and eyes that just pierced you. He was a reluctant Hunter recruit, but not out of fear—out of boredom. He was better than his peers on day one, he surpassed senior students with ease, and soon he could only train with fully-fledged Hunters.

"He spoke to few, aside from O'Hanlon. As they became teenagers, Falco grew cocky. He knew he was the best, and we, on the Council, knew he would be the one to take over from Hydo. He was the most gifted we had ever seen. He was arrogant and frustrated—nothing left to learn, no one left to challenge him. He picked fights and got in trouble on a daily basis. It wasn't just the other recruits he messed with—he taunted Hunters and Councilmen alike. No one could touch him.

"When Hydo came back from beyond the Grey, he told us Falco had gone rogue. He said the boy had finally snapped—killing a poor country family in a fire. Falco showed up not long after, wild-eyed, demanding the Blade. He attacked Hydo and we did what we thought was right—we defended the Lord. It had all seemed to make sense—many of us had thought Falco was headed toward a dark path, too powerful for his own good. We had no clue...

"O'Hanlon was unlucky enough to get in the way. Falco carved him up nicely, all the while calling him a traitor—all of us were betraying him, in his mind."

Jessop couldn't help but interrupt. "You *were* betraying him."

"Well, we didn't know that, did we? We thought he had snapped, that he had to be killed, and if any of us had been capable of it, he would have been. O'Hanlon got him pretty good, but only because Falco was hesitant to kill him. We thought maybe he would succumb to the wound...It wasn't long until we heard of the construction of a city, fortified by mage magic, being built by the most dangerous boy any had ever seen."

Jessop nodded slowly to the old Hunter. It was odd for her to hear about Falco from someone who had known him so well in childhood. She had met Falco as a young adolescent boy, and he had been arrogant, but not without reason. It had never bothered her, for she knew his plight—he felt entirely alone in the world.

"I understand how we all came to be where we are. What I do not understand is why Kohl, Hanson, and the others are still supporting Hydo." Urdo fixed his stare on her. "There is much you don't know about Hanson Knell...War, killing—it impacts everyone differently. Hanson went to a dark place once, a very dark place, and Hydo brought him back into the fold, forgiving him all his trespasses. Knell owes Hydo his loyalty."

Jessop wanted to know more, but knew better than to press the subject. She remembered what Falco had said to her, and what she had seen herself of Hanson; he did not indulge in any vices and showed no interests outside of Kohl. She would find out more about the old Hunter in time. "And Kohl?"

Urdo practically scoffed. "O'Hanlon didn't choose Hydo over Falco, he chose Hydo over *you*. You broke his heart. Humiliated him. How could he stay and serve under Falco all the while longing for you?"

Jessop shifted in her seat uncomfortably. "He could have tried. He knew what the right thing to do was."

Urdo laughed softly. "Jessop, I mean no disrespect, for I follow you into battle wholeheartedly and I follow Falco without question, but what do you really know about right and wrong? You're the wife of a warlord—I couldn't fathom how many have died on your blade. You betrayed a man who loved you; you killed, lied, and deceived to be where you are now."

Jessop felt her skin tingle, angered by his words—however true they were. "Hydo *forced* Falco and me into these lives. We had no choice but to become who we are today."

Urdo cocked his head at her, skeptical. "Didn't you? You're not the first people to lose your families, Jessop."

She turned away from him. Sentio or not, his ability to work his way into her mind wounded her.

CHAPTER 13

Bareduk was unchanged—a small, barren town on the outskirts of nothing. They landed in the dark, and disembarked swiftly. A small unit would be left behind to guard the Soar-Craft, but everyone else would make for Aranthol on foot with Jessop. Jessop studied the dark horizon, knowing that while Bareduk had not changed, *she* had. When she had last passed through the weigh station, she had been the wife of Falco Bane—now she was something much more. She led an army, and she was acknowledged as a powerful warrior—great enough to be a Hunter, to be much *more* than a Hunter. She had sought revenge and initiated a war that the whole of Daharia whispered about.

"Should we not make camp for the evening? It has been a long journey already," Mar'e suggested. Jessop didn't turn to her, instead keeping her gaze on the surrounding hills. She thought of Korend'a and knew that if they began their march now, they could be in Aranthol by morning. "No, we go now."

"But—"

At her rebuttal, Jessop snapped her gaze to the woman. Mar'e was silenced. Slowly, she turned from Jessop, and made her way back to the Soar-Craft to prepare. She knew they had travelled far, she knew the trip had been long already, but Korend'a had feared falling to Kohl's advances days ago—who knew what state he, and Aranthol, would be in by the morning.

* * * *

The army moved with ease through the darkness, with eyes like her own, adept for such settings. Urdo struggled the most, if he struggled at all. He moved with determination and experience, for he had led many battles. Jessop knew it best to focus only on Aranthol and Korend'a, but her mind wandered. She thought of Jeco and Falco, of Hanson's army, and of Kohl. Her hand danced over her abdomen as she saw his golden eyes in her mind.

She thought of the time they had spent together. She had remembered crying in his arms, winning him over with her supposed fear of his mentors. He had held her tightly, kissed her deeply, had whispered to her, *"You're with me now. I won't let them hurt you again."*

She thought of the way he saw her then and the way he saw her that day on the terrace. She remembered the look in his eyes, the confusion and the heartbreak. He had loved her, and she had destroyed him. She remembered the hatred in his voice as he had pierced her with the very blade he had designed for her. The blade she would take into battle against him. She wished that all she could remember was the last of their moments together; it would make hating him so much easier.

She remembered the taste of his lips, though, she remembered the way he had held her body close to his, she remembered how it felt to be wanted by him, loved by him. She remembered being surprised by his experience, the way he had kissed her neck and held her in his arms. She remembered hating herself—for caring for *him* when she loved Falco, for feeling like she betrayed them both. In truth, she felt it still, despite Falco's instructions for her—she had harmed both the men who loved her.

"You fear seeing him again?" Mar'e spoke, intuitive even without the abilities of Sentio.

Jessop kept her eyes trained forward, forcing foot after foot in the unforgiving sand. "I fear no one."

"There is a difference between fearing no fight and fearing no person, Jessop."

Jessop narrowed her eyes as a strong wind brought the sand up around them. They moved through the natural chaos silently, and when it abated, she glanced in the darkness to Mar'e. "Fear is fear. I have none for Kohl O'Hanlon."

"Would it be easier for you if he were dead?"

Jessop was somewhat taken aback by the question. It seemed unnatural, despite their ways, to discuss the notion of death with such ease. Unnatural did not mean untrue, though. She thought of her old friend's question. She had voiced it many times in the previous weeks—she did not believe Kohl deserved to die. Not for his attempt on her life, nor for his betrayal of Falco.

She thought of the feelings she had for him, however different they were from what she had for Falco, and she wished more than anything that they could be gone. She felt anger towards him, for being so gullible and reckless with his heart, for falling for her ruse so easily. She wanted to blame him for his heartbreak, despite knowing the fault lay solely with herself. She hated herself for caring about him, because it was an insult to her husband. She hated that Kohl knew of her what only Falco had ever known. Kohl was a living reminder of her great success against the Blade, which happened to also be the greatest mistake she had ever made. Perhaps, in truth, that was why she struggled so greatly. She had won her husband his throne, but at such a steep price it made her question herself. She could not help but wonder whether, if Kohl were dead, it would perhaps be easier to move on.

She thought of Urdo, though, and all he had said on their journey. She blamed Hydo for the life she led as she blamed Kohl for falling in love with her so easily. Jessop knew, though, that she was responsible for her own actions, and accepting that meant living with the guilt of her mistakes. She walked on a path created for her, but she did so without guidance. She felt amazed and horrified by her own abilities—she had become the sort of fighter who could contemplate living with the guilt of killing just to abate another, prior shame. Jessop had never been apologetic for who she was—all of Daharia feared Falco, but she felt as though, despite his actions, she *knew* him. Really knew him. In such a way that she could disconnect the man from the reputation, the boy she loved from the greatest dark leader Daharia had ever seen. In the same breath, she had begun to separate herself from her own actions, perhaps wrongly attributing them to the situation, and not the person.

She closed her eyes against the rising sands, and saw him. His golden mane, his silver star-shaped scar, his perfect hazel eyes. She saw him smile at her, a memory that tore at her heart. "No. It would not be easier for me if he were to die."

* * * *

They set up camp two miles out from the Aranthol gates, where the sky still shone light in the day and turned dark only at night. As the Kuroi rested, Jessop kept her eyes on the Aranthol region. All the territory that belonged to her and Falco could be distinguished by the sky. The Shadow City never experienced daylight—a blanket of constant night rested above it, extending a mile out around its perimeter. She noticed how Urdo stared at the border, where the mystical sky met the normal one, and where a belt of lighting formed the border in the clouds.

"He did this all for you," he whispered, shaking his head at the spectacle. Jessop looked upon the far-off city warmly, with its perpetual night, and smiled. Falco had reshaped nature just for her. There was nothing they wouldn't do for one another—whether it was to create a forever night, or break another's heart.

Mar'e appeared at her side. "The scouts have returned; they found no armies dwelling outside your city walls."

Urdo crossed his arms over his broad chest. "Which means they reside within Aranthol already."

Jessop knew she could lead an attack now. She expected the same of Urdo, but less so of the Kuroi. However capable, they needed their rest before entering battle. "We attack at dawn."

* * * *

Jessop woke before the milky sky broke light, her eyes fixed to the blanket of darkness over her city. Slowly, silent and ready, the Kuroi rose. They painted their faces with ochre and water, but they would not sing their war chant—this attack required stealth. They would descend on the Shadow City in silence.

Jessop led the troops, flanked by Mar'e and Urdo. She was happy to be moving before the sky was truly lit, and grateful to be leading Kuroi—who knew how to move in silence. The sandy terrain cushioned their steps, but there was little coverage to conceal them from any scouts. If Kohl was anticipating her attack, he would soon see her approaching. She hoped Korend'a had kept Kohl and his troops—whoever *they* were—too occupied to man the gates.

Within striking distance of the large onyx gates, she halted her army. Crouching low in the sand, her eyes travelled over the mystical barrier. She knew that the minute she revealed her scar to the gates, they would open. What she didn't know was what awaited them. Luck had been on their side allowing them such easy passage to the city—she did not believe it would remain so.

"Jessop," Urdo hissed, pulling her attention.

She glanced to him expectantly, impatient.

"What do you want us to do with O'Hanlon, if we find him before you?"

She felt the pang in her chest, the anticipation growing, knowing she was about to encounter Kohl for the first time since his escape. "He will find me long before you find him."

She turned her gaze back to the gate, ready to move forward.

"What if he doesn't, Jessop?"

She didn't turn back to Urdo. She knew what she had said to be true. Some part of her could feel his eyes on her already. She felt the target on her back, or more aptly, on her abdomen. After all, he had laid it there.

She stood slowly. "He will."

She took cautious steps towards the giant black gates. The doors were constructed of onyx and scrap metal. They stood some thirty feet high, where the edges of the welding tapered off in sharp prongs, pointing to the perimeter of electricity holding in the night sky above. The same border of electricity formed the mystical barrier around the city limits—were one to simply scale the gates, they would feel the assault of lightning.

She kept one hand on her hilt and used the other to loosen her leather vest and tunic. With a slight pause, she glanced back over her shoulder. Mar'e and Urdo were crouched, ready to run to her side with hundreds of Kuroi warriors behind them—swords drawn, shields raised, spears fixed forward.

She pulled her tunic low, tight between her breasts, revealing the scar which acted as a key to Aranthol. She knew that where she stood was in the sightline of a nearby guard tower. Typically, newcomers would elicit the presence of a guard, who could grant them entry to the City. Jessop knew no guard would appear for her, certain they had been called to fight Kohl's mercenaries.

After a brief moment, the massive gates began to drag open. She fixed her vest and drew her sword, taking a prepared stance as the gates drew a body-length apart. She took a deep breath, immediately thinking of how many mercenaries she could stop with Sentio, remembering the impact using such exhaustive methods had had on her that day on the terrace. She could hold back twenty perhaps, but she would fall to her knees doing it.

But as the gates fully parted, Jessop saw no one. The Gahaza Square was usually bustling with early morning traders and travelers. The Square wasn't just an area for merchants to make sales; it was also where newcomers received their residency paperwork, and where they looked for housing and labor. It was one of the busiest parts of the city, and yet, the dark street ahead was completely abandoned. The windows of black-stone buildings were boarded up with rotted, dark wood; the kiosks, typically swarming with merchants and consumers, were unmanned and without stock. The black-stone streets were wet with rain and stained with blood, home to the evidence of a battle Jessop had been too late to prevent—a discarded sword, a bloody cloth, a dented shield. She felt her skin prickle, rage running over her with ease, the feeling of betrayal, of violation, consuming her. Their home had fallen prey to a Hunter, the Arantholi people punished for her actions against the Blade.

Slowly, she took several steps towards the gate, raising her hand to indicate for the others to wait. She kept her eyes trained on the Square, darting about building corners and under kiosks, looking for any indication as to where anyone might be—mercenary or Arantholi. She took another step forward and while the smell of blood, dried and plentiful, overwhelmed her, she saw no one. She could imagine Kohl attacking the Square as soon as he got the gates opened. She could picture him, his Hunter's blade tight in hand, mercenaries instead of brethren at his side. It turned her stomach to picture it. Even though she knew Falco and Jeco were safe, and had been in the Blade when Kohl attacked, she felt sick to think an attack had happened to their family home. By breaching Aranthol, he had come too close to truly harming her once again.

As she stood at the entry of the Square, blood-stained stone beneath her feet, silence all about her, she indicated for the others to approach. They moved quickly and quietly, Mar'e and Urdo taking their respective places at her side. Jessop could hear Mar'e tighten her grip on her short sword. She looked to Jessop with concern. "Where is everyone?"

Jessop remained silent as they led their army further into the Square, unable to answer. She glanced to Urdo, hoping it would not take long for his eyes to adjust to the immediate darkness, but found he looked more concerned about the empty Square than the darkness. He pivoted about, looking up towards the building tops. She followed his gaze, but saw nothing.

"Jessop, we should move," he advised, his eyes darting from building top to building top.

"We are moving," she answered tightly, finding she was speaking in soft whispers.

He grabbed her arm with an urgency that rattled her. "Something's not right…Can't you sense it? We *aren't* alone."

She was about to close her eyes, about to focus on their surroundings more, to try to gauge what the older Hunter already sensed, when she heard the sound—the distinct stretch of a bow being pulled. "*Archers! Area'ha!*"

The Kuroi immediately brought their shields up as soldiers appeared over the edges of the rooftops, arrows trained on Jessop and her army. They wore no common uniform, many looking exactly like the Arantholi, but the weapons they carried—a random assortment of distinct pieces, fine bows in their hands, blades that cost more than they could rightfully afford on their hips—let her know they were, in fact, mercenaries. Before Jessop could lead her army out of the trap, the hired soldiers released, their arrows singing through the air.

As Urdo and Mar'e ducked low, Jessop threw her hand up in the air. She focused, zoning in on a single arrow, noting the way its metallic shaft and tapered end spun perfectly through the dark sky. She felt her energy traveling through her, snaking through her chest and down her arms, extending into the world around her. With easy focus, all of the arrows froze in a cloud of metal above her army.

She would not be able to stop a second wave without releasing the first. She looked back on her army of Kuroi. *"A've! Move!"*

At her order, the army dispersed. She kept the arrows frozen, knowing the mercenaries had likely had no warning of her abilities, knowing they watched her with torn focus. She followed Urdo with her eyes, watching as he used his abilities to scale a building wall, flipping over its lip onto the rooftop with the agility of a man half his age. With blade in hand, he engaged several fighters.

As fighting erupted all around her, Jessop scanned the rooftops, looking for the most populated. The roof top of the building nearest to the black gates held several archers. As her eyes locked on them, she saw them ready their bows, preparing to take aim at her. She took a deep breath and began to turn her fingers about, orchestrating the cloud of arrows she controlled to turn in a semi-circle. As the archers watched her, shock and amazement in their eyes, she couldn't help but softly smile. With a thrust of her forearm, she shot the arrows back at the group. She struck many; two leapt from the roof to the street, while others narrowly escaped.

Kohl hadn't warned his army of misfit killers about her—something she found interesting but unsurprising. He likely would have had to pay more coin to convince mercenaries to cross not only Falco Bane, but his deadly wife. She was astounded to realize that they hadn't already heard of her. As all reports seemed to have indicated, all of Daharia had heard of the woman with abilities greater than any Hunter.

She took a deep breath and ran full speed ahead at the nearest building. She leapt, and with one foot pushing off the stone wall, she flew well above the lip of the building, landing firmly on the rooftop. She spun her blade about her as she engaged several mercenary fighters. They did not move with the uniformity of soldiers, but that did not hamper their abilities. Typical of hired-soldiers, some were incredibly talented, and some were clearly novice. Whatever the span of their abilities, they were no match for Jessop—or Urdo, who in her periphery fought as many men as she did with masterful skill.

As she sprung about the Square, she worked quickly to inject herself in fight after fight between mercenary and Kuroi, feeling responsible for squashing the ambush. She had been a fool. On her first test, she had failed, leading her army—*Dezane's army*—into a trap that could have killed them all. She had been so confident in her own abilities she had forgotten the vulnerabilities of her cohorts. Her arrogance was blinding—and the realization made her feel ill. She had once made a similar claim against Hydo.

She had never led an army, never ruled a people—not as Falco had. She had spent her adult life focusing on her own abilities, her own fight, on Falco and on their son. She had never wanted to reign, never wanted to lead. She hadn't been trained by the Blade, hadn't been raised to always feel a loyalty to her brethren-in-arms. She saw them as more people she had to keep alive, and even in that task, she had nearly failed.

She ducked under a blade, spun about her attacker and kicked him squarely in the back. He flew off the rooftop with a loud cry. She turned, hearing the *thud* of his body collapsing on the street below. She sheathed her sword and leapt to a second rooftop. She grabbed the jaw of a mercenary she came up behind, and with an easy *snap* she let his lifeless body fall to the ground. She knew that she should have asked Urdo what he thought sooner—he had led countless armies.

She weaved around the mercenaries, and as a sword thrust past her abdomen, she grabbed the hilt, tugged it viciously out of the grasp of its owner, and flipped it around in her hand before skewering its possessor through the abdomen. She thought of what Falco would have done, and how he would have known to think for archers, how he would have sensed the trap.

Suddenly, Jessop's face was alight. Someone had struck her. She steadied herself, resisting raising a hand to her cheek. With all her might, she swung her arm out, backhanding the attacker across his jaw. As he stumbled away from her, she grabbed a dagger off her back. She flung it at him, piercing him in the chest as he scrambled for his weapon. She used Sentio to call her weapon back to her grasp, just in time to stab the third fighter in the diaphragm, catching his weapon-wielding wrist with her spare hand.

"Who are you?" he asked, blood trailing from the corners of his cracked mouth.

She ignored him, attacking him with her own questions as he fell to the ground. "Where is Kohl O'Hanlon? Where is the man who paid you?"

He was too close to death to answer. She wrenched her blade free from him, watching as he lay back on the roof top, his one hand pointing out behind him, towards her and Falco's home.

CHAPTER 14

Jessop kicked the door in with ease, the wood crunching beneath her boot. She led Mar'e, Urdo, and the Kuroi troops into the abandoned building, careful to scan the space first. Some were wounded, but few had died, thanks to Urdo. Jessop was thankful to find the building had a water source and linens on the boarded windows. She helped rip the material down, tearing the large pieces into strips for the wounded. As they settled in, she asked Urdo to speak in private, Mar'e following in tow. They found an adjacent room, covered in dust with parchment strewn about haphazardly, as though the space had been ransacked. Jessop stood at the room's one window, peeking through a crack in the boards.

"I cannot do this," she admitted, scanning the street through the dusty glass.

Urdo kicked over a wooden crate, fashioning himself a seat near her. "Do what?"

She turned to face them. Mar'e stood beside the old Hunter, a look of confusion on her face. Jessop crossed her arms, thinking her sentiment was apparent. "I can kill any who come against us, I can make it through the Shadow City on my own, I can do many things, but I cannot think about the safety of those warriors. It is not in my nature, it is not in my training."

Urdo shook his head at her. "If it's about the trap, don't let that discourage you—it's happened to the best of leaders."

She raised her hand to stop him from speaking further. "I'm not a leader, Urdo. I'm a killer."

Mar'e took a step towards her. "We have all killed, it is part of the job."

"It's not a job to me, Mar'e!"

Jessop's raised voice surprised herself as much as it did her companions. She thought of Falco, of Hydo, of all Urdo had said to her and all she had thought about. She knew what she was, and what she was responsible for. "This is no *job* to me. This is simply *me*. It is all I know. My proficiency with the blade, with Sentio—it does not make me a leader. Leaders have other qualities than a skilled sword hand."

Urdo shifted in his seat. "Do you think you're the first one to doubt their capability? Do you know how many Hunters I have trained, how many I have fought beside, who resist the position upon their first error? The hardest part about leading is taking responsibility for the path you forge."

She shook her head at him slowly, ignoring his pensive stare as best as she could. "I can't…I'm not one of your Hunters."

Urdo stood gruffly from the crate, a storm of dust exploding around him. "You want to go off and play rogue warrior, fine, we know we can't stop you. You want me to lead this army for you—*fine*. But you're going to help me find the rest of O'Hanlon's mercenaries first, because I am not going to be the one to tell Dezane DeHawn that I got half his army killed."

For the first time in years, she remembered what it felt like to be a child, admonished for her immaturity and selfishness. The last person to speak to her with any command had been her own parents, a lifetime ago. She looked at him, and while she saw Urdo, for the briefest of moments she heard her father's voice. Slowly, she nodded.

"Mar'e, go tell the troops we won't be staying here long. Jessop and I have Hunter business to attend to."

Mar'e scowled. "Why can't I stay and help? The troops are—"

Urdo raised a hand, silencing her. "This is *Hunter* business."

Mar'e tossed her hand out, pointing at Jessop. "You just heard her—she's not a *real* Hunter."

Her words kept Jessop in the past, remembering her life at ten and two years. Still dressed in ochre robes, still feeling inadequate around Mar'e Makenen. In childhood, she had lived with the knowledge that she wasn't *real* Kuroi, and in adulthood, no matter how much power she wielded, no matter how many she bested, she wasn't a *real* Hunter..

Urdo inclined his head slowly, his voice low. "I am *Master* Urdo Rendo, of the Taden people. I stopped Elias Rahut from accomplishing the Aren rebellion. I have been a Hunter for fifty-four years, a Councilman for twenty-eight. I believe I am somewhat more fit to decide who is and isn't a *real* Hunter than either of you. Jessop Bane is as real as they come."

Mar'e looked from Urdo to Jessop, but neither looked back to her. Jessop kept her gaze locked on Urdo, his warm eyes regarding her with confidence. She felt moved by him, and knew instantly that his powerful oration was why he had led so many armies. Jessop nodded to him slowly, prepared to do whatever he said, realizing that *his* ability was to remind others of their own.

* * * *

Jessop sat cross-legged, mirroring Urdo. He rested his hands, palms upwards, on his knees, taking deep breaths. "Take my hands," he instructed. She hesitated, always apprehensive of human contact, but as she took a deep breath, she rested her hands in his. His skin was warm and calloused, his hands hardened from years of the fight.

"We will search for them together," he explained, though Jessop was still confused. She could sense others with her abilities because her mind picked up on Sentio, but she could not just locate unknown persons.

"I've never done this before," she admitted.

Urdo opened his eyes slowly. "I have, and today you'll learn. It is something that nearly always requires several Hunters, but your abilities are great—they can carry us."

She didn't know if that were true or not. Around Urdo, Jessop felt like a pupil, knowing her arrogance had led her astray. For all of her and Falco's abilities, they had sincerely thought there was nothing of the blade or Sentio left to learn. She wondered what she may have learnt, had she spent her time in the Blade with an open mind as opposed to one fixed on an agenda.

As he closed his eyes, she did the same. They took deep breaths for what felt like several minutes. Jessop found that as they breathed, the noises around them died out. She could no longer hear the warriors rifling in the other room, she could not make out their Kuroi dialect. She did not still hear the wind, which had been so sharp around the corners of the building, so angry against the windows. She saw nothing in her mind. Not Falco, not Kohl, nothing but darkness. Far from alarming, she felt completely at peace. She wondered, for the briefest of moments, if it were the breathing that achieved this, or if it were an extension of Urdo's powers.

"View your abilities like a light, travelling out from our hands, searching the city." His voice was slow and deep, his instructions spoken through measured tones. She did as he said, envisioning her powers escaping out from her hands. Though she kept her eyes shut, she felt as though she could see the light moving from them both, dancing between them like a sandstorm before dashing out of the cracks in the windows and walls.

She could follow the light, like a bird, as it made its way through the Shadow City.

It swirled and grew larger, faster; it spread out, searching the shadows. Jessop's breath caught as she saw families hiding, raiders drinking in an abandoned tavern, people packing up their belongings. She was traveling through her city, and yet she hadn't left the floor from which she sat. The light moved past the Arantholi, for they were not who Jessop searched for. She followed it through the dark streets, under kiosks, down alleyways, and through cracked windows.

They moved deeper into the Shadow City, turning over errant baskets and crates, moving faster and faster. Their light grew in strength and determination, and Jessop realized that together, their powers were *hunting*.

"Push harder, we nearly have them, Jessop," Urdo urged her. She took a deep breath and exhaled deeply from her lungs. The light shifted, growing, moving through the streets not like a stream, but a wave. It washed around corners, it swam through buildings, it scaled walls and cleared alleys.

She saw the onyx tower. The light travelled to its very tip, and as it had no roof, it easily spilled through, devouring the black walls, searching, hungry, hunting...

Jessop opened her eyes, loosening her hold on Urdo's hands. "I know where they are."

* * * *

Jessop moved through the city with ease. Aranthol had been built for her, and few knew its back streets better. She travelled undetected, though there were none out in the streets to detect her. Kohl would know by now that she had arrived, and with an army. He would have heard how his ambush had failed. She wondered what he thought of, knowing she was so near, knowing he was no match for her with a blade, knowing it would be the first time he laid eyes on her since he had nearly killed her.

Jessop didn't know what Kohl sought to achieve by resisting Falco so boldly. She knew what Urdo had said, that it was not Falco he turned from, but her...It was difficult for her to believe that he would go to such lengths to punish her, difficult for her to live with the result of her actions against him. She leapt over an overturned kiosk and found herself standing before the black tower. Her heart raced, knowing he was near, sensing the powers of another nearby.

She could easily remember her first fight with Kohl—not one of blades, but one of heart. It had been the first time she tried to show him who she really was, what she could do. She had pleaded with him, but it had been futile.

"*Kohl, please—*"

"*I held you in my arms. I trained with you.*"

She had taken a step towards him, reaching out for him, but he resisted her.

"*I made love to you,*" he whispered, his voice thick with disgust.

Jessop had brought him to his knees, angry and embarrassed. She had taken his memories, knowing he couldn't ever see her for who she truly was.

Jessop suppressed the memory as she moved towards the onyx steps leading up to the great hall. Suddenly, her stomach convulsed violently. She struggled to catch her breath. She fell to her knee, sharply cutting skin on the edge of the step. She thought she would heave, when suddenly the world around her transformed. She was no longer on the stairs in Aranthol, no longer in the middle of a battle. She was back in the Blade.

She was naked, half-drowned, the eyes of all the Councilmen on her exhausted body. She was in his arms. He was trying to conceal her, trying to protect her. He was yelling at them, turning his back on them, for her. He carried her down the clinically clean halls. He kept her shivering, naked body pressed tightly against his. He looked down into her green eyes with his brilliant golden ones, and seemed to feel all the devastation imaginable. She could feel his instant love for her.

Jessop forced against the illusion, knowing it to be just another memory. She blinked and found she was back on the black stairs, her hands clutching the steps, her heart racing. Someone had forced themselves into her mind. She knew no one capable of the task; no Hunter alive had powers that exceeded her own. She scanned the streets, desperate to find her attacker. She looked up the stairs, scrambling on all fours. She saw no one. How was she being forced to—?

She was kissing him. She ran her hands through his golden hair, her strong legs tensing around his hips, her breast hot against his chest. He moved inside her, his breath warm on her lips, the taste of him fresh on her tongue. She wanted to hate it, she wanted it all to be a show, but it wasn't, it couldn't be. He had a practiced touch and she couldn't pretend that some part of her hadn't longed for him.

She was wrenched back to the moment. Sweat trailed down her brow as she fought to regain control of her mind. She scurried up the stairs. "*Stop!*"

She didn't care if she alerted an entire army to her presence—she couldn't stand to relive their memories, couldn't tolerate someone rifling around her mind, forcing thoughts and images to the surface. She ran up the remainder of the stairs, nearly collapsing against the heavy doors. She grabbed the massive metal handles and used all her might to force the giant black doors open. Her breath caught as she laid eyes on a man she had never seen before, standing in the great hall.

He wore blue robes, and while he had a shaved head, he possessed a long beard. The most distinguishing of his features, though, were his completely white eyes. He was a desert mage. The first she had faced since the one who shredded her back. The man regarded her without surprise or sympathy. "Collect yourself, woman—you do not know what I am capable of."

Jessop bristled at his words, taking angry step after angry step forward. She saw only his white eyes. She could feel the leather lashing her once more, her scars on fire. He looked so like the one who had once attacked her that Jessop felt nothing but rage. Nothing but the desire to demonstrate all she had become capable of. The mage attempted to force his way into her mind, but seeing the source of her agony gave Jessop focus, and with a wave of her arm, she cut through his abilities. The shock on his face brought joy to her heart. "I take it he didn't tell you what I was capable of, *fool*."

At her words, she twisted her hand sharply in the air, snapping the mage's neck. He fell to the ground, his lifeless body hitting the black stone with a satisfying *thump*.

She stared down at his body. She knew he wasn't the man who had attacked her, for Falco had long ago killed him, but he was a desert mage. He had the same powers, and however great, they had no control over her once she confronted them. As her breathing slowed, she realized that Kohl had procured a mage to do what he could not.

She didn't know why it surprised her, that he would have someone invade her mind—he had already tried to kill her twice—but nonetheless, it did. Jessop felt that while he had never really known her, she had known him, truly *known* him. She felt foolish once again. Clearly, she hadn't known the real Kohl O'Hanlon. Which was much easier to believe than the alternative—that she had broken him so greatly, he was simply no longer the same man he had once been.

As if on cue, she could feel him. She didn't turn around immediately, but she knew when he stood behind her. The sensation was similar to smooth cloth running slowly over bare skin. Her senses were sharp, teased by his presence. Her heart sped up and she focused on calming it once again, slowing her adrenaline. The time had finally come for them to be reunited. Despite having killed the desert mage, the memories flooded her mind.

His lips pulled softly at hers...She leaned against the wall and watched him watch her. His fingers ran softly over her lips, her chin, down her neck. He drew his hand across her bare chest...He ran a line down her with his hot fingers, moving from the base of her neck, between her bare breasts, down to her navel...

She forced the memory back and took deep breaths, trying to regain the sense of calm and focus Urdo had helped her find earlier. She could remember so vividly though, the way he kissed her collarbone, the strength of his hands as they held her hips, the heat of his breath against her...She shook her head, resisting the memories.

Slowly, he came around her, into view. He clapped slowly, derisively, before letting his hands fall to his sides. His blond hair was tied back in a knot, his lip was cut, and he had a bruise on his cheekbone. He wore a dirty white tunic under an open leather vest, though not his Hunter's leather, and dark breeches. His sword was sheathed at his hip. He looked the same, and yet different...In his golden eyes she saw no hope or youthfulness. He no longer carried himself with the same fresh optimism he once had—there was nothing young or immature in his gait. He was hardened, rugged, toughened by whatever life he had been living since fleeing the Blade.

He nodded at her slowly. "You look different too."

He, unlike his hired help, could not enter her mind without her permission. He simply knew her thoughts from once having known her.

She held his stare, and as the memories of his touch abated, her anger restored. "You would have a mage attack me."

He shrugged. "I simply wanted you to remember all we had."

"What we had wasn't real, Kohl," she shook her head.

"Of that, I am acutely aware!" he barked, throwing his hands out to the side.

She remained silent and still as he began to pace.

"You know, I've been all around this...*place*. This dark palace he built for you. I've seen where you trained, where you ate, where you slept...I've sat in Falco's dark throne. I met Corin—he says hello."

Jessop's fists clenched.

"I even lay in your bed. In the beginning, I didn't know why I wanted to come here so badly, why, when given the opportunity to escape you and Falco forever, I would find myself *needing* to get into the Shadow City. It came to me of course, as I got to see more of your life as it was here. I wanted to know *you* as you knew *me*. I wanted to see what was behind all the rage and treachery."

She bit the inside of her cheek, listening to him. She felt violated, as though he had taken from her something she had not offered up. She understood that this was how he had felt, sharing his life in the Blade with her, only to be made the fool.

He finally stopped pacing. "He made a city of darkness just for you." He seemed to think long on his words, as he looked up to dark sky above them. His golden gaze finally fell back to her. "I truly believe no two people were ever more suited to one another."

He walked past her, causing her to turn on her heel and follow him with her eyes. "I imagine Urdo showed you how to sense where my army was. An ability of the seasoned Hunter—obviously it would come easily to you."

He kept his eyes trained on the large doorway, out into the dark streets. She watched him warily. "Yes."

"Falco built Aranthol so that you both could live in the Shadows, like the dark lords you are, so that you could prosper at his side and never face the harsh light of fire ever again. How greatly you must hate Azgul."

She did not respond, but his drawn-out tone made her grow more cautious, and she rested a hand on her hilt. He was waiting on something, she knew as much. She wanted to cease being surprised by Kohl O'Hanlon, and yet, no matter all she knew, the hatred in his voice wounded her.

"How greatly you must hate me," he added, turning his head just enough to glance back at her.

The first of his words to sound soft and sincere, as they had always been with her *before*, pulled at her heart—though she did not loosen her grip on her hilt. "I've never hated you, Kohl."

He spun around at her words. "How can you say that to me? You destroyed my life and all we had."

She shook her head at him, frustrated and guilt-stricken. "We had nothing, Kohl."

"That is a lie! It might have all been a ruse to you, but *I* didn't know that, did I? It was real for me." His voice cracked over his words, emotion overwhelming him.

She nodded, and some part of her wanted to move towards him, to take his hand and apologize, the way she had wanted to so many times before. But she couldn't touch him. Not after the way she had touched him before. Not after the way he had nearly killed her. "Kohl, I'm sorry," she spoke, her own voice a whisper.

"Save your apologies, you cannot give me what I want," he spat, his anger still brimming.

"What is it you want? To know why I did it? To kill me? Falco? Tell me what you want—"

"*You*! I wanted you, Jessop."

She felt a wrenching pain in her chest. She wished for things to have been different between them. She wished she had sought out any other Hunter that day in the tavern, one whose heart hadn't been so easy to win over. No matter how many fell on her blade, it was the damage she had caused Kohl that tormented her. He haunted her dreams, his memory living forever at her side, pulling at her, nagging her to recall all they had shared.

"Kohl..." she began, but let her voice trail off. She didn't know what could be said.

He shook his head. "It's fine...If we can't have the life I wanted for us, I can do the next best thing."

She waited, her breath frozen in her lungs, her hand twitching—always ready to go for her blade.

"I can take the life he built for you," he whispered, turning back to face the doorway, his eyes on the dark streets. She looked past him but saw nothing. She took several steps towards him, looking over his shoulder, but still, she could not make out what he looked for. Then, something caught her eye. A bright light, something flickering in the distance. She narrowed her gaze on it, uncertain of what she was seeing. The light was growing in both hue and size as it became more distinct.

Then there was another...and another. They appeared throughout the city, illuminating the streets, surrounding the borders of Aranthol. Fire.

"Kohl, no!" she shrieked, attempting to dart past him, but he grabbed her with a surprising force and flung her back. She slid over the onyx floor, remembering his strength. He had once told her, with such seriousness, that he wasn't fragile. *"The hurt is intrinsic to my way of life..."* They had been his words but he hadn't known what kind of hurt had awaited him then.

"Your city will burn to the ground," he spoke, his voice low and serious. She got to her feet slowly, unable to ignore the smell of smoke that had already reached them. She could hear people screaming.

He reached for her, as though to touch her face, his hand falling just short. "And along with the city, all those you hold dear," he added. Suddenly, the sound of quick marching erupted all around her. His army, a band of hired swords, appeared from the hall hidden behind Falco's throne. Their emergence did not surprise her; she had known where they hid. She did not fear his army, and she did not fear him. All she could think of was Aranthol burning to the ground...until she heard *his* voice.

"Jessop!"

She pivoted around and saw Korend'a, his arms and legs bound, being carried by several mercenaries. Corin was being shuffled along beside him, gagged.

"Kohl—release them," she warned.

He shook his head slowly.

The sympathy she felt for him began to pale. She would not let harm come to Korend'a or Corin. She locked eyes with Kohl. "I warn you, I will kill you where you stand," she yelled, her voice loud and deep, echoing about the dark hall.

"Do it, then!" he screamed back, waving his hands out to the side, expanding his chest as he offered it up as a target for her.

"Don't test me, Kohl!"

"*Do it!*"

She understood then, what it was he wanted. He wanted to die. She reached over her shoulder, grabbed her short dagger, and flung it at him. With easy aim, she struck him in the shoulder, the blade thrusting deep into him. He fell to his knee, a look of agony painted across his face. He touched the hilt gingerly, contemplating pulling it out, but hesitated at the sensation of pain. With the strength of a Hunter, he slowly rose back to his feet. With an easy flick, Jessop released her second dagger, stabbing him in the opposite shoulder. He fell to the ground, grabbing his chest. The wounds would not kill him, but he would not get to his feet quickly.

"We are not done," she growled at him, and turning to face the mercenaries, she unsheathed her Hunter's blade.

CHAPTER 15

Jessop flung her arm out and a wave of the mercenary soldiers flew to the ground, visibly stunned. She raced through the minds of those who held Korend'a, and crippled them instantly. He rolled away from them, quick to begin working on the binds on his legs. She approached the wall of soldiers with confidence, alone, prepared to fight what would be an unwinnable battle to any other, for she was unable to rely on anyone—

"Stay back!"

Suddenly, Urdo Rendo came barreling past her, blade raised high as he threw himself into the battle, cutting down the soldier who had stood before her. Jessop hesitated, shocked. Urdo appearing in time to fight at her side had not been the plan—he was supposed to wait outside for those she drove out. And yet, he was with her.

Within seconds, Dezane's army swarmed the room. Chaos erupted as the mercenaries engaged with the Kuroi. Jessop leapt into the mix, striking down a man with a sword in place of where an arm might have once been, ducking under low-flying blades, dodging assaults. She sliced through mercenary after mercenary, until she was near Korend'a. He had his hands at his mouth, attempting to bite his binds away. She grabbed his wrists and cut the ties loose, quickly embracing him.

"Get Corin out of here!" she yelled, thrusting her sword up into the abdomen of another assailant.

"I can fight!" he shouted back, shaking his head. But she saw the cuts on his face, the swelling of bruises, the fatigue.

"You have already done your part, let me do mine," she insisted, leaping to her feet.

She offered him her forearm, helping him up. "Get Corin out of the city; we won't be far behind," she instructed. Korend'a nodded, quickly pulling her into another embrace. He let her go just as quickly, turned, and grabbed the frail Corin from the ground. With ease, he tossed the old man over his shoulder and ducked through the crowd, liberating him from the madness of the fight.

* * * *

Several Kuroi walked through the scene, killing those mercenaries who were mortally wounded, and tending to their kin. Jessop knelt, providing a swift death to one who would have agonized for several more hours before succumbing to his wounds. She stood slowly, her eyes darting over the bodies. The battle had not been a long one; the Kuroi had lived up to their reputation, as had she and Urdo. Kohl would have known his band of rebels wouldn't survive the fight—he had sent them to their certain death.

The smell of smoke was overwhelming—they didn't have long to escape the city. She looked about the room until her eyes fell on Kohl, leaning against Falco's black throne, breathing heavily and sweating profusely, her daggers still stuck in his shoulders. She crossed the room, stepping over dead bodies, sidewinding her way around the wounded, until she knelt before him.

"You don't look well," she remarked, crouching forward to examine the wounds.

"You stabbed me," he hissed, his eyes narrowing on her.

"Consider us even then," she said, reminding him of the wound he had inflicted on her not so long ago.

"Not remotely," he growled, looking away from her.

She looked to the doorway, noting the fires still burning in the dark streets. "How many people have you murdered just to ruin my home?"

He shrugged, but Jessop knew he was not truly ambivalent. After a moment of silence, uncomfortable under her unblinking stare, he spoke. "Most of the city had evacuated before today."

She nodded slowly, thankful that he didn't possess the hatred required for that kind of damage, relieved to know some part of him was still recognizable. "Stand up."

He ignored her, looking to the scene of the battle. She grabbed the collar of his leather vest and stood, wrenching him to his feet. He held his arms to his chest tightly, hissing with pain and leaning against Falco's throne to steady himself. She forced him towards the doorway. Her eyes fell to Urdo, who was speaking with one of the warriors. "Let's move."

As she stepped out into the dark city, she froze. Many of the fires had died out, leaving behind charred remains, but some still licked at buildings and flitted down streets. Everything was ashen. Everything was ruined. The smell of smoke was overwhelming to her. She fought at her memories, refusing to let them surface, knowing that was what he had intended. She would not think of the fire, she would not think of this being the second home she had lost to the flames. All she could consider was that she had failed. She hadn't been able to save the city he had made for her. She tightened her grip on Kohl's arm. "Falco is going to make you wish you were dead." She hadn't thought the sentiment through. He stared out at the city he had burned and then down to her.

"I already wish it."

* * * *

They moved through the city in silence. Those remaining were fleeing for the gates, their belongings in their arms, their fear forcing them forward blindly. She could not help them. She refused to let go of Kohl, though she knew the warriors could have guarded him well enough.

Kohl voiced a running commentary as they weaved around the worst of the flames. He showed no sense of fear, no regard for his pain or situation. "Can you smell that? It's like…burned meat," he mused. She kicked the back of his knee, lurching him forward as he fell to the ground. She wrenched his head back with a grab of his bun and ripped one dagger from his shoulder.

He cried out as she stepped around to face him. "How much leeway do you think my guilt buys you? Do you honestly believe that I won't kill you, that I won't let Falco kill you?"

She let him rise to his feet, his hand tight against his shoulder. "Do not pretend you let me live out of guilt, Jessop."

She hesitated at his implication. She realized the eyes of all the Kuroi, of Mar'e and Urdo, rested on them. "*Don't*, Kohl."

He took a step towards her, his eyes desperate. "Then stop pretending you don't lo—"

She tightened her hand into a fist at her side, and immediately, he began to choke, as though her fingers gripped his jugular. She constricted further and he fell once again to his knees, his hands grabbing at his throat, his eyes wide.

"Jessop," Urdo cautioned, taking a step closer.

She ignored him. She wouldn't hear it, not any more. She had betrayed him, but he had nearly killed her. He mocked her as he burned her home to the ground. She stared at him, without sympathy, without concern, as his face began to turn color.

"Jessop," Mar'e added, nearing Urdo.

He loved her and he hated her—she understood that. She knew there was something about Kohl that she did love, that she would always love, but it was not what she felt for Falco. She was *meant* to be with Falco, it was more than destiny, more than any familiarity, more than words could explain. They were one; the same soul. Whatever Kohl felt for her, and she for him, it was no comparison.

"Jessop!"

Urdo's voice drew her back to the moment. Back to the streets that burned, back to the smell of charred flesh, back to the home he had destroyed in the same manner that his false Lord had destroyed the first. She knelt before him, keeping her grip on him.

"You took my home from me, just as Hydo once did, and you think I could ever love you? You're pathetic," she hissed, and without warning, she wrenched her second dagger free. She might not have saved Aranthol for Falco, but she could deliver Kohl to him.

She turned and began to walk once again towards the gates. She ignored his coughing, the sound of Mar'e helping him to his feet, the stare she could feel from Urdo. She ignored it all, refusing to turn back. Refusing to close her eyes to the blackened ruins around her. Despite the tears, she would not look away from it.

* * * *

They set up camp a mile from the city walls. Many who had escaped the fires, those who hadn't evacuated before, joined their group. Jessop wished to return to the Soar-Craft immediately, eager to return to Falco, but the troops needed rest. She had set up a tent and resided inside, alone with her thoughts. All she could see were the flames.

Mar'e had brought her food and told her that she had mended Kohl's wounds. She had tried comforting Jessop about the loss of her city, but she didn't want to hear it. She knew failure when she saw it.

She had sat with Korend'a for a long time, and with Corin when he felt well enough. They too tried comforting her. "What he said was true, most of the city had been forced to evacuate before he set the fires," Corin spoke, sipping a liquor that was hot on his breath. Jessop imagined he had received it from Urdo.

"We can rebuild, Jessop. Aranthol still has a forever night sky—the fires could do nothing to that," Korend'a added. She nodded as they spoke, smiling when appropriate. The truth was Aranthol would never be the same, and it would likely never be her home again. Falco had to rule from the Blade. Jeco had to be trained in the Blade. She would spend the rest of her life in the Red City. It wasn't simply the destruction of the Shadow City that tormented her—it was *him*. By enlisting the desert mage and setting fire to her home, he had attacked her the same way Hydo would have.

She knew he had intended to harm her, to punish her. He had succeeded.

"Get some sleep, Jessop," Korend'a advised, embracing her tightly before disappearing from her tent. Just as he left, the tent flapped open once again.

Urdo stood before her, a leather flagon in hand, a look of apology in his eyes.

He held the canteen out for her, offering a share of his drink. Though she normally would abstain, she took it, and sipped heartily. The liquid burned her throat, it travelled down her like a small fire burning, and she both relished and despised the sensation. She handed it back to him, offering him a seat opposite her.

"O'Hanlon's wound has been mended," he spoke between sips of his drink.

Jessop nodded. "I'd heard as much."

He offered her the drink once again but she declined.

"I'm sorry for what he did to your city."

She offered him a half smile, thankful for his words, though they both knew nothing could be changed by them. "Everything he does, he does out of vengeance. He will not stop until he understands I do not, nor did I ever love him."

"Or perhaps he will stop once you admit the opposite."

She narrowed her gaze at the older Hunter, discomforted by his assertion. "I would do no such thing."

"Is it so untrue that you ever had any feelings for him?"

Jessop knew if it had been any other asking, she would have reacted with greater severity. Urdo had earned the right to speak to her candidly.

"You've seen Falco and me," she answered.

"Aye, we all have. If you put that man's hand in fire, I reckon the burn would show up on your fingers. I've never seen two people more destined to be together…" His voice trailed off, his mind clearly contemplating their relationship.

He quickly took a large sip from his drink. "But does that mean the boy never meant anything to you? If you say so, I'll believe it. But just because you weren't in love with him doesn't mean you didn't care."

She ran her hand over her dark braid, frustrated. "I've told him as much, Urdo. I cared. I apologized. He cannot accept things as they are…and Falco may not let him live much longer should he continue to persist."

Urdo nodded slowly. "Maybe that's for the best then."

His words surprised her, causing her to lean back.

He shrugged. "The boy doesn't wish to live. He cannot stop loving you and he cannot stop hating you for your inability to love him back. He was the wrong mark, Jessop. He wasn't built for heartbreak."

Jessop ground her teeth roughly against one another, her jaw clenching under the words of her Hunter comrade. She took a low breath. She wouldn't be responsible for his death unless she took the blade to his throat—if he forced Falco's hand, then he would be the cause of his own demise, and he alone. "If he wishes to die so badly, that is his prerogative, but it shall not be permitted until I know where Hydo Jesuin is."

* * * *

Jessop could feel Falco in her mind as she laid in her tent, waiting to hear the rest of the camp wake. They traded bits of information with one another. Her son was well. Both had fought their battles, both had experienced relative success and failure. She was hesitant to let him see the images of Aranthol on fire, and she sensed how he retreated somewhat when he did come across them. She knew, through her own excursion of his mind, that many had died in the streets of the Red City—she also knew that neither Hydo nor Hanson had been captured.

She rolled to her side, disappointment welling in her chest like an acidic liquor. She felt as though they had come so far, in so many regards, and yet things had not quite fallen into place like they had once envisioned. She knew they had been too hopeful, living under the belief that once Falco was in the Blade again, everyone would hear his story and pledge their fealty. Many had, but not enough it seemed, not enough to prevent war.

Jessop sat upright and began to fix her long plait. They would make it to the Soar-Craft swiftly, not carrying many wounded, and then she would be reunited with Falco and Jeco. She couldn't quite anticipate how the reunion between Falco and Kohl would go, though Falco knew he was coming. Falco understood that Kohl couldn't just be killed—he was one of the few people who knew how to find Hydo. Despite all that had been said and thought, she refused to believe that Kohl truly wished to die. Her love wasn't worth his life. She believed, instead, that he simply wanted Jessop to think he longed for death to punish her.

"Jessop?" Korend'a called her name from outside the tent.

"Come in," she answered, tying off the end of her hair with a leather band. She turned and found Korend'a ducking into the tent. He wore fresh clothes supplied from his Kuroi brethren and he appeared revitalized from a good night's rest and a break from battle.

She gestured for him to sit and he acquiesced. "The man, Kohl, he has been readied for our trek back. He is bandaged and his hands are bound. I brought you this," he spoke, and from behind his back he unsheathed Kohl's Hunter Blade.

Jessop reached out and slowly took the blade from him. She hadn't held it in such a long time—its unique blade, its hilt, perfectly shaped to Kohl's grip. She lowered it to the ground beside her, ensuring it rested on a blanket. "Thank you, Korend'a."

He stared at her for a long moment before speaking. "Falco wishes to kill him, but you do not?"

She regarded her old friend thoughtfully. How could she possibly explain that which made no sense to Falco, and no sense to herself, about Kohl's living or dying? "Falco wishes to kill him, but we need him to tell us where Hydo is first."

Korend'a nodded, though she could see skepticism in his eyes as he spoke. "Could you not force the knowledge from his mind and then kill him?"

She nodded, knowing his words were truthful. "Yes, and should it come to it, I will."

"Why waste the time? You could do it now, I could bring him to you—"

She raised her hand, indicating for him to stop. She could remember the night she had gone up the Blade with Kohl, she remembered all they had spoken of, she remembered how he had told her he wouldn't trespass the thoughts of another without true purpose...She had found that to be honorable. "His fate shall be determined by Falco." It was a half-truth, for she had Falco's ear, but should Kohl continue on his chosen path, Jessop believed that not even she could sustain his life. Or that she would want to.

Korend'a nodded and together they sat in silence. After many minutes, she spoke. "How did he clear out Aranthol? It is one of the most dangerous regions in Daharia —if not *the* most—but the city was practically abandoned by the time he...by the time the fires started."

He looked at her with surprise. "That Hunter is a very dangerous man, Jessop. Very dangerous. He arrived, fighting, with his army—many of whom had been in Aranthol before, given their trade—and he killed many. He was not met without resistance; resistance simply couldn't hold him back. Even I was overcome by him eventually, when he resorted to his use of Sentio."

Jessop felt, in that moment, shame. She and Falco had left Aranthol without protection against one with Sentio. Korend'a was commonly found to have no equal with a blade, barring herself or Falco, but when confronted with mind tricks, he was helpless. She thought of the mage who had forced his way into her mind, of his audacity and aggression, and she felt as though she had let down Korend'a, Corin, and their people.

She tried to picture Kohl as Korend'a described him, and despite his rugged appearance and skilled sword hand, she couldn't. He simply wasn't someone she had ever viewed as a threat. Perhaps her mistake, from the beginning, had been to underestimate him too greatly. "How many did he kill?"

Korend'a looked up at her with dark eyes. "Too many to bury."

* * * *

The warriors were ready to return to the Soar-Craft. Mar'e had seen to it that the entire camp was packed up neatly, Urdo looked weary but ready for the trek, and near him, hands bound and mouth gagged, was Kohl. His shoulders were heavily bandaged, and it appeared as though his face had been tended to as well. It seemed that Mar'e had been diligent in her care of him.

"Jessop!" Korend'a called after her, but she did not yield. She needed to know, she needed to *see*. Korend'a had been right, she could force her way in to Kohl's mind with ease, and why she felt the urge to resist, after all he had done, was unfathomable.

Jessop crossed the large dune, walking towards Kohl with determination. She held his golden gaze without interruption, stepping through the thick, rolling sand. She pushed into his mind and though he resisted, she found the images she sought for quickly. He fought through the dark streets, his blade covered in blood, cutting down any who stepped before him. He killed indiscriminately, breaking down doors and ordering people out of their homes, proclaiming Aranthol a dead city. Any who rose against him fell at his feet.

Jessop outstretched her hand, and with a flex of her fingers, she forced Kohl to kneel. She could see him striking Corin, letting the elderly man fall unconscious to the ground, before meeting Korend'a near the Pit. Korend'a fought with two blades, and as he battled Kohl, he also struck down several mercenaries. He was a wonder to watch. She could sense the extent to which Kohl was impressed by his opponent, and she could feel the fear growing inside him, telling him that with a blade alone he would not best this Kuroi warrior.

She watched as he brought Korend'a to his knees with Sentio, forcing his weapons from him. He ordered his mercenaries to bind him and gag him, to keep him locked away safe. She knew that Kohl had heard of the Kuroi man who had cared for Jessop for many years, he was right in believing it to be *this* Kuroi man. She could hear his thoughts, she could see how Kohl envisioned killing Korend'a before her as her city burned. She sensed his real plan, that she would kill him in order to save her Kuroi friend.

Jessop left Kohl's mind, reeling from the darkness of his thoughts, his blackened character. He truly had intended to die on her blade. He stared up at her indignantly as she ripped his tunic, revealing his scarred chest for all to see. As she had anticipated, atop his breast bone, was his newest scar. It was freshly pink and formed out of the letters of her son's name. He had seen her scar and realized it was the key to Aranthol. He had carved the mark into himself with a sharp blade. Jessop pushed her fingers firmly into his pectoral, and holding his stare, she wrenched her nails through his flesh, tearing down across the scar—destroying the mark.

He jerked away from her, but the damage was done. Four long nail marks crossed his chest, bleeding, hot and red. "You have no right to wear this mark."

As she turned from him, he yelled. "You've seen what I did—why won't you end it? Just kill me."

His voice had broken, tears falling over his cheeks as she turned to face him. She said nothing, her cheeks burning as she felt the eyes of her soldiers on them both.

"I tried to kill you. I burned your city to the ground. Just do it," he pleaded with her.

"No."

"Then don't tell me you don't love me—"

"I *don't*—"

"Don't say it. I can't live with it, Jessop. I can't *live* knowing it meant nothing to you."

She couldn't slow her heart. She couldn't deny, despite all he had done, that she wished to comfort him. Her home was gone. Her scar still fresh. Their mutual hatred was strong. Yet she couldn't stand to see him suffer her.

She pivoted on her heel, turning from him, leaving him in tears before her troops. Silently she pushed the thought into his mind—*It did mean something to me.*

CHAPTER 16

Jessop walked ahead, ignoring Kohl's futile attempts to push thoughts at her. She shouldn't have said anything to him. She could see the Soar-Craft in the distance, over one final sand ridge, and she told herself if she could just resist engaging with him again until they got there, everything would be alright. It had been many hours though, of him pushing and prodding at the periphery of her mind, and she grew weary.

"Stop it," she growled, barely loud enough for any to hear.

"Then speak to me," he answered, his voice just as muted, but keen in her focused ears.

"No," she hissed.

"Jessop?" Mar'e stared at her with confusion, having appeared at her side from the rear.

She shook her head, forcing herself to not think of Kohl's niggling prods. "Nothing. What is it?"

"I just wanted to check on you. Since we lost your city, you've been hostile."

Jessop shot an angry look at her. "I lost my home, Mar'e, I think anyone would be a little 'hostile' were they in my position."

Mar'e raised her hands defensively. "Just like that."

Jessop ran a hand over her brow. "I'm sorry."

Mar'e stared at her, her brow knitted. They walked in silence for a long minute before she spoke again. "I was thinking you could tell me more about Kohl?"

"Why would you want to know more about Kohl?"

She studied her friend, who stared back at her silently. Jessop stopped walking, forcing Mar'e to stop as well. She stared at her friend with a serious gaze. "Don't fall for the pretty face, Mar'e, you will find another. He's our *captive*...And he likely won't survive another full moon."

Mar'e cocked her head, her long dark braids falling over her shoulder. "Falco's going to kill him?"

Jessop started walking again, Mar'e sticking at her side. "After all he has done...His odds of survival aren't looking too promising."

Jessop ignored the look in her old friend's face. It was the look of disappointment. She ignored it and hoped beyond hope that her own face didn't appear the same every time she spoke of Kohl dying.

* * * *

Kohl sat opposite her on the Soar-Craft. He had chewed his gag into nothing more than a threadbare collar and slipped it down his jaw. Blood from his chest had stained his white tunic. Four claw marks stared at her throughout their journey. His hands remained bound and he had stared at her without blinking for what felt like an eternity.

"Why won't you speak to me?"

She rolled her head back against her seat, sick of his persistence. "We have nothing to discuss."

"You know I know you. I knew you would come to the city, I knew you would kill the mage—"

She glared at him, knowing where he was leading with this. "Yes, you knew I would come to save *my* city that *you* burned to the ground. You knew I would kill your mage, who trespassed my mind. These things don't prove you know me, Kohl, they prove you know how to antagonize your enemy."

His brow furrowed at her words. "You're not my enemy, Jessop."

She narrowed her eyes on him. "One minute you're trying to kill me, the next you're proclaiming your love. Which is it, Kohl?"

He looked offended by her words. "I've done nothing to you that you haven't done to me, Jessop *Bane*."

She cocked her head back at him. "Actually, I've never tried to kill you."

"Might as well have."

He stared at her in silence, she held his gaze with her own challenging stare. Finally, he leaned forward, closing the small space between them. "You know I remember seeing you for the first time as keenly as if it were this very morning."

She remained silent, refusing to be the first to turn away.

"I'd never seen anyone move like you."

She knew the look she gave him reflected what they both thought. *Falco.*
"Obviously, I know now you learned from him...I just, I wanted you
to know, I loved you from the very start."
She finally tore her gaze away, unable to hold it any longer. "I know."

* * * *

They landed the Soar-Craft late in the evening. It was the first time
she had been happy to see the dusty red sky, knowing it meant she was
that much closer to Falco and their son. Every minute she was away from
Falco left her feeling more doubt and self-hatred. She was ashamed and
felt as though her thoughts alone were a betrayal of him. She wanted to be
able to hate Kohl, she wanted to hate him for herself, she wanted to hate
him for Falco, for their Arantholi people—but she simply couldn't. She
told herself again and again that it was simply a matter of guilt, that she
forgave him his trespasses for she had set him on his destructive path. It
was the truth, to an extent. But there was also the other truth. That when
she was alone with her thoughts she remembered training with him,
laughing with him, watching him as he slept. She remembered fearing
for his life and regretting any harm she would bring to him. She cared,
more than she should have.

As they disembarked, she found Falco standing on the platform,
surrounded by white-clothed techs waiting to help unload the vessels.
She leapt from the Soar-Craft, quick to leave Kohl behind.

She jogged over to Falco, who held a sleeping Jeco in his arms. She
immediately kissed them both, lacing her arms around Falco, nuzzling
their son between them. She looked up into his welcoming gray eyes. He
had a cut above his brow, surrounded by a faint bruise.

"I'm fine," he insisted, offering her a half smile. She reached up and
touched the bruise with her cool fingers, almost recoiling at the natural
heat of his skin. She was always so much colder than him. He brushed his
face into her palm, welcoming her cool touch. She kissed him once more.

"These days apart have been too long," she whispered to him.

He used his free hand to pull her closer. "I feel the same, my love."

She wanted to return to their chambers, to be alone with him and Jeco.
She didn't wish to speak to any on the Council. She didn't wish to discuss
her failure or hear the details of Hanson's attack on the Red City.

"We can retire soon, my love, we have but one thing to attend to," Falco
spoke, hearing her thoughts.

She followed his gaze over her shoulder, turning to see where his gray eyes focused. Kohl stared at her with intensity, his golden eyes trailing over Jeco before fixing on her. He looked at her as though he had never seen her before. Instinctively, she took Jeco from Falco's arms. She knew what Falco intended. "I'll take Jeco to bed."

Falco didn't take long to join her in their chambers. She had put Jeco to sleep and bathed herself. He returned as she dried her body, seated on the edge of the bed. He quietly made his way to their bathing chamber. He said nothing, and in turn, she ignored the fresh blood on his knuckles. She had known he would hurt Kohl, but it wasn't Kohl she feared for. She feared what Falco might have seen in Kohl's mind, or what his old friend may have told him out of spite.

* * * *

She walked back into the bathing chamber, leaning against the wall as he cleaned himself. "Did he say anything?"

Falco turned under the stream of water to face her. "Many things, and at the same time, nothing."

She watched him step out of the water, remaining silent. She handed him fresh linens to dry with. He dabbed his face and wrapped the material around his body.

"He loves you still."

Her heart quickened. Any love she had for Kohl paled in comparison to what she felt for Falco. "All that matters is that I love you."

He was silent for a long moment before speaking. As though he contemplated her sentiment. "And I you."

She ran her finger down his chest, through the valley of his high muscular walls. "Falco—" she began, but he kissed her abruptly.

He leaned his forehead against hers. "I can't talk about it—him and you— not now, Jessop."

He pulled away from her, turning to their bedroom. Jessop felt her heart twist, as though seized by a firm grip. She loved him more than life itself and no matter what he said, no matter that the plan had been *his* plan, he was wounded. "Falco, there is no him and I."

He hesitated, but he did not look back.

She walked around him, standing before him and forcing him to face her. "Falco, we can't keep doing this. I'm in love with *you*."

"We have other things to discuss now. The battles—"

She stepped back from him, angry. "I don't care about the battles, Falco. None of it matters if it costs our relationship."

"I would never leave you."

"But would you look at me the same? Knowing what you know about—"

"About Kohl and you? Knowing you love him."

The words were a knife. She felt her hands unclench, never having realized she made fists. She saw the look in his gray eyes—the hurt.

"It is not what you think. I told you I cared for him."

"Like you care for me?"

"Not at all."

He crossed his arms over his bare chest. "He betrayed me. He tried to kill you. He burned our home to the ground. Does he need to kill me for you to change how you feel for him?"

"Don't speak like that."

"It's the truth, isn't it?"

"*No*! It's not the truth." She felt the tears as they streaked her face.

"Why am I not enough for you to forget him?"

"You are! You loved him once too. I cared for him, and I wish I hadn't. I wish I had never met him. But I did—I did it for *you*. I was never in love with him, I'm not now. But I cared for him and I wronged him and now I've lost him, as I feel I am losing you."

He grabbed her in his arms, tears streaming down his face. "It's I who fears losing you. You can't love him. I'll kill him. I will."

She pulled him tight into her embrace, his strong body heaving with sorrow. She said nothing to him. Perhaps Urdo was right. Perhaps if Kohl died, it would be for the best.

* * * *

Jessop hesitated in the mossy, dim-lit corridor. Falco had locked Kohl away in the Hollow. She did not know what version of him she would find, or what version of herself seeing him would bring forward. She didn't know what damage Falco might have inflicted, though she knew him well enough to know it could be devastating. She had never seen him as distraught as she had the night before. It pained her to think of it. She took a slow breath and carried forward, finding herself standing at the lip of the fighting arena.

Her eyes landed on him instantly. His arms were shackled to the stone wall. The manacles must have been placed in her absence. His white tunic was torn. His chest still bore her scratch marks. His head hung low, his blond hair damp and clinging to him. She saw, stained in the dirt at his feet, dark blood. She leapt from the edge, landing on bended knee several feet away from him.

He didn't move.

She slowly approached him, and though she expected him to look up at her or shift in his chains, he did not stir. She took a small step forward, knowing if she reached out just slightly, she could touch his golden crown of hair. For the briefest of moments, she wondered if he had died, but a slow rise of his back muscles let her know he breathed still.

Had Falco perhaps wounded him too greatly? Had heat and dehydration slowed his senses? She crossed her arms over her chest, resisting her urge to reach for him. She could never reconcile the feelings she had for him—the impulse to set him free coupled with the dark desire to wound him further. She wondered if she would feel the weight of such conflict for the rest of her life, another scar.

"I wondered when you would come," he whispered. His voice, cracked and dry, startled her.

She said nothing, watching as he slowly raised his head to face her. His golden tresses clung to the sweat and blood on his face, tangled over his eyes and scar. Falco had left him bruised and beaten, though it was nothing Kohl hadn't endured before, she knew. "I came to see if he had killed you."

He smiled at her with a bloodied grin. "Your concern warms my heart."

She shook her head at him. "You've brought this on yourself. Falco offered you a place at his side."

"Tell me, Jessop," he began, attempting to flick his hair out of his eyes as he spoke. "Do you truly live with a diminished sense of responsibility, or do I haunt your nightmares, as you do mine?"

She could resist no longer, reaching out and brushing his sticky hair out of his face. She let her hand fall from him, ignoring the peaceful expression her touch painted across his face. "I live with my guilt daily," she answered. She wondered what his nightmares entailed, she wondered if they mirrored her own.

"Tell me of your nightmares," she ordered, trying to soften her tone.

He held her in his gaze warmly. "In some, we live peacefully. In others…I kill you."

His words nipped her. She couldn't feel angered by them. Not when she lived with her own nightmares.

He locked his golden eyes on her. "Some part of me truly wished you had died that day."

She nodded, knowing what he meant. "Some part of me truly wishes you were dead right now."

He shrugged his tired shoulders. "If you wish me dead, kill me."

She shook her head slowly. "I don't really believe you deserve to die."

He arched his brow at her. Long gone was the hopeful tone in his voice. He did not push at her, did not ask her to admit her love. He seemed somewhat broken. "Then you must not think I deserve peace."

Before she could answer, she felt *him*. She knew Falco's gray eyes were set on her. She could feel his presence as keenly as if his hand touched her. She slowly turned, tilting her head up to see him standing on one of the steel beams.

"My love," she addressed him. He had a stern expression and narrowed eyes. Jessop wondered if he had watched her with Kohl for longer than she had sensed. He leapt down to the Hollow ground and approached them slowly.

He ran a hand up her back as he stood beside her, his eyes stuck on Kohl. "You may have realized my wife is somewhat more forgiving than I, old friend."

Kohl shook his head slowly, a skeptical look playing on his face. "I'm not sure about that, Falco. She's done more damage to me than you ever did."

A tight smile pulled on Falco's face. "Give me time, brother."

Kohl forced a smile back. "If you plan on torturing me more just have at it. I'm sick of waiting."

"It's not quite time for you and me, yet, but soon it will be."

Jessop turned at Falco's words, unsure what he implied, but he did not look to her, keeping his gaze on Kohl. "Last chance to tell me where Hydo is."

"I told you already. I don't know."

Falco grabbed Kohl's hair, wrenching his head back. "You lie. It matters not. You can't hide anything from Jessop."

Jessop bristled at his words. He would have her search Kohl's mind for the truth. As Korend'a had suggested from the start. She looked at Falco with a critical eye. He was just as capable of searching Kohl's mind. She knew he tasked her with it out of anger. But she would do it. If Falco needed her to, then she would.

He nodded to her encouragingly. "Find Hydo, my love. And make it swift."

* * * *

Jessop stepped away from him, letting her hands fall to the side, dizzy. She kept her eyes closed and focused on regaining her balance. It had been hours and she had found nothing, her rigorous search of his mind wearing on her. She had seen the early days, after he had nearly killed her, where he spoke with Hanson while Hydo regained his strength in some unknown part of the city. She had felt all his emotions, all his concerns, she had known how he despaired and how he agonized over his attack on her. He had gone countless sleepless nights wondering if she had survived his assault. Hanson had been the one to comfort him in the end, explaining that if he had killed her, Falco would have gone on the warpath already.

Once Hydo had recovered, they had planned their separate missions. Hanson would lead an assault on the Red City, while Kohl would attack Aranthol. Hanson had insisted that Kohl stay with him and fight by his side, but Hydo had refused. He said it was their time to part ways and they would find Kohl once the battles were done and they had succeeded in reclaiming the Blade. They had not succeeded though, and they had refused to tell Kohl where he could find them should they have failed.

Slowly, Jessop opened her eyes. Tears had streaked Kohl's face. His cracked lips were parted, though he had long since given up on asking her to stop. She felt a pang in her chest, seeing the pain she caused in his eyes once more, tenfold for her rampant, hours-long searching. "He knows nothing, Falco," she insisted again.

"Search *harder* then," he pressed back, leaning against the back wall of the Hollow.

She turned to face him. "It's been hours—I would have found something by now."

He pushed off the wall and approached her. "He's been trained to defend his mind against such raids, Jessop, don't be fooled."

"Not against the likes of me, Falco, and you know it," she argued, squaring off with him.

"You're restrained by your guilt—you do not wish to see him harmed further," he hissed, shaking his head at her.

She narrowed her gaze. "Twice now you have offended me with your words."

"As you offend me with your actions—do you not wish to find Hydo?"

She glared at him, but before either could say anything further, Kohl spoke. "Just kill me now." His tone was mocking, as though she and Falco irritated him.

Falco moved past her gruffly. Before she could say anything, he hit Kohl. He struck him violently, again and again.

"Falco," she warned, but he ignored her.

He raised his hand at the shackles and, using Sentio, he ripped them from the walls. With a forceful jerk, he threw Kohl across the Hollow. Kohl tried getting to his feet, but Falco was on him in an instant. He kicked him in the abdomen before pinning him to the ground, striking him again and again. She approached him slowly. "Falco, that's enough."

He hit Kohl once more, blood staining them both.

Jessop raised her hand and, using her own abilities, pushed Falco off Kohl.

He stared at her with anger, and for a moment, it was as though he weren't her husband. She held his gaze until his face calmed. He got to his feet slowly, and stood above Kohl. "It's been far too long since Azgul has had a public execution, brother. Know that your silence has been your death sentence."

CHAPTER 17

"*Public execution*? Really, Falco?"

He rounded on her as she closed their chamber doors behind them. His eyes were dark and wild, his hands covered in blood. They had left Kohl in the Hollow, instructing the guard who stood watch to fetch a medic to tend to his wounds.

"He's brought this on himself. He declined a spot at my side, he tried to kill you, he burned Aranthol to the ground—and now he resists helping us locate Hydo," he yelled. His words echoed around the room and she was thankful Jeco was with Trax still.

Jessop nearly hit the wall in her frustration, her hands tightened into fists. While Falco's words were true, they were also misleading. He refused a spot at Falco's side because of what she did to him, he tried to kill her because of what *she* did to *him*, he burned Aranthol to the ground out of vengeance. And he truly didn't know where Hanson or Hydo were.

Falco stared at her with amazement. "Stop defending him, Jessop!"

She took a step towards him, ignoring his anger. "He does not know where they are—do you really think he could hide such information from me?"

"I think you hesitate to hurt him—*hesitate to kill him*— because you still walk around with your guilt, despite all he has done."

She squared off with him, holding his angry stare. "And you leap at the opportunity to kill him because you cannot live with your own guilt! You are equally responsible for what transpired between Kohl and myself, *equally* responsible for what he did to exact vengeance on us, and now you wish to see him dead."

He turned from her, pacing. "And you do not?"

She hesitated, unable to answer. Her hands fell to her side as she took a slow breath. "We have killed indiscriminately for so many years, Falco. The fact that he loves me is not a good enough reason to kill him."

He shook his head at her. "It's also not a good enough reason to let him live in light of his trespasses. The decision remains with me. It is I who rules the Blade."

She took a step towards him. Her hands shook at her sides, her breathing slow to calm her racing heart. "Do not forget who gave you the Blade, my love."

* * * *

That night Falco did not come to bed and Jessop did not go in search of him. She lay with Jeco, brushing his hair back with her hand, soothing him into a slumber neither of them seemed interested in.

He put his small, pudgy hand on top of hers, wriggling in her arms. "Where Dada?"

She kissed his little fingers, squeezing him tighter. "He has work to do, my love."

He rolled around in her arms, turning to face her, directing his gray eyes on her. She marveled at how greatly he resembled his father already, though his eyes did not carry the burden of Falco's history. They had never argued before as they had that day. Always of one mind, they had never had any reason to, nothing to dispute. Kohl O'Hanlon was their first true point of contention. She knew Falco wished Kohl dead for the same reasons she wished him to live—to abate their guilt. He had been collateral damage, and while he was not the first to suffer from her and Falco's ambitions, he was the first to strike back against them so keenly.

Falco's anger only highlighted her remorse; with every strike he made against Kohl, she had to defend him. With every insistence on his death, she had an equally insistent claim for his life. She wished she could accept what Falco believed, what Urdo believed—that it simply would be for the best if Kohl died. She wished it not only for her sake, but for Falco's. His suffering was torment for her. She wanted to relieve his guilt, she wanted to restore their relationship, and yet, she could not let Kohl's life be the price for such repair. He simply didn't deserve it.

She looked down at her son and knew that it was at his birth that she had developed a conscience. Hydo had destroyed much of who Jessop was. She had felt nothing for anyone except Falco for so many long years. She had fought and killed. She had encouraged Falco to do whatever necessary for their lives, for their futures. She had never lost a single night's sleep over their decisions. Until Jeco. Her son had reminded her of the sanctity of life, and in his presence, she felt shame for relishing in violence, for harming others who did not deserve harm. He made her want to be better. And in advocating for Kohl's life, she believed she was achieving that.

She thought of Aranthol, though, and the fires. The many who had died on Kohl's sword. Perhaps the primary reason for her defense of him was her conscience—she truly didn't think he deserved death—but she also knew there was more to it. Had any other burned their city to the ground, she would have done more than just kill them. And Falco would have killed whoever responsible as soon as he knew they held no further knowledge he required...Perhaps, both she and her husband let him live for the same reason. Some part of them both loved him still.

She remembered sitting in the tent with Kohl in Okton Radon, arguing about his bond with his brothers. She remembered how he explained it to her. *"It's not that I love my brothers in the same way that I love you, because I obviously don't, and it's not that I love them more, because I have now begun to realize that that is not true either. It's simply that I loved them first."* She thought of her husband, who had told her time and again that for Hunters, before all else came their loyalty, their love for one another. She thought of how he had surprised them all, offering Kohl a place at his side. She thought of how often he had expressed such anger at his brother's refusal. He had sentenced Kohl to die at the hand of an executioner because he could not do it himself—some part of him still felt that loyalty, that love of his brethren, that love for his best friend.

"Dada," Jeco complained, wanting his father, his small voice sad and frustrated.

She nodded, kissing his forehead. "He'll be back soon." She pulled Jeco closer in her embrace, hoping her words were true, for the both of them.

* * * *

The next morning Jessop woke to the sound of heavy knocking on her door. Jeco stirred at the sound, causing her to leap from her bed. She immediately realized Falco's side of the bed was undisturbed. He hadn't returned that night.

She opened the door quickly, prepared to chastise whoever disturbed them, but the sight of Mar'e, visibly distraught, struck away her anger. Her Kuroi friend stared at her with red, swollen eyes. Her braids fell about her sad face without any of their usual order. She wore ochre robes, haphazardly pulled on.

"Mar'e, what's the matt—"

Mar'e grabbed the doorway, as if trying to support her own weight. "Is it true?"

Jessop glanced over her shoulder to see Jeco, still sleeping. She stepped towards Mar'e, forcing them out into the corridor. She closed the door quietly behind them. "Is *what* true?"

"The execution, Jessop," she answered. Her voice was hoarse and angry.

Jessop regarded her old friend, so clearly devastated by the news. She thought about how Mar'e had tended to Kohl's wounds and asked about him. Jessop didn't believe her former friend could have developed any real feelings for Kohl—she didn't even know him—but her distraught state warned Jessop off the thought.

"It's true," Jessop answered plainly.

Fresh tears sprung forth and Mar'e wiped her face quickly, clearly embarrassed. "Please change Falco's mind."

Jessop shook her head slowly. Her thoughts from the night before came back to her, the memories of their fight. The fact that he had not slept next to her that night. "I've tried."

Mar'e grabbed her wrist and pulled her closer. "Jessop, *please*," she begged, her eyes fearful.

Jessop pulled her arm free. She had her own fears. She feared that if she stayed speaking to Mar'e a minute longer, she too would break down in tears.

"I have already spoken to Falco."

She opened the door and began to retreat inside.

"But, but, Jessop…"

"My son needs me," she answered sternly, stepping further inside the room. She offered Mar'e a final glance. "I'm very sorry."

She closed the door behind her, turning and slowly lowering herself to the ground. She watched Jeco sleep, so peaceful and so unaware of the world falling apart around him. She kept her eyes on him as her vision blurred and her breath hastened, as she tried to hold back the tears she did not wish to show anyone.

* * * *

Long after Mar'e had left, Trax came for Jeco. He told Jessop that Falco had stayed up speaking with him that night. He told her that sadly, he knew all about Kohl's fate, and that he too had been unable to change Falco's mind.

"Few are as distraught as Mar'e," she remarked, finding Jeco's play swords and getting him ready for his time with Trax.

Trax shook his head with disapproval. "She has grown feelings for him most swiftly...Does she not understand the extent to which she could anger Falco?"

Jessop shrugged. "I do not know if what she feels for Kohl is sincere, or if she feels it merely to scorn me."

Trax nodded slowly, watching her with his golden eyes. "You do not think very highly of your friend."

Jessop hesitated as she handed Trax Jeco's sword. "No, I suppose I never have."

He picked Jeco up and smiled to him, telling him how they would spend the afternoon training. As he made his way to the door, he paused, turning to face her once more. "She may have real feelings for him. You cannot deny he is easy to love, Jessop."

She crossed her arms over her chest, silent, knowing any answer she gave would be a betrayal to either the truth or to Falco.

* * * *

For the second time in their recent history, Jessop found herself sharing a drink with Urdo Rendo. He had come to check on her, flask in hand. She had not wished to stay in her room any longer, and the two had gone to one of the highest points in the Blade, where she could pop open one of the many glass windows and sit on the ledge of the great building.

"This is his favorite spot," she explained, sipping the hot liquor.

"I know," Urdo nodded, taking the flask from her as she finished.

Her eyes trailed over the red city's horizon—the Soar-Craft weaving about one another through the dusty sky, the Levi-Hubs busy with travelers and traders, the street so far below that the people seemed like little dots. She had shared this view with him so long ago, and she couldn't quite believe all that had come to pass between them.

"I do not love him as I love Falco," she admitted, reaching for the drink once more.

Urdo nodded, letting her sip his liquor thirstily. "I know that, Jessop. We all do."

"Then what is wrong with me? Is it just the guilt...Why, when we have all killed so many, does his death bother me so greatly?" She studied Urdo's older face, and wise eyes, for answers. He had mentored her in many ways, teaching her new abilities and supporting her in battle. She knew that if any would know these answers, it would be him.

"Could you kill Trax or Korend'a, or even that odd old man, Corin?" Jessop shook her head. "Of course not."

He sipped his drink, turning his eyes to the red sky. "Love takes many shapes and forms, Jessop. Loving another does not mean you love Falco any less, and not being *in* love with Kohl does not mean you don't love him."

She felt the tears pressing at her eyes once more. Urdo offered her the flask, but she shook her head, afraid that if she spoke, she would once again find herself crying.

Urdo's large hand landed gruffly on her back. He patted her with inexpert movements. "Go to him, Jessop. Say your goodbyes while you still can."

* * * *

Falco had ordered more guards to the Hollow. They lined the dark corridor, and two rode perpetually up and down the only bullet that could reach the training area. She wondered if he feared Kohl's ability to escape, or another's interest in freeing him. She ignored the guards and they did not try to stop her from seeing him; there were few left who did not know who she was and what she was capable of.

She was surprised to see Kohl was no longer shackled to the wall. He had a clean tunic and his wounds had been tended to—though he did not look well. His face was blue and swollen from Falco's beating. There was a deep cut in the bridge of his nose, and his lip was black with dried blood and bruising. She turned her head at him softly, hardening her expression as she leapt down to the Hollow grounds.

He turned to her, his blond hair falling over his golden eyes, and he offered the smallest smile. She felt a fire growing in her chest, she felt the tears she had held back from Urdo rising once again. She saw all they had once shared, and she felt all the pain she had caused him. She felt all the pain he had caused her. He took a step towards her. "I knew you'd come. A guard told me it's tomorrow and—"

She raised her hand, silencing him as a single tear ran down her cheek. "Don't speak." He nodded at her order. They held one another's stares for the longest moment, and she knew he felt the same sense of loss that she did. She knew that as each memory of their relationship flashed before her, he saw it too. Without cue or command, they grabbed onto one another, embracing tightly, falling to their knees as they both cried.

She ran her hands over his back, sobbing heavily into his chest. His tears travelled down her neck, and his heavy body rocked back and forth in her strong arms. There was nothing left to be said, there was nothing left to be done. Everything that was ever going to come to pass between them already had. They could offer nothing but the strength of their embrace, nothing but a mutual understanding for one another's tears. Kohl O'Hanlon was going to die in the morning, and once again, her entire life would be changed because of him.

* * * *

Falco returned that evening. Jessop felt his eyes on her as she bathed. She didn't know how long she had been in the Hollow, but the tears, coupled with Urdo's drink, had brought a pain to her head. She did not wish to argue further with him. She wanted simply to rest, to somehow forget what the dawn would be bringing.

"I am sorry my decision wounds you so," he finally spoke. She did not turn to face him, instead facing the cascading water and letting it wash away any redness from her face.

"Jessop, can we speak?" He pressed again, approaching her slowly. Reluctantly, she pivoted around. She held his gray stare, her face stone cold to him. She loved him, as she always would, and he knew that. She did not blame Falco for the way he felt, but for the way in which he blamed her for how *she* felt.

She stepped out of the water and moved past him, only dropping his gaze at the last possible minute. He followed her into the bedroom quietly and sat on the bed as she began to dry her body. "Jessop...what do you want me to say?"

She fixed her stare on him. "Admit you love him still. Admit it wounds you that he did not return to your side. I want you to *admit* that you regret asking me to woo him of all the possible Hunters. Admit you wish to kill him because you cannot live with your decision, and you can't let him live with it either."

He stared at her in silence. His eyes were wide and pain filled his face. They both knew she was right.

"Jess—"

"Goodnight, Falco."

* * * *

When Jessop woke, Falco was sitting at the end of their bed, watching her. She rolled over and sat up slowly. She had to dress Jeco and take him to Trax, before the proceedings began.

"I already took him to Trax," Falco spoke, knowing all she thought, always.

She ignored him, slowly getting to her feet. She needed to dress. As she moved past him, he reached for her hand. She pulled away. "I do not wish to speak with you, Falco."

"But, Jessop..."

She glared down at him, disinterested in picking up where they had left off the previous night. She had felt as though Kohl's fate would always be in her hands, despite anything she had said to the contrary.

"Jessop, I thought about what—" Falco began, but was cut off by a loud rasping at the door.

"*Falco! Jessop!*"

It was Korend'a. Jessop ran to the door and threw it open. Korend'a was flanked by guards and out of breath.

She grabbed his arm, stunned to see him so shaken. He had sweat on his brow and his eyes told her something terrible had happened. He shook his head at her. "It's urgent—Trax, he's been attacked. There's blood everywhere."

Falco brushed past her, his brow knitted with concern and anger. "Take me to him."

Jessop tried to understand what Korend'a was saying. Trax was too great a warrior to be gravely wounded. He was the youngest Councilman in the Blade—who could possibly best him if not herself or Falco? It wasn't just because of their close friendship that she trusted him with their son...*Jeco*.

Jessop's heart raced and the blood seemed to drain from her. She felt faint, knowing instantly what horror Korend'a was reporting. Her knees buckled and she fell against the doorway, collapsing to the ground. Falco grabbed her arms, trying to pull her back up, obviously yet to understand what their friend was trying to tell them.

"Falco—it's your son. We can't find him."

CHAPTER 18

Jessop moved through the corridors, quick as a flame, forcing open every door she passed with a sweep of her hand, entering the minds of any she crossed, searching for those big, gray eyes. "*Jeco!*"

She had never known she could scream at such a volume.

There had been blood everywhere, more blood than she had ever seen in one of the Blade's sterile chambers. Trax had collapsed, face forward, surrounded in the crimson pool. He had been cut from lower hip to rib cage, up his back, with a wound that would have killed him had Falco arrived any later. His eyes had rolled back in his head, blood trailing from his mouth, and he had breathed two names aloud, barely audible. "*Jeco...Hanson...*"

Jessop had gone into his mind instantly, feeling the blade enter his back, reaching for his weapon futilely as the wound was deepened. He fell to his knees. "*Run Jeco! Run!*" He had lurched the boy forward in his arms. Jeco was crying, clinging to Trax as the old scarred hands grabbed him. "*Come with me, come now,*" the voice had commanded, and Jessop knew it well. It was the distinct voice of Hanson Knell.

That was all she had managed to get before leaving Falco to heal him. Korend'a had set all of the guards into motion; Mar'e had ordered the soldiers into the city, and Jessop was searching the Blade, stopping every passer-by who crossed her. No matter what comforts she voiced in her head, no matter how many times someone told her "*He's here somewhere—we will find him,*" she could not slow her heart. She felt an acidity in her stomach that rose into her throat; she felt a helplessness that one with great power never felt; she felt all the fear she had been incapable of feeling for all of her long years.

She stepped into the bullet and travelled down a floor, her eyes searching through the transparent chute for her dark-haired boy. Word had already gotten out—the Blade knew Falco Bane's son was missing. Hunters were searching, students were searching, techs were searching—anyone who wasn't looking for Jeco would answer to her and Falco. She stepped out of the bullet and crossed the pristine corridor quickly. Two guards came by her, holding idle conversation. She forced into the mind of one, and found nothing. Without thinking, she grabbed the other, placed her hand on his temple and rooted around angrily through his thoughts.

"What the—"

He tried to push her off but her grip was unbreakable, her strength fortified by her fear and determination.

When she found nothing, she released him. The guard stared at her with anger and confusion, his friend holding him steady to collect himself. "What are you doing?" he demanded of her.

Wasn't it obvious, she thought to herself. Searching for her son took precedent over everything, over everyone. "Finding my son," she growled back. When they did not move, she felt her rage spring forth. "Get to work! Go find a Hunter and receive instruction on how you can help—*now*."

They scurried around her, jogging in the direction of the bullet. She couldn't focus on the sheer incompetence of those surrounding her. She couldn't focus, in general. She *needed* him back. It was a feeling like no other, not knowing where her son was. The pain was indescribable—a severed limb. The confusion and suspicion unparalleled. She felt as though if she could do anything, say anything in that moment to get him back, she would do it, as certain as she ever could be that nothing had ever mattered more than him.

She flung doors open, nearly breaking their automatic motions. She entered rooms without announcement. She ignored the confused eyes and startled movements of tenants, she flipped over beds and searched bathing chambers, uttering nothing as she entered and exited, throwing occupants out of her way with a flick of her wrist. She carried down the corridor, searching room after room, yelling for her son to return to her.

She continued her hunt, floor after floor, until she felt the realization in her heart—he wasn't in the Blade any longer. Suddenly, it dawned on her. Would Hanson Knell really come so far for Jeco when there was another he cared for greatly? She pivoted around, her boots screeching on the immaculate floor as she raced for a bullet.

* * * *

His guards were all still standing watch. "Has anyone come for him?" she barked to the first, who stood with a blank expression at the entry of the dark corridor. "Answer me, has anyone attempted to rescue the prisoner?" Her voice was an echo in the small space, her anger and fear travelling around them with a violent force.

"No, no one has come," he answered, shaken by her.

She didn't believe it. If Jeco had been missing for an hour that was more than enough time for Hanson to have made his way to the Hollow. "Get out of my way," she growled, marching past the guards. She expected to find the training room empty, she expected the guards to have been duped by strong Sentio powers and a powerful Hunter's agenda...but *he* was still there.

His hands were bound in manacles that were fixed to the ground, only several feet away from a burning fire pit. He was wearing fresh clothes, all black, and his hair had been tied back with a leather. She had completely forgotten about the execution. He looked up to her with wide-eyed concern.

She flipped to the ground, landing just before him on bended knee. "Where is he, Kohl?"

He shook his head at her. "Jessop, what's going on? The guards won't tell me anything, but I can sense it, I can feel the chaos throughout the Blade—what's happened?"

She studied his hazel eyes and searched his confused face. His expression and voice were so sincere that she immediately wanted to believe him, and were it about any other matter, she likely would have. But things had changed—she had seen what Kohl was capable of. "Do not toy with me. Where is Hanson?"

He arched his brow at her. "*Hanson?*"

She struck him violently, the back of her hand searing against his cheek. "I said don't toy with me, Kohl! Hanson was here. What do you know? What have you kept from me?" She hit him again, and a third time, until his lips bled onto her throbbing fingers.

He swayed under her assaults. She struck him with each fist, demanding information. He gave her nothing. "I know nothing, Jessop. I know nothing." She kicked him in the chest and he fell back with a heavy thud. She leapt, like an animal, onto him, straddling his broad form. She grabbed his blond head of hair and focused, entering his mind without pause. She searched, moving from the most recent images of her attacking him, to when Falco had beaten him, to his time in Aranthol...She needed to get further back.

She forced her way through his mind, and some part of her could hear his audible screams, but she knew they did not matter. She trailed over hazy memories of his time recruiting mercenaries. She found every memory of speaking with Hydo and Hanson after Falco took the Blade. She lived through each, playing them over again and again before her, searching for clues. She found nothing, and sliced through several more memories. She felt him struggling beneath her, she could hear him screaming her name, but it did not sound like him...

She ignored it, pushing harder, faster. She saw him speaking with Hanson before Falco had ever arrived, before he knew of her deceit. The memories gave her no information—no mention of a plan, no word of her son. She knew she had gone too far back to find anything of value. She didn't understand. Why wouldn't Hanson have rescued him?

"*Jessop!*"

She was vaguely aware of the sensation of flying. Someone had jolted her from Kohl. She landed with a heavy *thud*, rolling several feet away, losing her grasp on Kohl's mind. She blinked several times as she regained her focus. Falco was kneeling beside Kohl, his hand on Kohl's forehead.

"Jessop, what were you doing to him?" he asked, assessing Kohl's wounds.

She looked from Kohl to Falco, but did not care to answer. "Have they found him? Is he back?"

Falco stood slowly, and shook his head—*no*.

Jessop felt the tears brimming and leapt to her feet. "Hanson would have come for *him*—not Jeco. Why is he not here? Where has he taken our son?"

She closed the gap between herself and Falco in an instant and struck him with all her might. He swayed under her forceful hit. "We will find him."

"Where is he, Falco? *Where!*" She pounded her fists against his chest, barely aware of the echoes of her screaming, her face numb as tears trailed down her cheeks, her throat on fire. She couldn't breathe. She couldn't think.

He grabbed her hands and tried to restrain her, but it was to no avail. Her sorrow could not be contained. "Find him! I want him back. I want him back *now*."

"Hanson took your son?"

The question, barely audible, slurred with blood, was voiced by Kohl. He was propped up on his arms, staring up at her through blood and his own tears.

"Don't pretend—" Jessop lunged at him, but Falco held her back.

Falco held her still. "He isn't pretending, Jessop. We have both searched his mind."

"I...I can help. Let me help," Kohl mumbled, getting back up to his knees.

"You've done enough—" she began, but Falco cut her off.

"How can you help, brother?"

* * * *

"The tavern owner's name is Derox, and there's no way he will meet with you," Kohl explained, sitting on the edge of the bed in the medic's ward. He had been instructed to hold a white garment that smelled distinctly of alcohol against his face for several minutes.

"He'll meet with me or I'll cut him limb from limb," Jessop spoke. The soldiers had found nothing, the Hunters had found no one, the guards had turned up empty handed. The streets were still being overturned, and everyone in the Blade had been rounded up and their whereabouts accounted for—Urdo was conducting the mind searches personally, checking for anyone who may have crossed paths with Hanson that morning. At this stage, Kohl was their best bet.

"They won't meet with *just* you. Derox doesn't do business with women. An opportunity to meet with Falco Bane, on the other hand..." Kohl explained, looking up to Falco.

"It's not *business*." She felt Falco's hand on her back, his attempt to support her. She shrugged it off.

Falco crossed his arms tightly over his chest. "Where can I find him?"

"I'll take you to him, brother," Kohl answered, lowering the white material from his cheeks. To Jessop's amazement, Kohl's wounds had healed. Gone were the bruises and cuts inflicted on him, first by Falco and then by Jessop. She listened to how Falco and Kohl spoke with one another—as though their brotherhood had been reinstated. Had it been her words, or Hanson's actions? She did not know and it did not matter then. All that mattered was Jeco.

"Then let's go," Jessop snapped.

* * * *

The streets had descended into utter chaos. Dezane and Falco's soldiers had stopped every passerby, turned over every kiosk, emptied out every building in search of Jeco. The street merchants lined the walls of their buildings, waiting to be interrogated. Women holding their own children, obviously concerned, waited outside their homes, allowing their belongings to be violently overturned. Jessop spotted several Hunters as they made their way, on foot, through Azgul. They were searching minds and interrogating passersby indiscriminately.

She hadn't traversed the Red City on foot since her first arrival there, in the days before she met Kohl. With crimson dirt dusting her boots and her eyes narrowing in the red sky and scarlet tinted city, she did not find any renewed sense of love. It was not her city—it was not her home. She would tear it to the ground in order to find Jeco.

"Jessop, can you slow down?" Kohl complained, winding a corner to catch up with her. "You don't even know which direction—"

Before he finished his sentence, she turned on him, pivoting tightly on her heel. She locked eyes with him and entered his mind quickly, searching for the tavern owner by name. As she found an old recollection—an introduction between an insalubrious looking bald fellow and Hanson— she found the location of the tavern quickly. She freed Kohl's mind from her grasp, ignoring the pained look on his face, ignoring the concern in Falco's eyes, and turned back to the street ahead.

With quick waves of her arms, kiosks went flying out of her way, crates exploded at her feet, doors flung open and windows shattered. Falco and Kohl stayed on her heel, quick to dodge the shrapnel her rage created. She wanted every Azguli to be terrified, to look upon her and know nothing but fear. She wanted them to be so afraid they would never dare cross her, so afraid they would never consider helping Hanson Knell or Hydo Jesuin take her child out of the city walls. She wanted to see their tears, to know they cowered—she wanted to see the very fear that she felt manifest in the people Falco ruled over.

She took a sharp corner and found herself looking at a dark scarlet-painted door. She recognized it from Kohl's mind. With a swing of her hand and a jolt from her mind, the door flung open, ripping off its hinges and sliding into the dark corridor. She waited for no one, stepping into the tavern without hesitation.

Despite the exterior, the inside of the tavern was quite modern. The bar was made entirely of shining metals, welded neatly together. The floors were a pristine white stone. The lights overhead were tucked into the ceiling tightly, emitting pointed blue rays in every odd direction. Five men were drinking throughout the room, several sitting at a table, two at the bar. Her eyes immediately fixed to the man *behind* the bar, though. He was bald, with a blue sword inked down the middle of his scalp. He was twice Jessop's age and had dark eyes. He was the man from Kohl's mind—he was Derox.

At her gruff entrance, the five men got to their feet, clearly loyal to their patron. Falco held out his hand, instantly paralyzing them all. As he clenched his fist, each man fell to his knees, helpless under his control. "We are here to speak to Derox," he announced.

The bald man with the blue inked sword came slowly around the side of the bar. "Falco Bane, I've been meaning to send my respects on the new dominion. Many of us have waited a long time to see you in power."

"We have no time for your flattery, Derox," Jessop hissed, narrowing her eyes on him.

"Your Hunter friend might have warned you, woman, I don't deal with the weaker sex," he barked angrily, barely looking at her.

Jessop moved so quickly none could forecast her actions. With an aggressive flick of her wrist, she had flung her short blade into Derox's thigh. The man growled in pain, buckling forward to support his wounded leg. Jessop spun on her ankle, turning her body low, and kicked the tavern owner square in the chest. He flipped back and landed on his bar. She closed the space between them with a large step, and ripped her blade free from his thick flesh. She brought it to his neck, "In this room, *you* are the weaker sex."

Despite all the hatred in his eyes, she saw also fear. He had heard of her, and now he witnessed her abilities to be true to the claims. She pressed the bloody point further against the soft skin of his throat. "What do you know of what happened today?"

He managed to look past her still, focusing on Falco instead of her. "I know nothing about today. You're the ones who have turned the city over for who knows what."

Falco took a step closer to them both. "Derox, it goes largely without saying, but my wife will slit you from that oozing thigh to your thick throat, and I will keep you alive long enough for her to do it again and again. Where is my son?"

"I already said, I know nothing," he answered quickly, tilting his throat away from Jessop's blade.

"It is in your best—" Kohl began, but Jessop had no time for this. She didn't need the man to speak. She grabbed his head and forced her way into his mind. She sailed through dark memories, illicit trades, late-night forays, a crying woman, the death of a man at this very bar, not several nights ago. She searched with wild aggression, not caring what damage she inflicted.

"*Make her stop!*" she heard him yell, feeling him wriggling to break free from her grasp.

She focused, burrowing herself further and further. She found an image that suddenly struck her…The Hunter's sigil, on a leather vest. The vest was draped over the bar. As hands curled over the vest, loud noises erupted. The streets were being emptied. She could hear speaking. *"Go quickly, before they get here. Golden Death Valley is several nights travel."*

Jessop released her hold on Derox. She blinked as her eyes readjusted to the blue lights of the tavern. The memory had been not several hours ago. She leapt on top of the bar and found what she was looking for, tucked beneath the countertop—a Hunter's leather vest. She grabbed it as she hopped down.

"Hanson was here," she growled, tossing the leather to Kohl.

Suddenly, Derox began to froth at the mouth. Jessop took a small step back from him. His skin began to turn red and his eyes bulged forward, seemingly too tight in their sockets. "He kept a death capsule in his teeth," Falco snapped, realizing what was occurring. They knew many mercenaries who did the same, preferring death over Hunter torture. Jessop grabbed Derox by the shoulders and shook him. "Tell me what happened—where is Golden Death Valley?"

She rattled the man violently, but it was too late. She felt the pulse disappear from his body. She turned slowly to see Falco, his gray eyes staring at her with hope and concern. "Golden Death Valley?"

She nodded to him. The only source they had found who could help find her son had died. She had never heard of any Golden Death Valley. Their armies had turned up nothing. The Hunters had found no leads. Her son, her perfect, only child, was gone. She may as well have had her heart cut from her chest. She couldn't think about it any longer, she couldn't feel any more pain. She knew the tears were coming, and she wanted to scream. She wanted to scream like she never had before. She grabbed her face, holding on so tightly it was as though she feared she may shatter.

With an explosion of rage, she threw her arms out to the side, and as though she were a mage, fire erupted in the tavern. The flames licked over the bar, and caught onto the two men frozen in their seats. She stared at them as they burned. She knew the fire was her doing, but she did not know how. She spun about, her hands trailing over the room, and everywhere they pointed, new flames were born.

"Jessop…" Falco's voice was barely a whisper. Kohl stared in shock. She knew this was not a natural progression of Hunter abilities. She knew she had never been able to create a flame—always feeling loath towards their presence. Had things been different, she might have felt fear at her newfound ability. She might have questioned it. She may have turned to her husband for guidance. But she felt nothing for herself, or any other. She felt nothing but the need to find Jeco—to learn where Golden Death Valley was. She moved past Falco and Kohl, ignoring their fearful regard of her. She crossed the blue lit pub as the smoke filled it, flames dancing on her heels, and stepped out into the streets.

She felt Kohl and Falco trailing just behind her as she made her way down the street. She needed to feel it again. To feel the release of her rage. To feel the sensation of the world burning at her behest. With an aggressive extension of her fingers, fire erupted over the buildings she passed. It felt *good*, it felt right, as though her body had found a way to cope with the pain. She did not stop to think about the how or the why—she did not ever consider that there had only ever been one Hunter before her who could wield fire as if it were magic.

CHAPTER 19

Dezane sat down slowly, lowering his body into the chair with a kind of deliberation that somehow aged him in Jessop's eyes. "I know where this place is," he said again. Jessop felt her heart lighten the smallest degree. Everyone remained silent, waiting for the tribal elder to say more. Trax was reclined on the bed, wheeled into the large room by medics. He wore a loose tunic, the fabric bunching around his many bandages. Falco had healed him, certainly saving his life, but the wounds had been great and he had needed further care from the medics to manage the tissue damage and pain.

Urdo stood leaning against the wall, his arms crossed over his broad chest. He looked both weary and determined. Korend'a stood at his side, eyes bloodshot, an impatient look stretched across his face. Jessop knew both men would help her find Jeco, both would go without sleep or provisions in order to bring her son back to her. She stood at the head of the table and could feel Kohl and Falco beside her, their eyes boring into her still. She knew she frightened them both; she knew the abilities she had displayed in the street had been more than either had ever anticipated her capable of. In truth, they were more than she had ever believed herself capable of. Abilities that Falco didn't even possess…She cared not if they were alarming, all she knew was that they could help her get her son back. She had long since grown accustomed to learning new powers—Sentio had diminished her sense of surprise for the mystical.

Mar'e stood in the corner of the room, behind Dezane and Trax. Teck Fay, whom Jessop had not seen in quite some time, stood off to her left, cloak pulled down low, tucked into the shadows. She turned her gaze back to Dezane. "Where is it then, Dezane, tell me," she commanded the elder.

Whatever love and allegiance she felt towards the man paled in comparison to the pressing need to have Jeco back in her arms.

"It is a forbidden and treacherous territory—not under the rule of Daharia," he answered, keeping his aged eyes on her.

"It belongs to another galaxy?" Kohl quipped.

Dezane shook his head. "It belongs to no one. It is a barren wasteland, nothing but sand dunes...It is where the Great War took place many thousands of years ago."

Jessop knew the Great War referred to the battle for Daharia, fought by both man and creature for the rights to the territory. The Bakora, a foreign tribe who ruled over the nearby galaxy of Bakoran, lost the Great War, leaving the Prince of Daharia, who had fought with the mighty Blade of Light, to claim the territory. She also knew that the Great War had been fought in a region of a very different name.

"The Great War was battled in Haren'dul Daku," she interjected.

"*Haren'dul Daku* is old Kuroi for Shimmering Death, as the sands of these places shone like diamonds painted in blood," Trax answered, keeping his eyes on the table. His voice was faint and he clearly struggled to speak. "The easier translation became Golden Death Valley."

Falco leaned forward, resting his hands on the table. "It is not ours and it is not Bakoran's?"

Dezane once again shook his head slowly. "It was agreed upon that such land was forever tainted—hosting the greatest loss of life Daharia and Bakoran had ever experienced. The land was deigned no man's."

Jessop could feel her hands shaking. "That monster has taken *my son* to a forbidden wasteland?"

The room was silent. It felt as though each one of them experienced a sense of personal guilt, and Jessop felt no urge to reprieve them of it. Jeco had been in the Blade, with the very people who surrounded her, and he had been taken. She had trusted these men and her son had paid the price. They had all, at one time or another, vouched for Hanson Knell. But not she. Jessop had never trusted the old man.

They group remained silent, but Jessop knew that more was left to be said. It was a silence that concealed some unspoken secret. She flicked her gaze over Dezane and Trax, to Mar'e, who seemed to turn herself further toward the wall. "What is it?" she demanded, her eyes turning to Korend'a and then Urdo.

Urdo looked to Trax and then back to her. "While you were gone, I discovered who helped Hanson get so far into the Blade without detection."

Jessop felt the heat rising in her once again, the pressure boiling under her skin, the urge to erupt in flames. "Who?"

"Jessop, you need to remember that Hanson's Sentio is great—he abused this person. They did not help willingly nor do they—"

"*Tell me*," she growled.

Once again, silence.

Jessop slammed her fist on the table. "I swear if—"

Mar'e stepped forward. Silent tears streaked her face, and her shoulders were shaking. "It was me."

Jessop felt the flame inside her chest. Of course, it had been Mar'e—weakest of them all. Her old friend who had come to the Blade with uncertain intentions, who turned her eye from Falco to Kohl, who questioned her every decision, who had been cruel to her in childhood.

She took a small step towards Jessop, her eyes wide and watery. "Jessop, I can't tell you how sorry I am. I don't remember any of it, I don't remember ever even seeing him, but—"

Jessop couldn't hear her speak. She saw the woman's mouth moving, but she heard no noise. She saw no one else in the room. She thought of nothing but retribution. She raised her hand over her shoulder, and with lightning speed, she threw her dagger. The blade sung through the air and lodged in her old friend's stomach. Mar'e lurched forward, falling to her knees. Her small hands hovered over the hilt of Jessop's dagger, wedged beneath her rib cage. Her eyes were bulging, her full lips parted; she was shocked. She was dying.

"*Jessop!*" Kohl hissed, leaping past her and kneeling beside Mar'e.

Trax appeared stunned, his mouth ajar, his eyes unblinking. Korend'a took two steps towards the injured Kuroi and then froze. Teck Fay stepped out of the shadows, his indigo eyes trained on Mar'e. Jessop felt Falco tense at her side. Dezane kept his eyes on Jessop only, his tired face showing no signs of surprise.

Jessop watched the blood pool, staining the ochre robes Mar'e wore, dripping to the floor like crimson rain. Her old friend looked at her with shock, with horror, and Jessop felt nothing. She could smell the blood, she could see the pain, but in her mind, all she heard was Jeco's laugh, all she saw was her son's eyes.

"Falco, heal her," Kohl begged, his hazel eyes on Falco as he held the dying woman in his arms.

Falco did not move. "Jessop wishes her dead."

"Jessop, please, *please*," Kohl pleaded, pulling Mar'e tighter against his own chest, soaking in her blood as her head fell back.

She stared at him and wondered how much pain her death would truly mean to him. She stared at him, the man who had proclaimed to love her and had tried to kill her, and wondered if *this* was the punishment he truly deserved. She felt her skin twitching at the thought. She knew she would not kill another to punish him.

"Heal her," she whispered, her voice barely a murmur, heard likely only by Falco. He nodded and crossed the room quickly, taking a knee beside Kohl. As Falco pulled the blade free and began to heal Mar'e, everyone watched in silence, captivated by the ability only he possessed—though Falco was no longer the only Hunter with a singular skill.

Jessop raised her hand out and used her mind to summon her dagger back to her. As it cut through the air, it ignited in bright orange flames. She caught the fiery hilt, and the attention of all in the room. The flames encircled her hand, but they did not burn her. It seemed she was impervious to her own flame. She felt their eyes, their shock and concern. There were few fire wielders in existence, and the men now knew her to be one of them.

Urdo took a step towards her, his eyes wide. She could sense his mind racing. She knew who he was thinking of. Korend'a fixed his gaze to her burning hand, a look of amazement in his eyes. He had likely never seen a fire wielder. Dezane nodded slowly, as though unsurprised by her newfound ability. Trax stared from his reclined spot, and she could sense that his thoughts mirrored Urdo's. *Hydo.*

She spun the blade around her fingers with expert ease. "We leave for Golden Death Valley at first light."

* * * *

They had been up all night preparing for their mission. If Hanson and Hydo had made camp in the Golden Death Valley, then their armies resided with them. They did not simply prepare to find Jeco—they prepared for war. Dezane had readied the Kuroi. Falco had rounded up his army. Urdo had enlisted three Hunters who he believed would be most beneficial to their journey, only one of whom Jessop had ever heard of. "Hode Avay," he introduced himself to her, lugging a small sleep sack over his shoulder as he appeared on the docking bay early that morning. She nodded to him. Hode Avay had led missions near Aranthol before, and Jessop knew him by reputation. The other two were much younger, though fiercely loyal and highly skilled, Urdo insisted.

She watched as the large Soar-Craft before her was packed to the brim with provisions—weapons, food, libations, bedding, and tents. The tools for war, she thought, watching as crate after crate was loaded up. Falco moved all around, snapping orders, lifting bags, packing up the vessels. They had barely spoken, barely looked at one another for longer than a second. No one had dared speak to her about the fire wielding. No one had dared speak to her at all, barring Korend'a and Urdo.

Jessop could sense *her* before she spoke. She turned and found Mar'e standing behind her, wide-eyed and fearful. Jessop looked her up and down and took a step closer to her. "What?"

"I wanted to…I wanted to apologize again," she spoke. Her voice was small and frail. Jessop crossed her arms over her chest. She had nearly killed Mar'e and yet, the woman returned, risking Jessop's temper once more.

"I don't remember any of it, Jessop, you must believe me. I have never had anyone enter my mind like that. I don't know when he found me, or how, or how long he kept me under his control. I cannot remember anything."

Jessop didn't care to hear more. She began to turn from Mar'e when the other woman grabbed her hand. "Jessop, *please*. My life is yours, I truly know that you can take it and that you spare it at your will. Please, let me help get Jeco back."

Jessop wrenched her hand free, holding the woman's stare. "Let me make this clear, *friend*, if your weak mind has cost my son his life, I'll finish what I started yesterday."

Mar'e nodded slowly, visibly saddened and silenced by Jessop. She could not bring herself to care. She would kill Mar'e if she wished to, she would turn on any who got between her and Jeco. She returned her gaze to the vessels and found Falco and Kohl in deep discussion near one of the Soar-Craft. They spoke in hushed tones, Kohl keeping his hand on Falco's shoulder, as though there had never been any threat of execution or hatred between the two. She watched them interact, and without willing it, her hands caught fire. She couldn't feel the burning. She couldn't feel anything.

CHAPTER 20

Jessop had found a seat next to Urdo, tucked against the metal wall. Each Soar-Craft was bursting with provisions and warriors. Soldiers filled seats and aisles, food parcels were stored in overhead compartments and underneath the canvas covered chairs, weapons were bound tightly together and piled up against the walls. Falco and Kohl had found seats nearer the front. Falco had asked her to join them when they first boarded, but she declined, knowing that if the fire was something she could not control, being near him and Kohl made her a danger to the entire vessel.

They had travelled for many hours already, the skies having changed from light to dark, and Jessop knew they neared Hara'agul, the southernmost weigh station in Daharia. The weigh station would typically be the last place any could stop before the hundreds of miles of barren land leading up to the border of their Daharian territory. She thought only of Jeco and Hanson, of how they had made this journey. She thought of every square space of territory far beneath that they flew over, and of how Jeco had already passed over it. She thought of all the ways Hanson would pay for his trespass. She had felt sorrow for him, the day she let Falco into the Blade. She had seen his look of disappointment, she had known the ways in which she betrayed him, having worked so long to win over his faith… but none of it compared to this.

Hanson did not know what rage he had unleashed. She was not the same woman he had seen when last in the Blade. She had walked and left fire in her wake. She would burn him alive given the opportunity. She would burn all of Daharia to the ground if that's what it took to get Jeco back.

"Jessop?"

She stirred, her attention pulled to the present. Falco stood in the aisle. She forced herself to look up into his gray eyes, the eyes her son had inherited, and found he looked awful. His eyes were bloodshot and circled in dark skin, his cheeks looked sunken, his dark hair was an untidy mess. She looked to the floor.

"Urdo, would you mind giving Jessop and me a moment?"

Jessop grabbed Urdo's forearm. "This is *his* seat, Falco, he doesn't have to move."

Urdo looked from her to him and back to her. "I'll return shortly." She removed her hand as he stood, his large frame taking up the entire aisle as he moved past Falco. Falco took his seat, leaning forward, his elbows on his knees. He waited in silence, and she knew he wished for her to look at him.

She felt the heat inside her expanding, her fingers tingling, her mind racing—searching for some release, some sense of peace. She took deep breaths, her eyes forced tightly shut, and tried to focus on her breathing. "Jessop," he pressed. She clenched her fingers over her knees, taking slow breaths, ignoring him. She knew that even if she could initiate the fire at will, it could also start on its own. She couldn't control it—she had never been trained by a Fire-wielder. She did not know their tricks.

Falco grabbed her hand, and quickly retracted, hissing in pain. She opened her eyes and saw that while there were no flames, he kept his hand close to his chest, clearly in pain. He looked at her with anger. "Your skin is hot as a flame."

She crossed her arms tightly over her chest, securing her hands against her sides. She felt no such heat. "Then don't touch me."

He sighed heavily and rested his hand on her knee, ignoring her anger. "We need to discuss this."

She refused to look at him, staring instead at his hand on her. "Discuss what?"

"The Fire-wielding," he answered. His voice was low and soft, as though he were trying to breach a difficult topic with kindness. She didn't need his kindness—she wasn't one of his indigent denizens.

"There's nothing to discuss. You're not a Fire-wielder, you know nothing of it," she snapped, flicking her gaze to him briefly.

"And you *are* and yet *you* know nothing of it. I don't know anyone who *becomes* a Fire-wielder. They're born with those abilities…It's incredibly dangerous, Jessop, it makes you that much more—"

"Volatile?"

He sighed heavily. "That's not the word I would use, but yes. We need to figure out how you can learn to control it."

She turned in her seat, focusing her angry stare on him. "What makes you think I can't control it on my own?"

He arched his brow at her. "You just burned my hand."

"Maybe it was on purpose."

They stared at one another, angry and indignant, silent. She had felt such rage it was difficult to discern truth from lies born of anger. She had acted in ways that she knew she previously never would have, but it seemed to be precisely that—*previously*. As in, *before* Jeco was taken. There was a before and an after, and she quite frankly no longer cared about who she was or what she did before. Nothing mattered but the present, nothing mattered but getting their son back.

"Do you think I don't feel the same?" Falco whispered, knowing her thoughts.

She shook her head at him. "Don't do that, Falco."

He shook his head at her. "Do what? Share a mind, as we always have?"

She held his stare. "Perhaps I no longer wish to share everything of mine with you."

He physically withdrew from her, recoiling his hand, narrowing his gaze. A part of her immediately regretted the words, but another part, the part where the fire resided within her, willed her to go on, urged her to hurt him further, as he had hurt her. "I have shared my entire life with you, I have shared my body with you, I have shared my abilities with you—I gave you our son. And what do I have to show for it? You have a throne and I have lost my child."

She felt the tears brimming, hot and plentiful in her eyes. Her throat was dry, as though the flames already licked her skin. She saw how her words wounded him, she saw the way he bit his cheek. "You blame me."

"This is *your* war, is it not? We took the Blade for you. We angered Hanson and Hydo for you. Now they have Jeco."

Her voice was louder than she had intended. Several warriors turned, their concerned eyes flicking between her and Falco. She cared not. She kept her focus on Falco. He stood and ran a hand over his face. "I won't speak with you when you're like this."

As he began to turn from her, she stood and grabbed his shoulder, lurching him around to face her. "Oh, you *will* speak to me. It is difficult to face the truth, isn't it? I did everything for you and now my boy is missing!"

"*Our* boy, Jessop! He's my son, too." Falco's voice was louder than hers, travelling about the cabin of the Soar-Craft, silencing any adjacent conversations, stilling any movements. Every eye was on them.

Urdo and Kohl quickly appeared in the aisle, alarmed by the arguing. Kohl raised his hands out slowly, as though gesturing peace to her. "Jessop, you cannot blame Falco for Hanson's misdeeds."

She turned her teary-eyed gaze to him. He looked at her with complete confidence, as though no matter how many times she attacked him, he believed their bond would keep him safe. She shook her head at him slowly. "Every time you speak to me, you risk your life. Hanson is *your* mentor. You helped him escape Falco's wrath when you nearly killed me. This is just as much your fault."

Kohl nodded slowly. "You're angry, that's understandable. But we will get Jeco back."

She shot him a warning stare. "Keep my son's name out of your mouth."

He was silenced, nodding at her slowly, gauging the extent of her anger. Urdo took a small step towards her. "Jessop, I know how mad you are, but you cannot appear to defy Falco before his soldiers, not days before he intends to lead them into another battle."

She shook her head at Urdo. "I can defy whomever I wish. Falco leads the rest of you because he is stronger than you all."

She turned her gaze back to her husband. To his tired gray eyes and his saddened face. "But you're not stronger than me, are you? It's becoming more apparent each day that my abilities have surpassed yours."

He nodded at her. "Perhaps you are stronger than me. Perhaps you're the strongest there's ever been. I don't care, Jessop. All I care about is you and getting Jeco back."

She shook her head at him, the tears silently streaking down her cheeks. "That's not true. It's never been true. Otherwise we would have never left Aranthol."

"We both wanted vengeance on Hydo, we both wanted to secure the Blade for our son."

She shook her head, unable to hold back the tears any longer. She felt the flames ignite, she could hear how they whipped about her wrists. She felt the despair that no words could describe, the hollowness in her chest, the pain of missing her child, so great that her body erupted in tangible heat when she thought of it. Nothing had ever mattered as much as he did. They had been so blinded by their revenge and their struggle for power and destiny, they had somehow lost their only son.

She lowered her head, crying heavily, her shoulders heaving as she fought for breath. The fire surrounding her fingers blurred in her teary-eyed vision. She tried to focus, she tried to take deep breaths. Falco was right and she knew it. She had no clue how to contain the flames that every eye on the vessel stared at with horror.

She felt hopeless. Helpless. She was more than a failure. She struggled for breath as the fire travelled up her arms, growing stronger and stronger. She could hear people calling her name but their voices sounded faint and far off, unrecognizable. She could smell smoke. The fire travelled around her torso, and she remembered the first fire, all those years ago. She remembered the cabin, and the screaming, and Hydo. The only Fire-wielder she had ever known. She could see him clearly controlling the flames, using his dark abilities to commit the murders that had initiated everything.

The memory made the pain worse, made her ability to focus that much more impaired. She bit her lip and struggled against the tears and despair. She needed to contain the flames, for however immune to their wicked burn she was, none surrounding her were equally invulnerable. She tried to keep her eyes on the fire, she tried to focus her attention, but all she could think about was the way the ashes had run through her fingers.

Suddenly, someone grabbed hold of both of her hands. The touch startled her, as fingers intertwined with her own, as she was pulled close to the chest of Falco. He held her tightly, burning in her flames. She tried to jerk free, she tried to move away from him, but he held her too tightly, refusing to let go.

He held her firmly against him, and she knew his agony was great. He ignored the burning of his own flesh, he ignored the pain, tucking his face against hers. He kissed her tears and whispered against her skin. "Come back to me, Jessop. Come back to me."

She had experienced it before. Falco's voice had the ability to cut through all the pain, a blade of his own, sharper than all the agony and chaos and mystical abilities. She heard his voice, and her heart needed him. He grounded her. She let her head rest against his chest, where she could hear the pounding of his heart.

"Come back to me," he whispered into her dark hair. The fires extinguished. He let go of her hands and she quickly wrapped them around him, holding him tightly. He locked his arms around her and held her against him. She sensed him healing as he held her, fixing the burns she had inflicted on him. *I'm sorry*, she pushed the small words across his mind. He shook his head, continuing to hold her.

Suddenly, the Soar-Craft jerked to the side, causing a stir amongst the passengers. Jessop pulled away from Falco, quick to grab hold of a chair to steady herself. She looked around to see everyone braced, holding onto items and walls, securing their positions against the turbulence. As soon as they seemed to recover, the vessel jerked in the opposite direction. A deafening sound filled the cabin, like wind whistling through a tight space. Then the Soar-Craft dropped. She felt the pressure change within the cabin as they were all lurched upward against the fall. She kept one hand on the chair, one on Falco. *What's happening?* She pushed the thought into his mind.

He looked around, seemingly as confused as everyone else. The Soar-Craft was still falling, beginning to tilt forward. Packs of bedding, food parcels, and weapons all began to tumble forward, collapsing against chairs, crushing people against cabin walls. As a massive crate came barreling towards them in the aisle, Jessop released her hold on the chair and threw her hand out, freezing the wooden box before it struck them. Falco locked his arms around her tightly, supporting her as she warded off falling items.

She knew what was happening and it terrified her.

As Falco held her upright, she flung oncoming items out of their way. "Falco—we're crashing!" she yelled, her voice battling against the whipping wind filling the cabin.

She felt him hold her tighter; he too knew the truth. Suddenly, Dezane appeared in the aisle, fighting his way against the falling debris and panicking passengers. Urdo grabbed the tribal elder and wrenched him up to where they stood. Dezane grabbed the seat beside Falco and Jessop. "We are under attack! Raiders in Hara'agul have shot the vessel—we're going down!"

Jessop turned in Falco's arms, looking from him to Dezane, and back to him. She looked into his perfect gray eyes as her heart raced, as the world around them began to soar past. They fell, faster and faster, hundreds of feet down. "Jeco!" she shouted to Falco, and he nodded at her, his gray eyes dark and serious, knowing her mind. They wouldn't die in this crash, they couldn't, not when they had their son to find.

She shifted in his tight embrace. "I need you to let go, Falco!"

He shook his head, staring at her as though she were insane. "Never."

She squeezed him tightly, "Do you trust me?"

He regarded her silently, slowly, as though he were at peace. "Of course."

She kissed him quickly, firmly, as if it were for the last time.

"Then let go..."

If you enjoyed *The Shadow City*, be sure not to miss the first book in Ryan Wieser's epic Hunters of Infinity series,

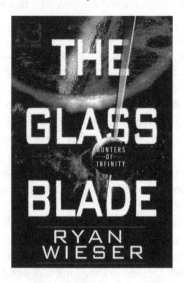

The Hunters of Infinity have been protecting the Daharian galaxy for years, but there has never been a female Hunter—until now.

In a seedy bar in the shadowy corners of Daharia, Jessop comes to the rescue of young Hunter Kohl O'Hanlon. Impressed by her remarkable sword-wielding skills, the Hunters invite her to their training facility, the Glass Blade, though not all are pleased with the intrusion. But they soon discover that Jessop learned to fight from the rogue leader of the Shadow City of Aranthol—and *escaped*. Now they want to use her intimate knowledge of their enemy to destroy him.

As Jessop grows closer to this elite brotherhood, their leader succumbs to a mysterious ailment, and Kohl learns that Jessop is hiding dark secrets, raising suspicions about the enigmatic woman who saved his life. Has the Hunters' security been breached—or do they have a traitor in their ranks?

Allegiances will be questioned.

Loyalties will be betrayed.
Vengeance will be brutal.

Read on for a special excerpt!

A Rebel Base Books e-book on sale now.

CHAPTER 1

The tavern was dark and quiet, barring the muted voices that filled the corners with whispers of quiet corruption and deceit. Hushed sounds traveled on thick smoke to the ceiling and her eyes trailed over the dimly lit corners and over the musty cloaked patrons. Dirty exchanges took place everywhere, too-young girls being offered coins and despair by corrupt travelers, whose lies traveled like fire across the alcohol on their lips. This wasn't a typical bar, this dark, underground dwelling in the heart of Azgul where there were more shadows than light, more smoke than air. It was a seedy, unsafe locale where illegal exchanges could occur. A place favored by those in the city's most important positions, for in this underground dwelling they could act as they truly wished.

From where she sat, with her cloak draped low over her face, she could easily make out the group of Aren. They were more discreet than she had anticipated, but few could go unseen to her well-trained eyes. They were scattered about the bar, donning the civilian attire of common Azgul nomad passerby. The Aren weren't common travelers though; they were fatalistic believers who waited anxiously for a supposed impending end. A doom and darkness that would swallow the entire Daharian galaxy whole—their belief in some unimagined state of horror for the universe made her certain that not a man amongst them had ever laid eyes on Aranthol.

She scanned the room, counting twelve of the zealots. Without their robes they appeared as normal men, barring their brand, which could be seen on the base of several of their necks. The tender nape of the neck was where all in Azgul had their brands. She knew that their mark was not well-known though, not as well-known as they would have liked it to be. Thinking of the brandings nearly had Jessop reaching for her own neck, certain she could almost feel the hot iron against her still. The smell of burning, blistering flesh unnaturally recoiling from heated metal filled her nostrils. She shivered at the putrid memory and forced it back to the depths of her mind, where she kept all her locked-away thoughts and all her darkness.

Suddenly, the oddest sensation roused her, overcoming her senses. She could feel silk running across her skin, dragging her fine hairs on end, exciting her cells. The energy of the room had completely changed, thickening the air more than any smoke or liquor could do. She had only ever been around one other of her kind, and to feel the changing electromagnetic charge in the room without *him* present was as compelling to her as it was terrifying. The draw was a beast's cry calling her in, feeding her need to find the one like her. It was a pull strong enough to grip her, strong enough to shoot adrenaline through her, to dilate her pupils and ready her muscles and tell her, without question, that Hunters were near.

She closed her eyes and narrowed in on their presence. She could smell the faintest scent of grease on one of them; it had an acidic air to it—like the oil slick found in the Western corner of the city. She could hear his voice though he did not speak. She could see the diminutive smudge of black slick over his boot though she did not open her eyes. Her senses—so refined—ensured she could see most of him without ever glancing his way.

And then she laid eyes on him.

She found herself staring at a silver star-shaped scar, a twisted knot of marred flesh the size of a plum carved into his cheekbone. He had a mess of blond hair that he wore pulled back and dark eyes that he scanned the bar with. His frame was large but he held one shoulder slightly higher—due to recent injury, she imagined. As one of his large hands curled around a drink, the other rested comfortably against the hilt of his blade. His eyes trailed over the room and for a moment she wondered if he sensed her presence too. His gaze returned to his drink, and he smiled with half his mouth, allowing the star-shaped scar to pull and glisten. He was beautifully flawed.

Her gaze fell to the man beside the young Hunter—an older man, another Hunter. The men dressed as she had expected. Their uniform consisted of black breeches and tunic, over which they wore a waist-length black leather vest, bound shut with the belt that carried their blade. The vest had their sigil imprinted over the heart. She watched as the older of the two pulled a stool out from the bar, slowly sitting as his well-trained eyes searched the corners of the establishment with practiced ease. His braid of silver hair rested down his back and as a rare flickering of light caught his face she saw his skin was mapped with the deep lines of worn scars. She had let her gaze hold him for less than a minute when she felt the whirring energy of his keen mind.

His age made him more attuned to the presence of those like him. He turned in his seat, searching the room—he could *sense* her. But Jessop didn't worry—he wouldn't be looking for *her*; he would be searching for a man. Just to be sure, though, she forced her thoughts down, quieting her mind and turning her gaze away.

She concentrated on her hand, on drumming her fingers on the table before her. She could feel her blood coursing, warm and rapid, through her veins, and her heart quickening, all for feeling the presence of those so like her so near. Her foot bounced against the floor, pumping adrenaline through her long legs. The silent room seemed to be getting louder and louder, she could hear her beating heart, swelling under her breast, her green eyes straining to stay down as anticipation welled inside her...

Through her periphery she could make out the lone Aren, moving swiftly towards the Hunters. He held a blade. He needed to be quick. Her beating heart was pulsing rhythmically, deafening her thoughts. Someone—a girl—seeing the knife, screamed, a shriek that set the room into motion. Jessop finally let herself look up. The Hunters moved quickly in the shadows, swift to unsheathe their weapons. The Aren formed their pack quickly; there were thirteen, not twelve. For a brief moment, she was surprised at how one could have passed under her sight. She threw her hood back, finally able to watch the scene unfold. As the zealots formed a semi-circle around the Hunters, backing them up against the bar, the tavern crumbled into pandemonium.

The young girls cried with an adolescent fear that nearly overwhelmed Jessop. But she had learnt long ago how to ignore pain—hers and theirs. Her eyes stayed set on the Hunters as the travelers and girls and workers all fought for the exits. The dark space that had offered them such safety from prying eyes minutes before now offered them danger and isolation from help. Quick to come for pleasure and quick to escape pain—Jessop had many criticisms for those who came to be in this part of Azgul.

The sound of a man dying refocused her attention. An Aren fell to the ground before the Hunters. Jessop watched the young fair one, his strong arm wielding his blade about him like an extension of himself. Something about his flesh appeared silvery to her, somehow reflective. She couldn't quite make it out. He spun low and struck with ease. He *was* good. Despite his well-rehearsed steps, he was still exciting to watch. The older Hunter had his fight memorized, a veteran warrior with a trusted blade, faster than one would have prepared for—*he* was exactly as Jessop had expected.

They were good—better than most she had ever seen. But there were simply too many Aren and she was uncertain what odds the Hunters, especially the young one, had fought against before. With every deflection and assault a new attack came down upon them. It seemed two against thirteen was an impossible fight for them to win without suffering serious harm.

The young Hunter was flung back against the bar as two Aren wrestled his strong arms back, a third moving towards him with a blade. Jessop knew she had little time to make her move.

She leaped from her seat, charging swiftly toward the Aren set on impaling the young Hunter. To the cloaked disciple's shock, she hooked her arm under his neck and kicked his feet out from underneath him. As he stumbled, she wrenched the blade from his grip. With a heavy throw, she lodged the small weapon expertly into the chest of one of the assailants holding the young Hunter's arm back.

The Hunter tore his surprised gaze from her to the dying Aren clinging to him, gargling blood. He shoved his attacker to the ground before gruffly elbowing the other man holding him, bloodying the Aren's nose before striking him in the chest. The Aren fell forward as the Hunter grabbed a bottle from the bar and beat it over the man's head. As glass shattered and liquor spurted across the bloodied floor, Jessop couldn't help but think him resourceful.

He shot Jessop a grateful, if not confused, glance, before grabbing his blade from the ground and continuing his fight. She watched him as he clashed with the fanatics—he moved with skill and grace, his star glass blade travelling silently through the air. The Hunters' blades were forged with the pressurized sediment left over from star formations. The blades appeared as glass, each slightly different in color, but were harder than any material found in Daharia. The young Hunter's sword was entirely transparent, crystal clear from base to deadly tip. It was beautiful.

She kept her eyes on him, while still easily deflecting any attack against her. Thirteen Aren against two Hunters was too many, thirteen against two Hunters and *her,* was just fine. She grabbed the shoulder of one Aren and quickly spun him around. He stared at her with shock.

"*What* are you doing?"

She didn't answer him. To see a woman intervene in an Azgul fight would be a surprise to any. She grabbed his wrist and disarmed him with a forceful twist of his hand. He lashed out with anger, hurling his spare fist towards her small face. She ducked and caught his arm with both hands, twisted at the hip, and kicked him viciously in the abdomen. He fell from her, winded. She knelt beside him and offered a vicious strike to his temple, leaving him unconscious.

She was on her feet instantly, turning just in time to grab the neck of the next Aren. She grabbed his wrist, holding his hand back, and then, quickly, released her hold on his neck, recoiled her hand, twisted her fingers into a fist, and struck back at the exposed flesh forcefully, punching him in the throat. The Aren coughed for air, grabbing at his windpipe. She took a step towards him, darted her arm past his face, and jerked it back, hitting him with her elbow. He fell to the ground.

She stepped over his writhing body and caught the eye of the young Hunter. He too had been watching her. A look of distinct admiration was in his eyes, despite being embroiled in his own fight; it was clear she had impressed him. She turned from him and found the hands of an Aren grabbing at her, coiling tightly around her neck. He lifted her off the ground and slammed her back against the bar. She could hear glasses shattering behind her, stools knocking against her legs and falling to the side.

She brought her arm up and over his hands, jerking downward until she leveraged his grip off of her. She kneed him in the abdomen, and as he buckled forward, she kneed him again, breaking his nose. He stumbled back and she crouched to the ground, spiraling with one leg extended and kicking his legs out from underneath him. She was standing, already in mid-motion for her next assault before he hit the ground. She kicked him swiftly and leapt over his body, her hands landing on the shoulders of one of the three Aren surrounding the older Hunter.

She spun him around and struck. She got his throat and elbowed his cheekbone. Holding his collar as she struck at him again, she looked to the old Hunter. "Get out of here—I've got this!" she yelled to him.

His aged cobalt eyes widened with suspicion. "Who are *you*?" He kicked one of the Aren back, seeming more concerned about Jessop than he was about his attacker.

The guttural cry of the young Hunter drew their attention—the young man was wounded. An Aren fell fatally from the Hunter's sword, but he had left a dagger stuck in the fair Hunter's side. The fight had gone on long enough. As the older Hunter ran past her to his wounded comrade, Jessop took a deep breath and closed her eyes; she concentrated on the feeling of electricity running through her, deep within her. The unadulterated power that she had long since learnt how to lose herself in—how to stay safe within the boundaries of.

She slowly exhaled. And with expert skill, she snapped the neck of the Aren before her, opening her eyes as he hit the ground.

She flicked her cloak to the side and found the hilt of her weapon. She drew the blade from its sheath and spun about, skillfully wielding the sword. The lethal piece was beautiful. Made of star glass, it was the only one of its kind—forged to be entirely onyx in color; the blade was black as night. She ducked low and spun on her knee, moving the sword around her in a circle, and came up behind an Aren attacker. She struck him down and stood as he fell from her weapon's lethal edge, slicing the sword with his crimson blood. She bent her knees and quickly jumped atop the bar, dancing over glasses as she made her way towards the Hunters.

She flipped from the edge, curving her blade out as she spun in the air. She landed on one knee, the Hunters safely behind her, the Aren before her. She remained crouched down as she brought her weapon's point up into the diaphragm of the next assailant. He stumbled towards her and she spun on her knee out to the side, liberating her weapon from his dying body as she stood. The two remaining Aren descended upon her swiftly. She twirled, her cloak flying about her as she landed a roundhouse kick against one. He fell to the ground as the other, with surprising might, grabbed her from behind. His strong forearm locked around her neck and pulled her back tightly. Her leather boot slipped in a thick pool of blood and she struggled to regain her footing as the other Aren recovered, steadying himself before her.

She backed into the man holding her and thrust her sword outward, connecting with the second Aren's side just enough to sting. He lunged at her, snarling wildly. She leaned back into her captor and kicked at the wounded man. She got his chin and forcefully sent him flying onto his back.

The silvery glint of the dagger caught her eye just in time.

The Aren holding her held his weapon high above her; ready to bring it down on her chest. She closed her eyes, concentrating on the energy between them—on her *power*—and, just as she had anticipated, the Aren shrieked in agony, dropping his blade to the ground, loosening his hold on her neck. Jessop snaked her sword about in her expert fingers, curved her body to the side, and thrust her sword inward, past her hip, into his abdomen.

She spun out of his grip, pulling her blade loose. He coughed, blood dripping from his lip, pooling in his gut. She remained in position with her sword extended out, perfectly parallel to the ground, her feet steadying themselves in the still-warm blood of her slain victims. She stood at the ready in a circle of the dead or dying. None of the attackers moved and she took a cautious breath, mentally assessing her body for injuries—she was mostly unharmed and the battle was over.

She cleaned her blade swiftly on her cloak and sheathed it before turning to the Hunters. The older was supporting the younger, applying pressure to his wound and they both stared at her with wild-eyed confusion, though the young one looked on through fluttering eyelashes.

The blue eyes of the old Hunter narrowed on her. "Tell me who you are," he ordered.

She looked away from him to his wounded companion. She could see the blood shining over his leather. His paling face and slowing breaths were poor signs. "Your friend needs treatment," she advised.

The silver-haired Hunter nodded, more concerned with his young friend than her identity. "Then help me get him some, girl."

Jessop flinched at the word, but nodded. She took a step towards the Hunters, and eased the young one's arm over her shoulder, slowly pulling him away from the bar. It was only once she was close enough to support his weight did she understand why his skin seemed to shimmer like silver to her—he was covered in hundreds of scars.

"You saved us," he whispered, his hazel eyes studying her. She smiled tightly at him, uncertain of how to respond, and then watched as he lost consciousness; his heart slowing caused her own to speed up.

About the Author

Ryan Wieser completed her B.A. in Sociology and Socio-Legal Studies before going on to complete her MSc. in Experimental Psychology. Having been raised in Africa and educated across multiple countries, Ryan has a passion for travel and an interest in diverse cultures. For more, please visit www.ryanwieserbooks.com.

Printed in the United States
by Baker & Taylor Publisher Services